MAGAZINE

Tin House

Volume 18, Number 3

"An addict alone is in bad company."

—Alcoholics Anonymous adage

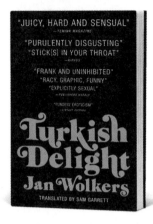

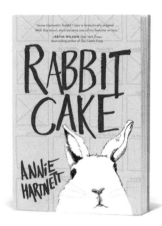

TURKISH DELIGHT

by Jan Wolkers
new translation by Sam Garrett

Upon its original publication in 1969, *Turkish Delight* was a sensation and a scandal. Its graphic language and explicit sex scenes had an explosive effect, but just as revolutionary was its frank, colloquial style. The more straitlaced critics condemned the book, but readers saw a novel that reflected the way they spoke, thought, and felt.

Turkish Delight opens with a screed: a sculptor in his studio, raging against the love he lost and describing, in gory detail, the state of his life since she left him. Our narrator alternates between the story of his relationship with Olga—its passion and affection, but also its obsessiveness and abuse—and the dark days that followed, as he attempts to recapture what they had when they lived together, "happy as beasts."

"Like Henry Miller, Wolkers writes with a tremendous appetite for life and a painterly approach to the sensuous. He is a refreshing stylist."

—*New York Times Book Review*

RABBIT CAKE

by Annie Hartnett

Elvis Babbitt has a head for the facts: she knows science proves yellow is the happiest color, she knows a healthy male giraffe weighs about 3,000 pounds, and she knows that the naked mole rat is the longest-living rodent. She also knows she plans to grieve her mother, who has recently drowned while sleepwalking, for exactly eighteen months. But there are things Elvis doesn't yet know—like how to keep her sister Lizzie from poisoning herself while sleep-eating or why her father has started wearing her mother's silk bathrobe around the house.

Elvis investigates the strange circumstances of her mother's death and finds comfort, if not answers, in the people—and animals—of Freedom, Alabama. As hilarious a storyteller as she is heartbreakingly honest, Elvis is a truly original voice in this exploration of grief, family, and the endurance of humor after loss.

"A brilliant book . . . Charming and beautifully written."

—*Kirkus*, Starred Review

Available March 2017

Available March 2017

LITTLE SISTER

by Barbara Gowdy

Thunderstorms are rolling across the summer sky. Every time one breaks, Rose Bowan loses consciousness and has vivid, realistic dreams about being in another woman's body.

Is Rose merely dreaming? Or is she, in fact, inhabiting a stranger? Disturbed yet entranced, she sets out to discover what is happening to her. Meanwhile her mother is in the early stages of dementia, and has begun to speak for the first time in decades about another haunting presence: Rose's younger sister.

In *Little Sister*, one woman fights to help someone she has never met, and to come to terms with a death for which she always felt responsible. With the elegant prose and groundbreaking imagination that have earned her international acclaim, Barbara Gowdy explores the astonishing power of empathy, the question of where we end and others begin, and the fierce bonds of motherhood and sisterhood.

"Gowdy's storytelling is fearless, inventive, and dazzling."

—HEATHER O'NEILL, author of *The Girl Who Was Saturday Night*

Available May 2017

NATURE POEM

by Tommy Pico

Nature Poem follows Teebs—a young, queer, American Indian (or NDN) poet—who can't bring himself to write a nature poem. For the reservation-born, urban-dwelling hipster, the exercise feels stereotypical, reductive, and boring. He hates nature. He prefers city lights to the night sky. He'd slap a tree across the face. He'd rather write a mountain of hashtag punchlines about death and give head in a pizza-parlor bathroom; he'd rather write odes to Aretha Franklin and Hole. While he's adamant—bratty even—about his distaste for the word "natural," over the course of the book we see him confronting the assimilationist, historical, colonial-white ideas that collude NDN people with nature. The closer his people were identified with the "natural world," he figures, the easier it was to mow them down like the underbrush. But Teebs gradually learns how to interpret constellations through his own lens, along with human nature, sexuality, language, music, and Twitter. Even while he reckons with manifest destiny and genocide and centuries of disenfranchisement, he learns how to have faith in his own voice.

Available May 2017

HORSETHIEF BOOKS

OUT IN FEB 2017

Our books are hardback covers wrapped in Pearl Linen fabric with foil stamped type. The interiors are printed on 60# Cream Tradebook.

OUR LANDS ARE NOT SO DIFFER ENT

Michael Bazzett

Elizabeth Scanlon

LONESOME GNOSIS

www.horsethiefbooks.com

Tin House

MAGAZINE

EDITOR IN CHIEF / PUBLISHER
Win McCormack

EDITOR	Rob Spillman
DEPUTY PUBLISHER	Holly MacArthur
ART DIRECTOR	Diane Chonette
MANAGING EDITOR	Cheston Knapp
EXECUTIVE EDITOR	Michelle Wildgen
POETRY EDITOR	Matthew Dickman
ASSISTANT POETRY EDITOR	Camille T. Dungy
EDITOR-AT-LARGE	Elissa Schappell
PARIS EDITOR	Heather Hartley
ASSOCIATE EDITOR	Emma Komlos-Hrobsky
ASSISTANT EDITOR	Thomas Ross
COPY EDITOR	Meg Storey
DESIGNER	Jakob Vala

CONTRIBUTING EDITORS: Dorothy Allison, Steve Almond, Aimee Bender, Charles D'Ambrosio, Anthony Doerr, Nick Flynn, Matthea Harvey, Jeanne McCulloch, Rick Moody, Whitney Otto, D. A. Powell, Jon Raymond, Helen Schulman, Jim Shepard, Karen Shepard

INTERNS: Olivia Boone, Austin Bridgen, Benjamin Buckingham, Devyn Defoe, Alanna Faelan, Kathryn Holmstrom

READERS: Leslie Marie Aguilar, William Clifford, M. V. Fierce, Selin Gökçesu, Paris Gravely, Todd Gray, Lisa Grgas, Dahlia Grossman-Heinz, Carol Keeley, Louise Wareham Leonard, Su-Yee Lin, Alyssa Persons, Sean Quinn, Lauren Roberts, Gordon Smith, Jennifer Taylor, J. R. Toriseva, Lin Woolman, Charlotte Wyatt

Tin House Magazine (ISSN 1541-521X) is published quarterly by McCormack Communications LLC, 2601 Northwest Thurman Street, Portland, OR 97210. Vol. 18, No. 3, Spring 2017. Printed by Versa Press, Inc. Send submissions (with SASE) to Tin House, P.O. Box 10500, Portland, OR 97296-0500. ©2017 McCormack Communications LLC. All rights reserved. No part of this publication may be reproduced, stored in a retrieval system, or transmitted in any form or by any means, electronic, mechanical, photocopying, recording, or otherwise, without the prior written permission of McCormack Communications LLC. Visit our Web site at **www.tinhouse.com**.

Basic subscription price: one year, $50.00. For subscription requests, write to P.O. Box 469049, Escondido, CA 92046-9049, or e-mail tinhouse@pcspublink.com, or call 1-800-786-3424. Circulation management by Circulation Specialists, Inc.

Periodicals postage paid at Portland, OR 97210 and additional mailing offices.

Postmaster: Send address changes to Tin House Magazine, P.O. Box 469049, Escondido, CA 92046-9049.

Newsstand distribution through Disticor Magazine Distribution Services (disticor.com). If you are a retailer and would like to order Tin House, call 905-619-6565, fax 905-619-2903, or e-mail Melanie Raucci at mraucci@disticor.com. For trade copies, contact W. W. Norton & Company at 800-233-4830.

America has always been the land of invention and reinvention. We hold on to the belief that people forged in the fires of misadventure or tragedy or just plain stupidity can save themselves if they are willing to accept responsibility for their misdeeds and make amends. But can we ever truly hit reset, go back to a pure state? The search for lost innocence has fueled many a quest, both personal and artistic. In this issue we explore some of the ways in which we try to restore the mind and heart. Leslie Jamison, in her essay "Confessions of an Unredeemed Fan," explores her fascination with the trainwreck life of Amy Winehouse as well as her own battles with the drug that consumed the late pop star. In "The First Wife," Aimee Bender reimagines and rehabilitates Bluebeard, while Alyssa Knickerbocker draws on the strength of Rogue, Jean Grey, Psylocke, Storm, and Jubilee (duh, the female X-Men) to return her power postpartum. Is there any redemption for hospital food? Jenni Ferrari-Adler makes the case in her Readable Feast. And former *Tin House* New Voice Jenn Shapland returns with "Illness Is Metaphor," about the history of consumptives who sought European-style nature cures in the pure New Mexico mountains. The poets will break your heart with their struggles, from pills and booze to blood and the religious ecstatic. Elissa Schappell argues that this country wants to shift back to a fantasia *Happy Days* '50s, while Peter Crabapple's photos document rural Vermont reenactors portraying German and Soviet troops on the Eastern Front during World War II. Hardly innocent or pure, the subjects are transported back to a state of intense clear feeling, theirs and also not quite their own, and just for a moment. Yet, sometimes that is enough. We hope that while reading this issue you have more than a few moments of true feeling. Or maybe one pure, bright moment of clarity that makes you forget all of the darkness.

CONTENTS

ISSUE #71 / REHAB

Fiction

Jennifer Tseng

To Drink from the Lion's Mouth ⁘ *Tabitha came home from kindergarten and demanded to know what "passive-aggressive" meant.* 12

Aimee Bender

The First Wife ⁘ *Shortly after we were married, my husband gave me a ring of keys to the castle.* 56

Rita Bullwinkel

Decor ⁘ *There was a period of my life in which my primary source of income came from being a piece of furniture.* 113

Ariel Djanikian

A Spot in the Pinewood ⁘ *My sister was born when I was three years old. I don't remember life before her, which is my loss.* 162

J. P. Gritton

Wyoming ⁘ *I'll tell you what happened and then you can go ahead and decide.* 174

Poetry

Kaveh Akbar

AGAINST DYING 24
AGAINST HELL 26
EVERY DRUNK WANTS TO DIE SOBER
IT'S HOW WE BEAT THE GAME 28

Jerry Williams

MY LITTLE PROBLEM 68

Peter LaBerge

RELIQUARY (AUGUST) 83
APHELION 85

Marie Howe

FRAGMENT: HOLY SATURDAY 95
MAGDALENE: AT THE GRAVE 96

Dorothea Lasky

GHOST FLIGHT TO THE MOON 128
THE DREAM 130
WINTER PLUMS 133

Brandon Courtney

LAZARETTO 169
AFTERWORLD 173

Leila Chatti

SARCOMA 207

Nonfiction

Leslie Jamison

CONFESSIONS OF AN UNREDEEMED FAN - *Her fans loved her as long as she broke down so they could watch.* 29

Alyssa Knickerbocker

X-Men + *I wasn't supposed to be having a baby. I was supposed to be writing a novel.* 45

Meehan Crist

Methods + *I have begun to think that the human head is not the safest place to house the human brain.* 69

Amy Bloom

The Car Wash of the Dead + *Not every dead person goes through the car wash. Not everyone needs to.* 89

Peter Crabtree

On the Eastern Front + *Mary Ruefle introduces these haunting portraits of World War II reenactors.* 139

Kara Thompson

Injury and Invitation + *Once disability becomes a time-sequenced narrative, one tends to sentimentalize it.* 150

Jenn Shapland

Illness Is Metaphor + *I moved to New Mexico in June 2016 with my partner, and at the time I didn't think of it as a cure outright.* 194

Relapse

Elissa Schappell

Fifties 41

Sarah Manguso

Karaoke 86

Benjamin Percy

Last Breath 136

Michael W. Clune

Not in the Eyes! 191

Lost & Found

Adam Wilson

On John Berryman's *Recovery* - *Berryman has little interest in the highs and lows of the drinking life, or even the anguish of detox.* 98

Micah Perks

On Mary Rowlandson's *A Narrative of the Captivity and Restoration of Mrs. Mary Rowlandson* - *This is the story of your fierce voice, the one that reaches out over three hundred years with that slap upside the head.* 101

Laura Bogart

On Keri Hulme's *The Bone People* - *Hulme's work is a remarkable immersion into the hellscape of rage and shame inside the batterer's mind.* 105

Alix Ohlin

On Barbara Trapido's *Brother of the More Famous Jack* - *Trapido's sentences are both intensely pleasurable to read and are about pleasure of many kinds: sexual, intellectual, aesthetic.* 107

Santi Elijah Holley

On Leonard Michaels's *A Cat* - *What were these sentimental musings, these schmaltzy witticisms? What was with the accompanying doodle-like line drawings?* 110

Readable Feast

Jenni Ferrari-Adler

Hospital Food - *Isn't it nice when someone brings you breakfast in bed?* 208

The Last Word

Peter Orner

Reading Gordon Bowker's Biography of Joyce - *Joyce accompanied his daughter, Lucia, to her first appointment with Carl Jung.* 213

FICTION

To Drink from the Lion's Mouth

Jennifer Tseng

Tabitha came home from kindergarten bursting, as always, with suitable non sequiturs and demanded to know what "passive-aggressive" meant. I laughed and thought, *Why don't you ask Daddy, that's his department?*, but I said, "Where'd you hear that?" "Mrs. Lockwood told me I was being passive-aggressive at circle time." "Mrs. Lockwood's an idiot. You're five. How's that supposed to help you?" She shrugged then lurched toward me. "First she said I was being passive-aggressive, then she asked if I knew what it meant and I said yes because I didn't want her to know I didn't know. So can you tell me?"

Her cheeks were pink with agitation and unbelievably full. Much of the fat from my thighs, tummy, and rear had been transferred to her cheeks via my nipples—the closest thing to a Catholic miracle I've seen in my lifetime. Over the course of four years, while I lay passively on the bed, a child lay next to me, aggressively shaping us.

"First, tell me what happened." I was trying to buy time. It seemed passive-aggressive to give her examples like "You know how Daddy always says he doesn't mind giving us a ride and then he yells at us in the car?" or "Have you noticed every time Grandma takes us out to dinner, she forgets her wallet?" I could have used myself as an example, the way sometimes, at the end of the night, I did the dishes, but angrily. Without knowing what Tabitha had done, I felt exposed, uneasy at the thought that she may have learned whatever it was from me.

My own mother is aggressive, always yelling at strangers who are in her way or insisting to see the manager at restaurants and stores, while my father is so passive the silence between us threatens to become eternal if I don't speak. To punish him, Ma calls him P-A-P-A, spelling it out like the BE AGGRESSIVE cheer.

JENNIFER TSENG

"What did I do wrong?" Tabitha whimpered. She was getting hungry.

"Probably nothing." I sighed and handed her a granola bar. I knelt down; I held her miraculous cheeks.

Before Tabitha was born, I worked as a tailor in a shop, doing alterations mostly. On occasion I helped the owner, Ms. von Almassy, sew costumes for local productions. When I quit, people told me I should set up a home business while I still had the clientele. Do it now, before everyone forgets you, they said. But not one of those people had ever tried sewing a button on a shirt, much less altering an expensive antique wedding dress on a deadline, with Tabitha in their arms.

Tabitha preferred a clean, open lap; she fussed when I tried to do other things. She was like one of those cats that sits on the newspaper you're reading. But she was a marvelous baby, a happy baby. Because I held her all the time, she almost never cried. When I was pregnant, I read that for centuries Native American women wore their babies everywhere—in the woods, in the fields, while they were cooking or sewing. The babies could drink milk whenever they needed to, so they didn't cry. The women just kept going. I liked the way that sounded. I tried it and it worked, though I wasn't quite as adept as the Indians at the keeping going part.

> **Men were out of the question. His rule was simple: "No one with a penis."**

My husband didn't allow anyone but me to babysit her. "How about Miranda?" I would say. Miranda is his best friend from high school.

"I don't trust Miranda."

"You don't trust Miranda?! How can you not trust Miranda?"

"It's pretty easy."

"What about Aunt Lilly?" His aunt Lilly teaches kids with special needs.

"I don't trust her either."

Men were out of the question. His rule was simple: "No one with a penis." If I suggested someone indisputably trustworthy and penis-less, like his mother, he would say, "I don't think Tabitha is quite old enough for a babysitter." He would go on artfully making his pressed sandwich or rolling his organic cigarette or opening his craft beer while he refused me, not once sitting down or taking off his glasses or even slightly furrowing his brow to give the appearance of considering my suggestions. If he had simply said, "You are the only person in the world I trust with our child," I may have been more inclined to embrace the privilege he'd granted me.

Shakespeare wrote, "It is a wise father that knows his own child." (Ms. von Almassy and I once sewed costumes for *The Merchant of Venice*.) Perhaps it was wise of my husband to forbid a babysitter. As I've mentioned, Tabitha was a happy baby. She wanted to be with me. Most young children prefer the company of their parents.

But do they? I never wanted to be around mine. It always surprises me when Tabitha says, "I want to stay home with you, Mama." It is both touching and unfathomable to me. Shouldn't she, on some deep biological level, want to escape me and all my neuroses?

> I always dreamed of having a little girl but I never imagined the father being there.

I always dreamed of having a little girl but I never imagined the father being there, a man who was equally responsible for her and who disagreed with everything I said. I also dreamed of sewing my imagined daughter's clothes. I never dreamed we would live in a world where there's a surplus of clothing made by low-paid factory workers under horrible conditions, a world in which cotton is typically grown with pesticides. I try not to perpetuate the problem; I avoid buying new fabric and sweatshop-manufactured clothes. I do, however, make clothing and quilts for charity out of remnants left over from my shop days. For inexplicable, likely passive-aggressive reasons, I enjoy sewing dresses for strangers in need, using my last yards of silk, my best buttons and trim, dresses for women whose faces I'll never see and blankets for babies whose cries I'll never hear. I can't pray, but I can sew. Somewhere there's a woman who can do both, but it isn't me.

Now that Tabitha's in school, I should do something with my time but obviously sewing clothes is not the answer. Ms. von Almassy's shop closed two years ago; I'm fairly certain our clientele has forgotten me and I can't say I want to be remembered. What does one do with a bachelor's degree in psychology in the twenty-first century, I wonder?

My husband earns a good salary working a job he says he hates. I don't envy him that. Selling real estate requires he exploit his capacity to be like my mother: a master of aggressive social interactions that verge on spectacle. He once sold a house to a couple—close friends of mine—who had come to our home for dinner. Before we sat to down to eat whatever mediocre meal I had prepared (though my husband was a supertaster, he reserved his cooking skills for his own lunches, doomed to subsist on my ordinary dinners) he convinced them to drive over with him to see the property, which had a stunning view of the city at night. By the time we were eating our store-bought cake, the papers had been signed. Another wife might have been proud of her husband's agility, but I found it embarrassing, sexually unappetizing even; it struck me as somehow promiscuous. There's no nice way to say that to a person. The thought of climbing into bed with a man like that.

When I was a child, we couldn't afford family vacations, but my father liked to eat dinners out. Often, just as my mother was tying her apron on, after she'd arranged all her ingredients on the kitchen counter, he would say softly, sweetly—he too was like a cat, he could charm us easily with the slightest attention—"Let's go out." My brother, Howie, and I would shriek with happiness, "Yeah! Let's go out!" We would roll around on the floor like two puppies at his feet while our mother silently hung up her apron and put the food back in the cupboard.

Then, I thought this was our father's way of giving our mother a night off, but later I wondered about her silence. She's proud of her cooking, of her reputation in the Chinese community as an excellent chef, and she generally frowns upon restaurant fare. "Greasy! Overcooked! Such small portions!" Ma is oddly more forgiving of Chinese restaurants, especially if the owner happens to be from her province. Whether because of this or to add insult to injury, our father usually chose Golden Dragon, whose owner, Mr. Lee, was from her home province of Szechwan.

As soon as we were seated, Howie and I would rip open our chopsticks and start tapping on the small cups of tea, playing along with the Chinese folk music being piped in from the back. Or we'd read aloud from the paper place mats that explained the twelve signs of the Chinese zodiac— each one's strengths and downfalls, each one's fate. Regardless of how plain or extravagant it may have been, the meal our mother had begun to prepare at home would be forgotten. She'd give the appearance of having moved on; she would chatter away in Chinese with waitstaff and patrons alike, sometimes getting up to visit another booth to greet friends.

"Tell me something special tonight!" she would command Mr. Lee loudly, in English, while Howie and I repressed our laughter. Nothing provokes her anger more than someone pointing out a mistake she has made. Our father would sit placidly, smiling the nearly imperceptible smile of a cat who will soon be fed, and wait for his wife to order in Chinese. She would order our favorite dishes and then say, unsmiling, "Wéixiào yīgè yǐn dāo de bèihòu" which translates to: "Behind the smile, a hidden knife." Of all the Chinese our mother had taught us, this was her most commonly uttered phrase.

Fridays I ate lunch with Tabitha and her class in the school cafeteria. I was afraid she'd be embarrassed to have me eating next to her at the kindergarten table. But as soon as I arrived, she'd pounce on me. The other kids were clearly impressed by, even jealous of, my presence. As if during school hours, each child existed alone, solely within the confines of the school, whereas Tabitha had proof of her own existence in the greater world, proof of being loved. She is well liked; my visits only increased her stature. Inviting your mother to lunch became the fun thing to do. Though not many mothers had the time or the interest. A couple of women tried to coordinate with me, hoping we could all eat together some Friday, but it only worked out once or twice.

One day, as I was turning to go, Tabitha wouldn't let go of my hand. She pleaded with me to stay and visit her class. On a whim, I did and was disturbed by what I discovered.

A Southerner who abandoned the South, Mrs. Lockwood seemed almost a foreigner in our northeastern midst. She retained a heavy accent and wore an air of weary hospitality, like a once splendid mansion left to ruin. Her clothes were pristine but rumpled, as if the sheer volume of fabric necessary to clothe her large body was beyond her power to control. Using karate as a theme, she devised a competitive system to measure the kindergartners' progress playing various musical instruments. They played songs of ascending difficulty in order to earn yellow belts, green belts, black belts, etc. Before entering the classroom, they were required to bow to her and for the duration of the class they were required to call her "Master." Her interest in karate may have simply been a means to an end, though I like to think she might be a practitioner.

"Master" swooned bombastically over a boy named Danny, telling the group (most of whom had brown or black hair and brown eyes), in a voice gone unsettlingly husky, that because of Danny's "bee-yoo-tee-ful" blond hair and blue eyes, he would be "a real heartbreaker" someday. She devoted the remainder of the period to forbidding the children to touch their instruments and to punishing them when they disobeyed. Mrs. Lockwood looked pleased to have me as a visitor and showed no signs of shame or hesitation in my presence. If this was how she behaved with a visitor in the classroom, who knew what she'd be up to unsupervised.

Tabitha had complained about Mrs. Lockwood since the first day of school. After my impromptu visit, I felt guilty for not taking her more seriously. I saw now that our child had been unusually kind and diplomatic when she'd explained, "I like her as a person. I just don't like her as a teacher." She never said, "I hate Mrs. Lockwood." But sometimes she said, "I wish I had Miss Calle."

If Tabitha ever needed to confide in an adult at school, she could turn to "the feelings teacher," Mary. Small groups of children take turns having lunch with Mary in her office. She uses puppets to talk to them about their feelings. Tabitha had little patience for these lunches and regularly remarked, "Who cares about puppets and their problems?"

The other kids were clearly impressed by, even jealous of, my presence.

Tabitha loves animals. Her favorite weekend outing is going to the zoo. What she likes best are the snow leopards and polar bears, their silver and white pelts so evocative of the places they came from. She's named the female snow leopard Sugar. She pities Sugar being so far from home, a visitor who can never take off her coat, who spends her days pacing the man-made habitat, dozing, waiting for the keepers to bring her next slab of meat. "Sugar really loves me," Tabitha says. "But our world isn't cold enough." Tabitha doesn't yet pity the animal population as a whole. If she could add an animal that's missing from our zoo it would be the panda. One summer, we visited the pandas in D.C. and ever since, she's been talking about how the three Chinese bears looked just like the three of us dressed for a party. Sometimes, her imagination kills me.

Despite her passion for live animals, the thing she does with the most gusto is drink from the lion-shaped drinking fountain just inside the zoo's entrance. The lion's mouth is wide open, its sharp, white teeth are bared, and in order to take a drink you must put your head between its jaws. Ma's smile and knife in reverse. Rare the knife that hides a smile, or the beast that carries within it a hidden spring. Some children are afraid to take a drink, but not Tabitha.

Almost everything sounds passive-aggressive if I think about it long enough. Whenever I went to the grocery store I'd ask my husband if he wanted anything. He'd always say, "No thanks, I don't need anything," but then he'd eat everything I'd bought for Tabitha's lunches. If you want turkey, why not just come out and say it? Why pretend? I try to consider it from another woman's point of view. Another woman might think, "Well, that's easy! I don't need to get him a thing!" But what would this theoretical woman say about waking up on Monday morning to find all the lunch meat has been eaten?

I wonder if he wasn't playing a game with me, a hidden-knife game, American style. Perhaps he was pretending to be Chinese and I was supposed to keep asking him and asking him until he finally says yes. But why would he do that?

> Tabitha claims she's had many other parents before us, in her past lives.

Ms. von Almassy once observed, "Your husband is more Chinese than you are. He's so inscrutable." By "inscrutable" I think she meant he was silent when he dropped me off and picked me up. As for the Chinese part, she never met my effervescent mother. Although I resented Ms. von Almassy's narrow thinking, it was true I did not know my own husband. He is a frozen sea I have yet to find the axe for.

My husband is superstitious. He's afraid of seeing black cats on the streets, of getting the number 666 on store receipts. He believes if you speak about something terrible you're liable to make it happen and if you speak about something good you'll prevent it from happening. To use his words, you'll jinx it. Sometimes when I told him I loved him, his face darkened. When I asked him what was wrong he said, "Saying 'I love you' implies there's a lack of love and you're saying the words to make up for it."

Under his influence, Tabitha has developed her own superstitions. If you want something, wish for its opposite. For example, say, "I hope it rains tomorrow!" if you have an important outdoor event to attend. Or "I hope Samantha can't come over!" if you really want her to. The two of them are godless supplicants in a constant state of prayer. Perhaps it was a mistake never to bring her to Mass. When it comes to cultivating a spiritual life, she's been left to fend for herself in a wilderness.

Tabitha claims she's had many other parents before us, in her past lives. Last time she was given a choice and out of all the couples in the world, she chose us to be her new parents. Maybe because she handpicked us, we are the best ones she's ever had. She's decided she wants to be with us forever.

"He's your husband," my mother says. "You should obey him, even if it hurts." Since she and my father moved to Las Vegas last year, they know very little about my life.

"You know that's sexist, right?" I can hear her scrubbing a burner plate while she cradles the landline. She always saves the burner plates for last. The steel wool, her abrasive finale.

"Male, female, doesn't matter. Husband and wife sacrifice each other."

I imagine wrapping my husband in newspaper and leaving him on an altar with a few handfuls of Joss paper on top for good luck. "I know, I know. But what if there's a knife hidden behind his smile?"

"No such a thing. We are talking about married couple."

"Ma! You think only nonmarried people hide knives behind their smiles?"

"This is not the point," she snaps. Which reminds me of something my husband said about marriage before we were married: "If you aren't going to raise a family, then what's the point?" I thought, *What the hell is that supposed to mean?* but I didn't ask.

"How's P-A-P-A?" I ask.

"Oh, he's taking swimming lesson. They have free classes for seniors! Isn't that something?"

"I thought he already knew how to swim." P-A-P-A always manages to be at a swim lesson or a tennis match when I make my weekly call.

"Las Vegas is a wonderful place. You should think about it. Everything is cheaper here. And when you get old, lots of senior discounts."

"My husband doesn't like the heat," I lie.

"This is nonsense. He can get used to it, no problem. When you're hot, you go swimming, it's very simple. Tabitha will love it! The three of you can stay at our place while you look for apartment."

I don't know how we came to this juncture in the conversation but as long as it absolves me from talking about what's really happening in my life, I'm willing to participate. "How's my granddaughter?" Ma asks her question and rinses the burner plate at the same time. I hear her turn the tap on full blast and picture the blue suds being washed away, the clean steel reflecting the three lines that appear between her eyebrows whenever she concentrates.

I think, *You're so good at whatever you do, Ma. It's such a waste.* But I say, "Her teacher told her she was being passive-aggressive."

Ma laughs a hearty laugh.

"Be serious! Tabitha? What's new?"

"I *was* being serious."

"Something is wrong with this teacher. Is she American?"

"Yes, but . . ."

"Americans have things confused. Passive-aggressive not same thing as indirect. Tabitha probably just indirect. She acts like this. Be polite, not say directly is good habit. She's good girl." Ma doesn't even ask me what Tabitha did. She doesn't care.

Tabitha never did tell me what it was she'd been scolded for. While I was pacing the kitchen, racking my brain for an appropriate explanation, she announced, "Mama, I'm hungry! I need a meal!" She took a box of macaroni and cheese off the pantry shelf and shook it like a maraca in my face—her culinary equivalent of a rain dance. She hates macaroni and cheese. She receives my attempts to feed her packaged food as insults. When her hunger reaches its apex, she shakes the box and runs around the kitchen. It is her way of telling me to cook.

I remember the morning perfectly. The day was bright. It was snowing gently, the kind of snow you can walk in ecstatically without feeling cold. I had just woken up and was watching the snow fall. I watched it pile up on the eaves, on the branches of our mysterious apple tree that blooms every year but never makes fruit. I was studying the skiffs of snow that collect in the crooks between the trunk and the branches when I noticed a faint trail of footprints leading from our house to the tree to the road. One of the prints was deeper than the rest, though it too was quickly being filled in. As the snow fell, the trail vanished. I thought of the snow leopards and polar bears at the zoo, of their hard-earned comfort on a day like this. How many months of heat had they endured to reach this arctic dream? I must have looked down or turned my head slightly because something in my peripheral vision caught my eye. It was the unusually smooth white pillowcase belonging to my husband, who usually rose an hour after I did. I knew at once that he hadn't touched it all night and that he would never touch it again.

I got up to verify my suspicion though I needn't have bothered. He and all his things were gone. There was a lavish breakfast on the table. A plate of my favorite potato pancakes seasoned with smoked Gouda and scallions, a bowl of blackberries, an herbed quiche he must have spent half the night making and that was still vaguely warm. Frantically, I paced the kitchen in search of the right way to explain his departure to Tabitha. I was tempted to invent a story, to pretend for my own sake and for hers. But I kept thinking about the proverb. I didn't want to hide the knife.

"Hi," I said when she came into the kitchen, her hair like a tumbleweed around her face. "Your father has left us," I said quietly, with sudden confidence.

"I know," she said and nodded and was silent.

We ate the meal as if it were our usual porridge. In silence, we dressed for school. But when I opened the front door, before we stepped off the porch and into the freshly fallen snow, she screamed the agonizing scream of a wild animal in a cage. "I wish you two would get divorced! I'm glad he's gone and I hope he never comes back!"

For a moment, I was chastened by her incantation. I thought of the rain dances she performed to woo the sun, her fondness for blackberries, and the one other person in the world who, on the occasion of a farewell breakfast, might think to put some in a bowl for her. But then I saw the jaws of opportunity and I was thirsty, so I stuck my head in.

"You think *you're* glad!" I screamed back. "You have no idea how happy this makes me! I thought he'd never leave!" She kicked me hard in the shin. Her eyes turned placid, inscrutable. She was the very picture of her father. I bent down to rub my leg. "That hurt," I said. "If only Mrs. Lockwood could see you now."

Tabitha smiled and the frozen sea within me cracked a little. I jumped down off the porch and she followed, snow dusting up around us as our boots hit the ground.

From some invisible, inexhaustible source, more snow fell. It drifted down like confetti through the air and landed on our hats, on the shoulders of our coats; it erased the path before us as we walked. I mentioned my lifelong dream of visiting Mongolia. Tabitha talked about Sugar, wanted to know if I'd ever noticed her eyes looked like ancient scrolls, yellow and amazing. 🜚

AGAINST DYING

if the body is just a parable
about the body if breath
is a leash to hold the mind
then staying alive should be
easier than it is most sick
things become dead things
at twenty-four my liver was
already covered in fatty
rot my mother filled a tiny
coffin with picture frames
I spent the year drinking
from test tubes weeping
wherever I went somehow
it happened wellness crept
into me like a roach nibbling
through an eardrum for
a time the half minutes
of fire in my brainstem
made me want to pull out
my spine but even those
have become bearable so
how shall I live now
in the unexpected present
I spent so long in a lover's
quarrel with my flesh

the peace seems overcautious
too-polite I say
stop being cold or *make*
that blue bluer and it does
we speak to each other
in this code where every word
means *obey* I sit under
a poplar tree with a thermos
of chamomile feeling
useless as an oath against
dying I put a sugar cube
on my tongue and
swallow it like a pill

AGAINST HELL

With sensitive enough instruments even uprooting a shrub
becomes a seismic event. So much of living is about understanding
scale—a tiny crystal dropped in a river turns the entire river

red. The hands that folded me into my body were not punishing me
nor could they ever be punished, while the hands of the idol sculptor
were cut off and tossed to the dogs. This is proof of something,

but what? Maybe that retribution has grown vulgar, with sin now
inevitable as summer sweat. Most days I try hard to act human, to breathe
like a human and speak with the same flat language, but often

my kindness is clumsy—I stop a stranger to tie his shoe and
end up kissing his knees. I believe in luck and am barely troubled
by its volatility. I remember too well the knife held to my gut, the beehive

I once spat at for hours without getting stung. The charm of this
particular dilemma: faith begins where knowing ends. The undertaker
spills his midday latte on a corpse, a chariot wheel flies off

and kills a slave, and nobody asks for a refund. The unexpected
happens, then what? The next thing. I feel most like a person when
I am forcing something to be silent, holding a rat underwater or twining

shut the jaw of a lamb before it's roast on the spit. It's only natural to smell smoke and feel hungry, to lean into the confusion of tongues. If I am to be punished for any of this, it will be thousands of years too late.

EVERY DRUNK WANTS TO DIE SOBER IT'S HOW WE BEAT THE GAME

Hazrat Ali son-in-law of the prophet was martyred by a poisoned sword
while saying his evening prayers his final words *I am successful*   I am
successful I want to carve it in my forehead I've been cut into before
it barely hurt I found my body to be hard and bloodless as
glass still for effect I tore my shirt to tourniquets   let me now be
calm for one fucking second let me be open to revision eternity looms
in the corner like a home invader saying *don't mind me I'm just here to watch you nap*
if you throw prayer beads at a ghost they will cut through him soft
as a sabre through silk   I finally have answers to the questions I taught
my mother not to ask but now she won't ask them   as a child I was so tiny
and sweet she would tuck me in saying *moosh bokhoradet* a mouse
should eat you I melted away that sweet like sugar in water like once-fresh
honey dripping down a thigh   today I lean on habit and rarely unstrap
my muzzle it's hard to speak of something so gauche as ambition
while the whole wheezing mosaic chips away but let it be known
I do hope one day to be free of this body's dry wood   if living proves
anything it's that such astonishment is possible   the kite loosed
from its string outpaces its shadow an olive tree explodes
into the sky dazzling even the night   I don't understand the words
I babble in home movies from Tehran but I assume
they were lovely I have always been a tangle of tongue and pretty
want   in Islam there are prayers to return almost anything even
prayers to return faith I have been going through book after book pushing
the sounds through my crooked teeth   I will keep making these noises
as long as deemed necessary until there is nothing left of me to forgive

CONFESSIONS OF AN UNREDEEMED FAN

Leslie Jamison

On Amy Winehouse

Amy Winehouse's last big concert was in Belgrade, a month before she died. This was June of 2011. Billed as the beginning of her comeback tour, the gig turned into one of her most infamous train wrecks: when she came on stage, she was drunk beyond the point of making sense, beyond the point of standing—tripping and crouching, sitting down to take off her shoes, leaning into her bass guitarist and holding his hand. The crowd started heckling her early and didn't let up. "Sing!" they shouted. "Sing! Sing!"

Her eyes were as large as a child's, as if she'd been dropped into a life she had no idea how to live. Her life had been unmanageable for years. But the thing was, she had all this management: a promoter, a producer, a father. She was asleep when they put her on the plane to Serbia. She slept for the whole flight, woke up to her own life, and heard: *Sing!* Her fans loved her as long as she gave them what they needed—as long as she broke down so they could watch, as long as she picked herself back up again so she could give them her

voice. Her backup guys in their orange suits didn't know what to do with her.

The footage of Belgrade is nearly impossible to believe, but there it is, happening over and over again, as many times as you want to click the YouTube refresh button. Amy stumbles along in her tiny yellow dress with ragged stripes of black, a bruised banana. When she falls off an amp, her drummer's smile stretches into something more like a grimace. Is this an *oh-those-self-destructive-music-legends-how-they-fuck-up* moment or an *actually-this-woman-is-basically-committing-suicide-right-in-front-of-you* moment? He isn't sure what face to make. The public didn't know what face to make for years. "She's shit-faced," says a voice on the YouTube video. "She doesn't know where she is." And then: "Look at her. Look at her." At a certain point, her face changes. She's not confused anymore, or scared. She's smirking. Her smirk seems to say, *I'm done with this.* She throws the mic. Someone hands her another. One voice cries out: "Sing or give me my money back!"

She finally does sing, her voice barely audible above her music—above the song she'd written to turn her heartbreak into something beautiful, something profitable, *your love goes and my love grows*, the music that had turned her into a tabloid sensation it never seemed like she wanted to be. At a certain point, her voice is no longer audible

> The public loved to see Amy fucking up. They loved to hate her, loved to judge her, loved to feel bad for her.

above the noise of the crowd, the sounds of their frustration and desire, their voices reminding her of the words to her own song.

• • •

The public loved to see Amy fucking up. They loved to hate her, loved to judge her, loved to feel bad for her. They loved to *relate* to her, whatever the terms of that relation, because it brought them closer to her, and what they wanted most was access. The public loved to watch her falling apart. The darkness inside her was always spilling out. They got more of it than they wanted: She couldn't sing for them in Belgrade. She couldn't stay alive for them in London.

At a concert on the Isle of Wight, where she slurred her mumbled words behind a wheel bearing the title *HMS Winehouse*, she sang "Rehab," her unrepentant rallying cry, and drank from a plastic cup of wine held close to her mouth. She had to choose between drinking and singing—moment by moment, on a physical, literal level: she couldn't do both at once. She was already drunk. At the end of the song, she threw the cup and an arc of booze sprayed across the stage, streaking it like paint. *No, no, no*, she sang. She wouldn't go to rehab. Instead, she was doing this.

There are thousands of comments on her YouTube clips, full of taffy strands of pity: *It's really sad to see a human being like this.* Or else harsh strokes of judgment: *She is the definition of trash, nice voice or not! She is a disgrace to music and all the hard-working musicians around the globe.* Fifty years after the emergence of Morton Jellinek's disease model of alcoholism, people are still trying to figure out if it's a sickness or a sin: *Addiction = retardation . . . the crowd was right to boo her . . . So many people dream of being a Singer and being on stage and Amy just threw it all away.*

Someone else: *I see someone with a broken heart.*

After Belgrade, one newscaster wondered: "Why do they keep putting her on stage? Surely they know she has a problem." Another said: "This was supposed to be a comeback. And she TOTALLY. BLEW. IT."

Something about her addiction made people angry. But that anger wasn't simple. The woman who wrote, *Amy just threw it all away,* had a story of her own: *As for accidentally OD'ing that's bullshit. My dad didn't have a fucking accident when he overdosed on heroin . . . Me and my brothers just stood and watched as the paramedics revived him.*

Someone else just had a question: *Does she want to go back to rehab now ;P*

• • •

The soap opera version of the story went something like this: Amy's drinking got out of control after a breakup with Blake,

> It was unending, our collective fascination with the self-inflicted weakness of a beautiful woman.

her no-good junkie boyfriend, and then her friends tried to make her go to rehab. She said, *no, no, no,* and then she wrote an album that blew up, fueled by the anthem of her refusal to get better. Her career went through the stratosphere and Blake fought to get her back. They were madly in love. They got married in Miami, and hugely addicted to crack back home in London. At the peak of her use, she was spending £16,000 a week on hard drugs.

After Amy almost overdosed, her friends and family staged an intervention at a Four Seasons in Hampshire. The doctor said if she had another seizure, she'd die. But she went on her US tour anyway. She and Blake kept doing drugs together till he went to prison. She won five Grammys but she wasn't allowed to attend the ceremony because of all the drugs. In her acceptance speech—delivered at a club in London, where she was watching from afar—she said: "For my Blake, my Blake incarcerated."

A YouTube video from six months after Blake's incarceration shows Amy high on crack, playing with a bunch of newborn mice. Watching it is like falling into someone else's terrible dream. "This one has a message for Blake," Amy says, holding one of the wriggling furless mice on her finger. She gives us a squeaky mouse-voice, pleading: "Blake, please don't divorce me." The mouse-voice says: "I'm only a day old but I know what love is."

Even after Amy finally stopped the hard drugs, she kept drinking. She and Blake got divorced, mouse pleas notwithstanding. She kept drinking, and kept singing, but never made another record. She stopped drinking, kept drinking, stopped drinking, kept drinking—until her body finally just gave up. When she died, her blood alcohol content was over .4 percent, five times the legal limit for drunk driving. The coroner ruled it "death by misadventure."

. . .

The paparazzi loved Amy. They couldn't get enough of her. They loved her beauty. They loved its blemishing even more. They didn't just want her beehive hair; they wanted it ratty. They didn't just want her eyeliner cat's-eyes; they wanted them smeared. Their photos tried to zoom in on her cuts and bruises; the damage from her crack binges and booze benders. Little wounds were like openings in the tent flaps of her privacy. The camera got close on her wet flesh as if it were trying to get inside the wounds themselves, the closest thing to fucking that a camera could manage. The paparazzi wanted to get right into her bloodstream.

Amy once said to her husband: *I want to feel what you feel.* And that's what the public wanted from her—to know what she felt, to get under her skin. But also they wanted to jump away again, hide under the safe cover of irony: *What crawled into her*

hair and died there? one comedian wanted to know. *She looks like a campaign poster for neglected horses.* Her broke-down addict self was irritating. It was *so fucking sad.* OMG, it was funny.

Her addiction kept delivering physical evidence of her vulnerability, her bruises and her gashes and her emaciated body, and comedians kept delivering jokes so everyone could metabolize the horror of what was happening, like a five-year-long video of someone slowly dying in public. One paparazzi photographer took a photo of her getting into a car and started snapping shots closer and closer on her crotch, then posted these photos as proof that she was wearing diapers—that she'd started wearing them because she couldn't control her bodily functions. It was unending, our collective fascination with the self-inflicted weakness of a beautiful woman.

Why were we obsessed with her anti-rehab anthem? It's a great song, straight-up and flat-out, jaunty and sublime, Amy's singular voice all acrobatic and vaulting and rich, like vinyl and leather; the chorus blunt and surprising, full of defiance where you might expect to find the keeling croon of self-pity. The song finds hope and energy in its own rhythms. It's not interested in self-care. The *no, no, no* of refusing rehab echoes another kind of assertion: *Yes I been black, but when I come back, you'll know, know, know.* No turns into *know*: resistance becomes knowledge. This isn't just refusal; it's a declaration of presence.

The unrepentant junkie had been a beloved figure for a long time, an unleashed alternative to the good little sober boy. William Burroughs's 1953 cult classic, *Junkie*, was subtitled *Confessions of an Unredeemed Drug Addict*. It offered an appealing antidote to the bow-tied conversion narrative.

During the same decade, just as federal legislation against "narcotic addicts" was growing more draconian—mandating minimum sentences and constructing the addict as villain—people created another vision of the addict in stark opposition to these moralizing measures: someone who wasn't apologizing for anything, who was spinning something defiant or even beautiful from the darkness of their compulsion. Elizabeth Hardwick loved to imagine that Billie Holiday faced the wreckage of her life with unrepentant grandeur. She admired Holiday's "luminous self-destruction," and her refusal to play nice: "there did not seem to be any pleading need to quit, to modify." But that was its own myth; Holiday tried to kick her habit many times.

Perhaps with Amy, decades later, it was liberating to see someone who didn't want to get better; who seemed to say, *Fuck it, let's DRINK. Let's roll the foil and smoke.* If Amy was an unredeemed addict, then "Rehab" was her battle cry: She sang it over and over and over again. She sang it and stumbled; she sang it and drank; she sang it and spilled her wine. She tripped over her skyscraper heels. "I'm not gonna spend ten weeks," she sang. "Have everyone think I'm on the mend."

It was exciting to hear her resist the solace of mending and its easy answers, to hear her reject gift-wrapped redemption, refuse to give it to us—the public act of recuperating pain by performing its transcendence. She refused to get better.

But maybe "unrepentant" wasn't an alternative to the fantasy of conversion so much as another flavor of fantasy. Maybe *fuck it* was a fantasy. Maybe our collective vision of her alchemy—ache altered into chorus—depended on a myth that wasn't quite true. As the poet John Berryman put it, even *he* had to fight the "delusion that my art depended on my drinking." That delusion was what he had to break, he felt, if he ever wanted to get sober.

Amy launched her career on refusing rehab, but she actually went to rehab four times. On a home video from her first stint at an island rehab mansion called the Causeway Retreat, Blake taunts her to sing a revised version of "Rehab." Can she still sing, *no, no, no,* now that she's actually in treatment? Will she have to sing, *yes?*

But she doesn't seem particularly drawn to the joke. She tells him: "I don't mind it here, actually."

• • •

Amy Winehouse was born in London in September of 1983, three months after I was born across an ocean. When she was twenty-seven, she died from too much booze in her blood. When I was twenty-seven, I gave up booze entirely. Maybe these correspondences are part of the reason I grew so obsessed with her life, and with the possibility of what her life might have looked like sober. Or maybe these correspondences are just the little pieces of her I'd like to claim for myself. People love claiming little pieces of Amy for themselves: "Everyone wanted a piece of her," said her friend Nick, her first manager.

By the time I found myself wanting a piece of Amy, in memoriam, I'd been sober for years. But I could still remember what it had felt like to be unsober—gloriously, unapologetically unsober: drinking whiskey by a bonfire, feeling the sluice of heat down my throat, its rhyme with the flames at my fingertips. I remembered how drinking felt like constant apology; how a blackout could drop inside your life like hostile terrain, behind enemy lines, and how getting drunk also felt absolutely necessary, the only horizon of relief—like the perspective point in a painting, the crucial pivot everything else referred to. I remembered how the prospect of sobriety seemed like unrelenting gray, after luminous, disjunctive nights— a bleak horizon, a shirt washed so many times it had lost all its color. What could the straight line of *on the mend* hold that might rival the dark, sparkling sweep of falling apart?

• • •

When I imagined sobriety, before I got sober, I imagined *The Shining*: Jack Nicholson playing a writer white-knuckling his way through bitter sobriety in an empty mountain resort—the opposite of rehab, solitary confinement instead of company—or else a rehab full of ghosts. He spent his days punching a single sentence into his typewriter, over and over: *All work and no play makes Jack a dull boy.*

On the night she won five Grammys, Amy told one of her best friends: "Jules, this is so boring without drugs."

Part of me wants to tell her: *You were wrong. It wasn't boring without drugs. You just needed to learn how to live sober.* Part of me wants to tell her about church basements and evening coffee dates in diners, about the primal thrill of sitting across from someone who has felt some version of what you've felt—the fear of boredom, the urge to flee pain, or dissolve self, or *permit* self— and hear them say it out loud, how liberating that feels, in recovery, resonance not as easy moral or redemption but as a sense of outward possibility, drawing a door on something that looked like a wall.

That is part of me. Another part of me knows I'm drawn to watching her destroy herself. In one short story about an alcoholic going to rehab, Raymond Carver writes: "Part of me wanted help. But there was another part."

This was the other part: drugs and booze were part of why Amy's life was so *interesting*, to me and to everyone. They

Amy launched her career on refusing rehab, but she actually went to rehab four times.

were part of why we wanted to keep getting closer, wanted to bring our magnifying glasses and our microscopes, our telephoto lenses, to give ourselves a better view of her heartbreak.

Even the title of Asif Kapadia's 2015 documentary about her life confesses our collective desire for proximity: just *Amy*. As if we all knew her; or could still *get* to know her, even after she was dead, maybe because she had died. As if she were still available to us; as if she had ever been.

Amy. It's ridiculous I call her that. But I find it hard to call her anything else. The film summons the fantasy of intimacy but also ironizes it. It's full of paparazzi shouting: "Amy! Amy! Amy!" like the chorus to another song.

Off their tongues, in their mouths, her first name doesn't summon intimacy but its distortion; not private relation but its violation. "Cheer up, Amy!" one tabloid guy calls out, after she shoves a few of his colleagues out of the way. Then a year later, when her body is being carried out of her Camden mansion, a voice says, "Rest in peace, Amy," a perfect stranger, still on a first-name basis.

· · ·

Every story about a dead girl needs a villain, and *Amy* dangles a few suspects: Maybe her promoter killed her by keeping the machinery of her fame running even when her body was getting crushed by it. Maybe her father killed her by not giving her the love she needed when she was young. Maybe her husband killed her by giving her the thing that numbed the pain her father had already caused, and by causing even more pain that needed numbing.

The film offers Amy as victim-addict and Blake as villain-addict: the woman who got sucked into crack; the man who dragged her into its thrall. We don't have to reconcile these types: addict as victim; addict as villain. We're allowed to project them across two conveniently discrete human bodies.

When the documentary shows Blake coming back into Amy's life, after her album about their breakup made her a star, it visually frames his return as a literal emergence from darkness: he materializes from a dark doorway across a series of paparazzi shots. He's like a demon, ready to take her back: *Back to Black*. A doctor who consulted with both of them said: "It was a common case of one person having a situation that was very beneficial to his using . . . not wanting the other person to get better for fear of losing the gravy train."

Of Amy, the doctor said simply: "She was a very vulnerable woman."

Amy's addiction meant she was vulnerable, while Blake's addiction meant he preyed on someone vulnerable. Amy needed to be protected; Blake needed to be protected *from*. But Blake needed crack

> Celebrity was an ally to Amy's addiction, and an enemy to her art.

for reasons of his own: "It literally eradicates any kind of negative feeling," he said once. This was a man who had tried to slit his wrists as a boy, at the age of nine. Was that not vulnerability as well?

. . .

Really the film's greatest villain is celebrity itself: *we* killed her. Celebrity was an ally to Amy's addiction, and an enemy to her art. It kept her in gigs rather than in the studio. Kapadia's documentary has an uneasy relationship to the paparazzi it documents. They are its villains—all menace and flash, shutters like staccato gunfire—but also its collaborators. The film is built largely from their footage. At one point we see Amy closing a curtain; gazing out her window warily, protecting herself from view. But we can only witness that violation because the violation gave us a record of her resistance.

The film critiques the paparazzi's hunger for access, but also raises the stakes on this hunger—effectively, implicitly—by promising to take us deeper inside Amy's wounds than the paparazzi ever did. By showing the harsh glare and invasive constancy of paparazzi as *one kind* of access, heartless and shallow, the film invites us to think of its exploration as another kind of access entirely, full of depth and compassion. We want to feel better about our hunger, but it's still hunger: We're still after her, still sniffing the trail of her blood. We still just want *in*.

Or I should say: I wanted in. I'm not pleased or proud—but there it was, that

desire. Winehouse's life was gone, *Amy's* life was gone, and that only made me want to get deeper inside what her life had been. My own drunk life was gone and sometimes I wanted to get back inside it, too. Sometimes I didn't feel done with it. When I saw ten empty champagne flutes in front of her on a tabletop in St. Lucia, I felt sad for her, and I felt shame—shame at my own desire for proximity—and I also felt thirsty. Even the empty vodka bottles cluttering her home; all of it made me remember that old *fuck it* feeling. She'd followed it somewhere else.

When I watched the public obsession on film, an endless fuel driving the celebrity that killed her, their eager hands buying the magazines the paparazzi peppered with their eager angles, I hated that public. I also knew I was part of it. The fact of the film itself was almost sickening: we had outlived her, and we were still obsessed with her.

At one point, the film gives us the photo collage of a bender, after Amy's first stint in rehab: her face darkened by smeared mascara, Blake's whole face covered in streaks of blood; his arms in bandages, holding his cigarettes; her ballet flats covered in splotches of red. He'd cut himself with a bottle and she had to do it, too, because she wanted to feel whatever he felt, and we want to see the blood on her, so we can feel what she felt, too, or convince ourselves we've gotten close.

The film describes the bathroom at her recording studio after she'd covered it with her own vomit; the white towels darkened by mascara where she'd wiped her face. The film narrates these details while showing a video of Amy playing guitar in the studio: she is binging on booze and purging beauty, still metabolizing the pain, still turning it into song.

It was uncomfortable to watch the film because it was exposing a fixation and exploiting it at once. I cried when I watched it, and I wanted it to end. Then I wanted to watch it from the beginning, so I could cry again. I watched the end of the film at least twenty times, the haunting piano composition that plays as her corpse is carried from her house to a private ambulance in the street, as a doctor's voice speculates that years of starving and purging and drinking "just made her heart stop." I watched mourners gathering awkwardly in the street, after her funeral service: a man in a kippah standing with his head bowed in grief, one hand to his face; her mother using a cane to get into her car. I thought: *Who filmed this private grief?* I thought: *Who am I, watching it?*

"I died a hundred times," Amy sings in one of her torch songs, and I kept hitting rewind—to watch her die again.

• • •

"This isn't Amy," her mother said in 2007. "It's as if her whole life's turned into a stage performance." Amy always had a sense of humor about the dark silhouette she cast, the ways in which she had become an archetype. When the *Guardian* asked, "What keeps you awake at night?" She said:

"Being sober." She was self-aware about her "issues" and their public performance. "What is your most unappealing habit?" she was asked once. She said: "Being an abusive drunk."

She seemed to get a kick out of performing a kind of ironized self-destruction, spelling Blake's name on her stomach with a shard of glass while Terry Richardson snapped photographs. She called it "chickenscratch on her tummy," but it wasn't just performance. She'd really cut herself for years. Her arms were covered with scars.

Mos Def remembers watching Amy smoke crack one night and thinking: *This is someone who is trying to disappear.* Near the end, her doctor asked her: "Do you want to die?" She said: "No, I don't want to die." Her bodyguard said she didn't want to do that final gig in Belgrade: "Can't go anywhere. Can't hide anywhere. She needed an escape." He said, "Then the drinking . . . Escape route, innit?"

• • •

When I watched Amy change across the course of the documentary, watched her body shrink across the years, I felt as if I were watching the disappearance Mos Def described her craving. She went from a voluptuous girl to an emaciated creature; from plump to skeletal. Her beehive got so huge. Her body got so tiny.

Her tiny body was part of the outsized myth, too, our collective awe at how the force of her voice—and the chaos of her feverish dysfunction—was somehow held by the slip and twigs of her body. Her *Rolling Stone* cover profile started with her size: "Alongside the world's tallest free-standing tower, one of the world's tiniest pop stars is crouched next to a garbage pail, collecting a pile of eyeliner pencils and mascara tubes between her hands." It's all there: She was tiny. She was obsessed with her own beauty. She was close to the garbage.

In that profile, she says she wanted a different kind of life: "I know I'm talented, but I wasn't put here to sing. I was put here to be a wife and a mom and look after my family." She told one newspaper she wanted to be remembered as *genuine*.

Billie Holiday may have been beloved for what Hardwick called "the sheer enormity of her vices . . . the outrageousness of them," but she had other dreams: She wanted to buy a farm in the country and take in orphans. She once tried to adopt a child in Boston, but the judge wouldn't let her because of her drug record. Hardwick loved the absence of "any pleading need to quit, to modify" in Holiday, and admired that she spoke with "cold anger" of "various cures that had been forced upon her. But Holiday wasn't entirely resistant to quitting or to cures. Her anger was directed at the particular kind of "cure" that involved arrest and incarceration, persecution at the hands of federal agents. As a black woman,

her addiction made her more vulnerable to being treated as a criminal: she spent nearly a year in a West Virginia prison, and died handcuffed to her hospital bed. She hated that *cure*, but as for the junk itself? She tried to quit over and over again. To her pianist she said: "Carl, don't you ever use this shit! It's no good for you! Stay away from it! You don't want to end up like me!"

. . .

If Amy had gone to rehab that first time, we might have never gotten *Back to Black*, but I wonder what we would have gotten instead. I would have loved to hear her sing sober. Not just two weeks sober, but three years sober, twenty years sober. "She had the complete gift," Tony Bennett once said of her. "If she had lived, I would have said, 'Life teaches you, really, how to live it; if you live long enough.'"

I never lived Amy's life and she never lived mine, but I know that when I see her on that stage in Belgrade, as if she's been air-dropped into a moment she can't possibly fathom, I think of coming out of a blackout into the strange new world of a Mexican bathroom stall, or a dirt basement, wearing handcuffs, tasting gin and citrus, or some breezeless bedroom where it was easier to let a man finish fucking me than it was to stop him.

I know that when I watch Amy stumbling across that stage in Belgrade, and

> She seemed to get a kick out of performing a kind of ironized self-destruction.

finally squatting there—still and quiet, smiling—just waiting for something to happen or something to stop happening, I feel less that I know what is happening in her and more that her eyes know something that happened in me. I feel sad she didn't get years of ordinary coffee dates and people saying, *I get that*, that she was doomed to her singularity and her vodka-thinned blood and all her drunken stumbling under the broken tower of her beehive, hair like a pagoda on her head and her body barely holding the weight—until it wasn't, until it couldn't any longer. 🔹

Fifties

We were so cocky—we thought we had kicked the 1950s.

Racism! We've got a black president living in the White House!

Sexism! We've got our first female presidential candidate!

Homophobia! We've got marriage equality!

Xenophobia! We've got passports with stamps from many nations!

Isolationism! We opposed Brexit! Team Cameron forever!

We heard the Republicans, their skinny white lips chapped from blowing on their dog whistles, but it seems the joyful noise of gay weddings, sounds of Stevie Wonder and Paul McCartney Ebony-and-Ivorying made us deaf to the music of jackboots.

Donald Trump's campaign slogan, "Make America Great Again!," was pure '50s cornball. A bellicose cri de coeur for the long-gone "Golden Age" of America, post WWII, when industry was booming, the middle class was expanding, no one knew that cigarettes killed or what was in a Twinkie, and voters gobbled up that nostalgia like fried pork rinds.

How did we not see it coming?

Elissa Schappell

Cast an eyeball at history and you'll see that championing equality across races, genders, religions, and sexualities really sticks in the craw of folks infected with the irrational belief that being born straight, white, and Christian should come with certain privileges. Like bombing and burning black churches and neighborhoods and killing people, particularly black men, they just don't like the look of, with impunity.

Hell, it was the Civil Rights Movement in the late '50s that reignited the KKK, the prospect of black equality that called the Imperial Wizards, Grand Dragons, and Exalted Cyclops out of the woods for a race war.

Looking forward, we can expect the new president's sheet to have an obscenely high thread count and the Trump Hotel monogram. Reportedly, the White House tailor is already measuring Trump's cabinet picks for their own robes.

Here is the trippiest part—how to reconcile our Cold War nostalgia terror of Communism and the Red Menace with the new terror evidenced by Trump and Putin swapping Siberian-tiger-skin friendship bracelets and Russia's role in throwing the election to Trump?

Despite Trump's embrace of the '50s, his hard-on for celebrity approval makes the chance of him blacklisting famous entertainers low. However, conservative groups, inflamed by the GOP cultural warriors, have begun monitoring universities and compiling "professor watchlists" of those teachers who are simply too liberal to be patriotic Americans.

What kills me about our relapse was all the effort put in to save and protect the planet, hoping to eke out enough time for a generation or two of grandkids and great-grandkids to live on the surface of the earth, and it was working! We were rebuilding the ozone layer! We saved the giant panda!

But let's look on the sunny side. We still have our stuffed panda, and now that it's the '50s pre-EPA we can go back to treating the earth like a trash can. Tossing unfiltered cigarette butts and Coke cans out the window of our exhaust-spewing cars and gallons of gene-altering toxic waste into our waters. Finally, we can go back to eating koala steaks.

Trump *did* promise to bring back coal. If only to hasten the deaths of poor people who are sitting on land that would make a fantastic golf course. Or maybe he means he's bringing coal back like Justin Timberlake brought sexy back?

Maybe he is secretly planning to open a new hotel/tourist attraction/ Cracker Barrel. Ride the scariest coal-car roller coaster in the world! (Those tracks are made of Chinese steel!) Test your puny strength swinging a pickax! Hawk up a gob of black phlegm and see how far you can spit it.

And because what is the point of strip-mining if there aren't strippers? Trump's "Canaries" will be working the best, tallest stripper poles in the world, huuuge poles hundred-feet-high, wearing nothing but ash.

At least in 2017 we can get a prefab Building-Bomb-Shelters-for-Dummies kit on Amazon. Whether it's Kim Jong-un drunk tweeting that Trump's hair looks like it was made in South Korea or a lover's quarrel between Donnie and Pootie, we will be ready. Our schoolchildren, in bulletproof vests and bike helmets participating in air-raid drills, being mindful not to discharge their handguns when they crawl under their desks, will be ready.

Despite the party and the vice president elect's aversion to homosexuality, we can be assured that returning to the age of gay witch-hunts is not going to affect the rights of the LGBT community much. When you look at the '50s, before there was any LGBT (just a lot of Q), you'll see there are almost no gay people. And, fingers crossed, if the Trump-Pence gay teen conversion therapy centers—which sell themselves as musical theater camps—are successful, there won't be any more need for gay rights.

The good news for women, with this "Führer Knows Best" style of Republican government, is there always a man, (a whole gang of strongmen) on hand to tell a woman what to do and how to think and behave. Ready to criticize her for not being thinner or prettier, for not smiling enough. Ready to shame her for dressing like some kind of slattern, for having sex—worst of all, enjoying sex. Strong fathers who can tell a gal when she's *actually* been raped, when she's pregnant, and whether she can or cannot have an abortion (Heck no!). Who else is going to remind girls to lock their chastity belts before school and bed and give their daddy the key, if not the GOP?

While the GOP is dangerously fetishizing the '50s, working women should relax. We are returning to the happy days of harmless *Mad Men*-style fanny patting and pussy groping. And if a gal can't stand the heat in the office kitchen, if she doesn't want to play ball, her bosses will happily show her the door.

Regardless of the era, be it the 1950s or 2017, one thing has not changed. The person with the power to hire also has the power to fire. If screaming, "You're fired!" doesn't come naturally to you, may I suggest you imitate the man who made it his catchphrase: the most powerful reality TV show host in history and our president, Donald Trump. Don't worry—it will be on TV. In the 1950s there were only three channels and in 2017 *The Apprentice* will run continuously on all three.

Whether our grim '50s flashback is a result of H-Bomb fever, doing shots of snake oil or failing to engage in the electoral process, this much is certain, if we don't resist society's backsliding, if we don't vote ourselves out of the past, the future is going to kill us.

X-MEN

Alyssa Knickerbocker

On childbirth and the death of my imagination

It is a terrible thing
To be so open: it is as if my heart
Put on a face and walked into the world.
　　　　　—SYLVIA PLATH, "Three Women"

When my son was born, I became afraid. I pushed him out onto a bath towel on the floor of our living room—screamed him out, actually, wildly kicking one leg, as if I could swim away from the pain. He emerged a deep blue-purple that turned rapidly from white to pink to red, like a flower blossoming in fast-forward. A snake of meconium slipped out of him, hot and black.

The midwife rubbed him with a towel, and I sat there naked in a widening circle of blood while he shrieked, a hoarse cry that seemed familiar even though I'd never heard it before, the way certain songs can. When I lifted him he was so small but so heavy, with his wobbliness and his human density, and something flipped. The dreamy haze of protection that had enveloped me throughout my pregnancy—the easy certainty of his galloping heartbeat on the Doppler, his small movements inside me at night, the warmth of all that extra blood rushing around

my body—burned away, leaving behind a feral, possessive panic. I smelled his head, that alcoholic, pungent, amniotic smell; I wanted to lick him; I did. The world, I suddenly understood, was ruthless and random. How arrogant I'd been, to think I'd have any kind of power to protect him.

. . .

I wasn't supposed to be having a baby. I was supposed to be writing a novel. I'd just started a two-year writing fellowship in Louisville when I got pregnant halfway on purpose, halfway not, the baby an accident we courted and feared. I didn't tell anyone at the university. I didn't want them to think what I suspected was true—that having a baby would infringe on my ability to complete a book, which was the entire point of the fellowship. I was already aware that I was an idiot, pissing away this opportunity that so many other people had wanted; I didn't need to see it reflected in their faces. I wore loose tops, made my husband drink all my drinks after I'd taken one theatrical sip. One night, at a dinner party where I slid wine after beer after bourbon his way, he got drunker than I have ever seen him before or since. "Where are you taking me!" he cried on the way home, flailing in the passenger seat, as I pulled into what was obviously our own driveway. It didn't matter. Soon, I wouldn't be able to hide it. Such a typical, ordinary,

> As crazy as I thought giving birth would be, it was crazier.

sheeplike thing to do—to make a baby instead of a book.

As crazy as I thought giving birth would be, it was crazier. Birth became the only story I wanted to tell. I threw myself into describing it, trying out different ways each time to truly capture the experience. It was like aggressively revising a short story, needing to get across some intangible feeling but not quite hitting it, trying again. I ignored visitors' cues that they did not want to hear every gory detail. If someone gently attempted to steer the conversation to another topic, I steered it back, undeterred. I needed people to understand what labor and birth felt like. That there was a stretchy, interminable period of time in which not only could I not speak, to say "I am cold" or "I need some socks," but also where words—language in its entirety, really—had been erased. There was nothing but that clean, bright pain that swelled and swelled. That animal place made me question who I was— *what* I was. I had always felt that my *self* somehow occupied my body like a figure in a tower. But at a certain point during childbirth, my rational mind—that human consciousness I'd always identified as *me*— unhooked itself and dropped away.

. . .

When we were kids, my younger brother collected X-Men comic books. This was the early '90s, before the movies, when the X-Men were still a little obscure—peripheral superheroes, in terms of pop culture. Their story line hadn't yet been smoothed out for mainstream audiences, and their world was deep, expansive, complex, often contradictory, the characters depicted different ways by different writers and artists. I never bought any of the comic books myself. I fancied myself a serious reader, and spent most of my time reading Emily Dickinson and writing Dickinson-esque poems full of dashes and capital letters and death. But I eagerly read every comic my brother brought home.

I was particularly obsessed with the female X-Men: Rogue, Jean Grey, Psylocke, and Storm. There was also Jubilee, but her immaturity and relative weakness disinterested me, even though I should have liked her the most—a young teenager like me, a girl, insecure and seeking approval. Jubilee hung out in malls, wore a pink crop top, big hoop earrings, and a yellow coat. Her superpower was a little pathetic—she could make unimpressive fireworks with her hands—which was sort of the point, I guess, that she felt lesser, in comparison to the others. Every once in a while there was some consolation story line where Jubilee got to save the day, in an anticlimactic kind of way, by distracting the villain with her mini pyrotechnics so that one of the stronger

> I was desperate to start writing again—who was I, if I was not writing?—but I tried to be patient.

mutants could finish him off. Half the time, though, she couldn't muster up anything, and her power fizzled like a defective Roman candle. *Pfaff pfaff*, went a little sparkler between her palms—a cool trick, but not much of a power.

The other female X-Men were forces to be reckoned with. In the '90s-era art by Jim Lee, they were Amazonian, like the supermodels of that decade: tall, muscular, and voluptuous, with Cindy Crawford eyes, Cindy Crawford hair, Cindy Crawford thighs. Their uniforms were shiny and metallic, their breasts like missiles. I was mesmerized by them, and spent hours studying their inked contours. Their powers were strong and lethal, and they often suffered because of them. Psylocke, my favorite, possessed a "psychic knife," depicted in the comics as a translucent pink blade that extended from her wrist, against her clenched fist, and which she used to disable and read the mind of her opponent by jamming it into the base of his skull. In one instance, she used a special helmet to amplify her telepathic powers, only to have it overload and back up on her, leaving her writhing on the floor in her skimpy pink bathrobe. Storm, when her emotions got the better of her, created weather that was too much for her to control—electrical storms that threatened to destroy her. And Jean Grey, a telepath, could float and read minds, but always seemed depleted by it. She was often drawn bent over in pain, gripping her head with her hands, overwhelmed by her own abilities.

It's interesting to me now that so many of the female characters were given powers that are essentially a literalization of empathy: extending oneself into the mind, or even body, of another. Consider Rogue, the X-Man who can "borrow" someone else's powers simply by touching him with her bare hand. The downside to this is that she absorbs personalities and memories as well—entire identities—at the expense of her own. Sometimes it's something she can control—keeping the other person's entity apart from hers, holding the two together, yet separate. Other times her power becomes too much for her. Her identity is subsumed by the other, her memories, emotions, concerns replaced with theirs. In essence, she becomes the other person.

In *The Uncanny X-Men* No. 305, Rogue removes her glove to touch the bare skin of a silent, inscrutable prisoner the X-Men have captured. She intends to absorb his personality, read his mind, understand who he is and what he wants. But as soon as she touches him, he starts to laugh, those big comic book *ha ha has* blooming out of the illustration cells, and she realizes that something has gone horribly wrong, that he is barely human, some kind of decoy sent to destroy her. He explodes. She, a mirror to him now, begins to self-destruct. She unravels, literally, like a skein of yarn. Her arms, legs, and torso unspool into ribbons as she screams.

• • •

Our son needed to be constantly held, rocked, bounced, swaddled. He chomped on my breasts until my nipples bled, until I sobbed in pain. He was colicky and screamed and spat up, waking us every hour or two, fracturing our sleep, our thoughts. We blasted white noise and passed him back and forth, zombies, in love and shattered.

I was desperate to start writing again—who was I, if I was not writing?—but I tried to be patient. I e-mailed my adviser from grad school, a writer and mother herself, who had warned me against having a baby, whom I had ignored. She wrote back: *You will not be able to write in any real way but take notes on every little thing that seems like nothing right now and then someday you will look back and see what an interesting story it might make.* And so I took notes. So many notes! What on earth to do with all the notes?

I forget about him, that he exists. He is still so new. I wake up, and there is the white ceiling, the sunlight coming through the shutters in hot, shimmering stripes. Then I turn my head, and there he is. Oh my God.

We stand at the window, me holding him, watching the cars go by. Days since I've been outside. I put my hand on the glass, to feel if it's hot or cold, to remember what season we're in.

I was taking some other notes, too. A different kind. I had a Word document on my computer called THE BAD THINGS I IMAGINE HAPPENING. It was single-spaced and went on for pages and pages. I opened it whenever I was gripped with some vision I couldn't shake and typed it out.

I imagine waking up and finding him very still in the bassinet.

I imagine him falling from the deck of a ferry, the kind we used to take all the time in Seattle. Disappearing into the churning wake. I would jump in, but of course, I would never be able to find him.

I imagine having to kill him to spare him from a fate worse than death. Would I be able to do it, if the time came? In what situation, exactly, would I do it? How would I do it? What would be the fastest, most painless way? What if I did it and then it turned out I didn't really need to do it? What if I hesitated, did it only halfway? What would I be thinking right before I did it? Would I be thinking anything, or would some kind of nameless, wordless, desperate animal-me take over? What would I sing to him while I was doing it?

I should have been writing a novel; instead I was writing this. This is what I did with my imagination, which I had once used on a craft that pleased me, fulfilled me, before I became a mother. Maybe I just couldn't help it. Maybe it was an involuntary reflex, to burn up all of my creative energies each day in a bonfire of fear so there was nothing left to work with.

You would think that fiction would have been the perfect escape. That after a day of diapers and nursing and pacing around and around and around the same room I would have jumped at the chance to depart, mentally, and transport myself to another time and place, into another person completely, as I had always loved to do. There were plenty of instances—little scraps of time here and there—that I could have done something with, had I had the capacity. Time I spent sitting at the desk with the computer open while the baby napped in a vibrating bouncy chair in front of the running dishwasher, lulled by the rinse cycle. In the same room where I'd knelt on the floor to push out my baby, Post-its still clung to the walls, full of notes for my book. I couldn't decipher them anymore. I could barely remember why I'd wanted to write the thing, much less manage to travel back into the world of the book. I tried to call up the characters I had been so taken with just before his birth, the setting and plot that had once obsessed me, but nothing stirred. Perhaps imagination was not limitless, as I'd always thought—there was a specific amount that had been doled out to me, and I was using it up on these dark fantasies.

I wondered if what I was experiencing was normal, if all new mothers had it—the way we all had "weak pelvic floors" and leaked when we sneezed. One day I read an article in the *Washington Post* about parents who accidentally left their babies in hot cars to die, because they forgot the baby was in the car seat in the back, sleeping. I stayed up all night in the bathroom, crying until I threw up.

It happened over and over: a piece on the mothers and children of the Holocaust; a podcast about a woman, a survivor of Pol Pot's regime, taken to the Killing Fields with her two children. Every hour some atrocity, flying up out of history to remind me that the world was an open wound;

turning me into each mother, my own son into each baby. Even though it wasn't happening to me, right this moment, it was happening to *someone*; it had happened and would happen. I had always known this, of course, but now I understood it. I felt it in my body—what had once been a sort of empathetic concern that I could turn on and off, or at least push away for a while, had become an inescapable physical state.

I tried to erase these visions, to instead think up a short story or two, or a new chapter, but the visions grew back, swift and invasive. I Googled "postpartum depression." *Excessive crying*, perhaps, applied to me, but one symptom from a long list didn't seem like enough. I was not hopeless, numb, angry, guilty. I did not feel "disconnected" from my baby. My baby was a gorgeous little tyrant, with his satin skin and milk breath, his eyes locked on mine, his small hands on my face—he was perfect, intoxicating. All of this was a shadow to the sunlight of my love for him. What I was experiencing was not described in any pamphlet. *Excess of empathy* was not a bullet point on the Mayo Clinic web page, nor was *Feels like every mother who ever lived*.

I'd thought my main writing challenge would be prioritizing it. I had heard so many cautionary tales from women who let the baby become the main thing, let motherhood take over. (*Let it*. We use that phrase, implying that these women were

> Perhaps imagination was not limitless, as I'd always thought.

weak or not vigilant, that they forgetfully left a door open and allowed something in, something that filled up every room in the house, every room in your heart, all the room in your head.) I could no longer shapeshift into the narrator of my novel, but I effortlessly became every parent in every news article. I didn't write, but I added to my list of horrible things.

I imagine someone (who?) putting him into the washing machine, closing the lid, turning it on. I would have to watch (why?).

Sometimes, now, I tell people about that list. I make it a funny story, about how crazy new parents are. Washing machine! I mean, come on, it's a little funny, that someone would spend a year dreaming up this shit instead of writing a book.

I'm embarrassed to admit it, but I thought I would be better at it than other women. I thought I knew how to protect against that loss of self: take the time you need to write; equal partnership with the father. We had those things down. My husband rushed home from work, took the baby from me, and booted me out of the house, to the coffee shop across the street, where I sat with my fingertips on the keyboard, eyes closed, listening to the Bible group meetings full of young tattooed Christians, my breasts slowly filling with milk. Here was the time, so where were the words?

Words themselves—the great bank of them I had always been able to draw from—had been swallowed up into a kind of fog. I knew they were there, but I couldn't get to them. When speaking to people, I paused a lot midsentence, trying to find that perfect word that had once been *right there*.

In one famous, long-running plot line from the original *X-Men*, Jean Grey pushes her powers to their limits by extending a telekinetic bubble around a shuttle that contains the other X-Men and carrying it to safety. In the process, she weakens herself and is exposed to deadly levels of radiation. She dies. Eventually she is resurrected, a kind of clone of herself called the Phoenix. The Phoenix mistakenly believes she is the real Jean Grey, and is more powerful than Jean Grey ever was. But when the Phoenix realizes that Jean Grey is actually dead, she goes insane, becomes the Dark Phoenix, and attempts to destroy the universe. The other X-Men are forced to kill her—this copy of a person they once loved.

My little superpower, the power of words and imagination and expression—which had once been so much a part of me that I had taken it for granted, like the taste of water or the presence of air—had blown up into something huge and uncontrollable, like the Dark Phoenix, and then reduced itself to ash.

・ ・ ・

What had happened to the writer I'd been? She had self-destructed.

The fellowship ended—the one I had hoped to use writing a novel—and all I had was a couple of chapters and a wall full of Post-its. It wasn't a total wash: I'd been a good teacher, an obsessive mother, a terrible writer. On the whole, I'd kept my head above water, just barely. We moved again. I had another shot at a fellowship: writing, teaching. The baby was one—I knew I should have already made my way out of the fog. I would focus. Buckle down.

Dutifully, I wrote. I put in the hours. I thought I could write my way back into writing, that if I just kept going I would get somewhere. But I remained unable to transport myself. I wrote bland, useless scenes, descriptions of trees, flashbacks into the misty past. There was no conflict. Nothing bad happened to anyone. The imagination—that workhorse room inside my brain—remained dark, shut down. I wondered if I had damaged it irrevocably by imagining all those horrible things—or if I was now afraid to use it again, like someone who's been bucked off a horse and broken a bone. Once, I'd written fast, driven by visions. The scenes I saw in my mind were alive, moving. Somehow, giving birth—both the physical act of it and the more intangible process of becoming a mother—had ripped that ability away.

My husband got a teaching job on an island west of Seattle, and we moved into his family's cottage on the Kitsap Peninsula. I thought about quitting writing. I thought maybe everyone had been wrong about me, that I should face facts and pick another career. I stopped going places where I might meet new people or see old friends. I dreaded the question *What do you do?* I didn't want to have to reply, *Nothing*. I didn't want to have to admit that I'd been devoured by motherhood. Worse, I didn't want some well-meaning friend to tell people I was a writer. I had almost been one, once. But I wasn't anymore.

I didn't stop putting words down, but I didn't consider it *writing*. I wasn't making anything I could use. It was just to stay afloat.

One day my son, age two, left a sippy cup of water upside down on top of my closed laptop and it sat there all night, slowly draining into the motherboard. I didn't even try to figure out how much writing was gone—didn't check to see what was backed up and what wasn't. I knew I'd lost a lot, maybe a year of work. I didn't really care.

What had happened to the writer I'd been? She had self-destructed. She was gone.

• • •

In the world of the X-Men, death is rarely permanent. Resurrection is always an option. Jean Grey, years after morphing into the Dark Phoenix and being destroyed, appears again. She's been asleep the whole time, suspended in a kind of cocoon, waiting for the right time to return.

Eventually, the excess of empathy I was suffering from started to wear off, like an old spell. I stopped crying all night on the bathroom floor. I started sleeping. I grew a skin again, that barrier between oneself and the world that is necessary for survival. Was there something I could have done to fix myself faster? I would love to say that I took action, that I had some kind of agency. But I just waited. It didn't seem as if I had any other choice. It was something beyond me, outside of my control. It was a fog; it lifted.

• • •

I throw away the old novel draft, hundreds and hundreds of pages banged out by someone who couldn't imagine anything but bogeymen. It feels good and awful.

When I start writing again, it's halting, tentative. I'm afraid of what I might imagine, what I might feel. It had never occurred to me that I would someday have to be careful— that empathy could consume me, like the Dark Phoenix consuming a star, a universe, herself. It never occurred to me that the well of imagination might not be bottomless; that in fact I could burn through it like fire through oil, use it all up on horrible things, and have nothing left over for anything else.

We have friends over for dinner, and I talk about how much I dislike playing imaginary games with my kid. It surprises me, since I was an imaginative child myself and have become a writer—a person who depends on her imagination to do the work she cares about. And yet I can't stand doing it with blocks and dinosaurs and Lego minifigs.

"I just feel like I can't use up all my imagination on a war between Batman and the medieval knights," I say, and everybody laughs.

"That's crazy," my husband says. "Imagination isn't a finite resource."

"Yes it fucking is!" I yell, slamming my hand on the table, startling everyone.

Maybe it is crazy to think of imagination this way, like a well that can run dry. Either way, I guard it, miserly, doling it out to myself like water in a drought, pouring it only on the good things now.

Sometimes I still test myself, just to check—I read an essay, one that once utterly undid me; I thumb through the news, scanning for something about mothers and babies, something that will crack my heart open, immolate me. I almost want it to happen. These things horrify me, but now I can hold them at arm's length. The sensation is dulled, distant.

I told a friend recently that I was relieved, yet also sorry. Relieved because I didn't think it was possible to go on like that, feeling so much, so constantly. Sorry because, for a short time, a portal had opened up to me that was now closed. It felt like a superpower—to be able to feel so deeply, to completely dissolve the boundaries between myself and others— but it was one I couldn't contain. It was too much.

I realize that calling it a superpower sounds nuts. But to label it *postpartum depression*, if that's the other option, makes

me sad. It is such a small, clinical phrase, reducing the experience itself to something small and clinical. I can't bear it, to box it all up or think of it as something you can have or not have, like a head cold. It didn't feel like a sickness. It felt as if I could see something that nobody else could see. It felt like standing inside truth, bright and burning. It felt like being anyone, anywhere on earth; like being a time traveler, like being a god.

Does that sound insane? Maybe it will sound less insane if I say that I would never wish it on myself again. At the same time, though, I'm not sorry it happened.

· · ·

There's not really a neat way to wrap all this up except to say that my son is now five years old, that I had another baby, and it didn't happen again. This time when I went into that wordless, animal place, I knew that I would come out the other side.

He emerged in the caul: the amniotic sac still intact, which—depending on whom you ask—means he will have good luck, or be protected from drowning, or become the next Dalai Lama. The midwife tore the sac with a small hook, bursting the balloon of warm water onto my legs, and unwrapped him from his cord, which was looped once around his neck, once around his armpits. She laid him on my stomach, long and purple, and he looked up at me, his little face swollen from being shoved out into the world so roughly. It must be wild to be a baby being born—the sudden explosion of light and sound and sensation, your lungs filling with air for the very first time.

In *The Uncanny X-Men No. 305*, Rogue doesn't stay unraveled forever. She does finally recover, shocked back into her body by another mutant who has bio-electricity running through his body, not unlike an electric eel. He gives her a jolt, and the loose spools—the messy pile of her—coil back together, form back into the shape of a woman. She becomes herself again, though shattered and confused. She is more wary, now, of using her powers—more judicious about sliding off her glove again and touching someone else's skin with her bare hand, slipping into their memories and emotions and becoming them. Now she knows it can destroy her.

No. 305, along with all the others, is—as far as I know—still under my brother's bed, in a plastic sleeve, in a cardboard box. Somewhere in there, Psylocke lifts her hands to her temples, her purple hair streaming, pink butterfly wings radiating from her head as she reaches out with her mind. Jean Grey slips on Cerebro, the helmet that amplifies her telepathy, and zooms through the lives of hundreds of suffering people. Rogue pulls her glove off, extends her hand. They all grimace and writhe; they clutch their heads, stuck inside someone else's pain. On another page, Jubilee is humming, snapping bubble gum. She lounges in her pink sunglasses, making fireworks with her palms. 🛡

FICTION

The First Wife

Aimee Bender

Shortly after we were married, my husband gave me a ring of keys to the castle. It was not a real castle, of course, but a house built in the twenties in the style of one, even with small turrets that we (he) had to pay extra for a roofer to fix after a leaky rain. It was, however, architecturally stunning, though not in the way most houses are in this town, with their large glassy fish-tank modern living rooms, with their recessed lighting and matte-silver refrigerators. His was an old craftsman, dim, woodsy, dark green, cedar-scented, and filled with a surprising amount of small rooms. First, the usuals: the living room, the attendant dining room with its wrought-iron chandelier, the master bedroom with the claw-foot tub in the bathroom that he had shown me, radiant, when I'd bemoaned the broken hot water knob on mine. The series of homemade bath salts in glass jars, soaked in scents he had custom-ordered based on the flowers I liked the day we toured the botanical gardens. The guest room, furnished for out-of-town visitors, though we never did host any, but where I put most of the items that I brought with me from my old apartment, since they were so few, and so out of step with the otherwise general level of expense: one deep brown splintery bookshelf from my childhood that I still loved, a lamp from my mother, made of mauve glass in a curvy shape, that flickered, a photographic print of a man walking far in the distance in a field of tall grass given to me by my brother the year before he was born again and moved to a megachurch thousands of miles away.

But there were other rooms , too, and exploring them was like unpacking gift after gift—next to the kitchen, beside the laundry/pantry area, was a narrow door, almost half the height of a usual door, and once a person squeezed through it opened onto a small artist's room, in which my husband, knowing we both liked to spend time painting, had set up two easels facing a window looking out upon the yard, next to a small speaker of a stereo that we could program to any music we liked. He had stacked paint tubes of all colors on shelves and when he ushered me in tears of thankfulness rushed to my eyes as we lay together on the floor, which was a kind of soft vinyl, good for standing on while painting, fine for us, too. He was ugly, my husband, which is why no woman had seemed to be drawn to him yet, with his paleness and small hands, and unpleasantly feminine nose, with the odd indigo tone to his goatee, lending him a drawn-looking, shadowy air. I could see it, the unattractiveness, but I found him kind, and endlessly generous, and he was willing to undo all my student loans, and didn't care about my brittle, dispersed family, and no one had treated me as he did, as if I were I a delicate egg, a prize to be cherished. I had spent my twenties going from depressed person to depressed person, and never dining out and never really having much sex and coaxing out terribly sad stories

> I was starting to wonder just what sort of poison ran through me when I met B.

to which I tried to listen with great seriousness, and delivering what I thought were helpful pep talks, only to lose each one to the next partner and receiving, over several years, a series of almost identical e-mails about how the new person "makes me feel so alive" and "I never would've known I could feel like this" and "thank you for leading me to this new phase of my life" and so on. Partners who claimed no interest in having children now having several, another who had refused to go in a boat or even near a marina falling for a sailor, the non-traveler moving to Mozambique, all the excess circumstance falling away and revealing the mismatch of me. I was starting to wonder just what sort of poison ran through me when I met B. in the library. He found me in the romance section, searching for a new book. He did not make a joke. He told me he admired my scarf, that it brought out the sea color in my eyes, something no one had ever told me before. "But—" "The sea at night," he said. At the front desk, by all the flyers, he asked me out for that evening, and took me to a steakhouse first thing, and kissed me at my door, with grip, and authority, and told me he desired me, all of me, but waited a few more dates until I was ready for more. He was older than anyone I'd dated before, at least twenty years my senior, and yet without any personal photographs in his house, seemingly unhistoried, and he was also much more active than anyone I'd ever been with romantically, running his own tech company, with hobbies of cooking and racquetball, and a burgeoning interest in portraiture. My lease was up in a few weeks, coincidentally, and on our fifth date, he asked me to move in, to be his wife, and no one had ever asked me that either, he on a knee, three weeks into meeting him, caressing my hand at his cheek, telling me he adored me. Before we'd met, I had been checking out well-reviewed self-help audio books at the library, spending my mornings before work walking around the neighborhood with earphones in listening to so many recordings that said it might be better to do and regret later than to never do, and so I did, and such a lightness inside as I dropped my apartment key in the old rusting mail slot and wrote the landlady that she could keep her deposit. And into a house like I'd never seen, where the sconces—a word I hadn't even heard before—of twining vines were appropriate to the time period of the original building, where the doorknobs had been sourced, where the wood beneath my feet creaked in a way that made me feel like the heroine of a thick novel, and where he held my hand tight and said that all he'd ever wanted was for me to share it with him forever. We married at city hall, the only witness a florist there to renew a business license. "Bless you," she said, reaching into her pink bag, "have a rose," and he and I kissed with it nestled between us like our first most gorgeous child. My friends, uninvited, and my stepfather, who lived in Texas, were skeptical about the speed of things, and about him, too—his sometimes brusque manner on the telephone, and also his softness, his unworn and overly worn corners, his sense of slipperiness—but I told them I loved him, and I did.

He said if we were in the mood for regular sex, then we would use the master bed.

There were two other hidden doors—one tucked inside the master bathroom's bath, this one halved in height, that required actual crawling through, and needed a key, and revealed a small room with just a king-sized mattress set in the middle of the floor, where he said we could enact fantasies "if we liked." "Please," I said, and he pulled me to the mattress and said he wanted it first in the middle of the room like a raft, as he wanted us to seem to be floating, and he set the timer of a light above us so it grew hot, very hot, dry as a sauna, and a pair of inset speakers projected the sounds of waves crashing and we were about to die of dehydration but gave each other our last. After, covered in sweat, the room cooling, my head reeling, he said if we were in the mood for regular sex, then we would use the master bed, but if I wanted to be a princess or a knight or a man or a wounded soldier or a thief, or whatever, and he wanted to be what he wanted, sometimes a waiter, sometimes a killer, sometimes a very small mole (the animal, he clarified), we would go to that small room and perform it on one another. Our chamber of secrets. When, later, I bathed in the tub in mounds of gardenia bubbles and looked at the door, I smiled to myself, at our most intimate of sharings. We never spoke of it otherwise. He even programmed the speakers for door slamming when I told him, once, in a whisper, that I yearned for that, for the jarring start I felt when a door slammed, something I did remember from childhood, now a soundtrack to my pleasure.

The other door was off the guest room, and locked as well. Of a regular size. When he gave me the keys, when I first moved in, the day we married, he showed me how he had strung them on a sterling silver key chain, and he had chosen special colors for each of the keys, a rainbow collection— purple for the house key, green for the garage, red for the sex room, pink for the jewelry safe, and so on. The final key was blue, and it was the same size as the others. He pressed my hand as he showed it to me.

"Please, my love," he said. "Do not open this door. I beg of you."

"What's in it?" I let the keys fall over my hand, the colors glinting under the light of the wrought-iron chandelier, as we sat for our first meal as a married couple together. He had prepared it early in the morning, before our trip to city hall: pheasant under glass. He used actual glass bells, bought online from a specialty shop. I had laughed in disbelief when he brought me my plate with its crisped brown bird visible under the dome. Who lived like this anymore? His face glowing under my appreciation.

"It is my private space," he said in a low voice. "It is the core of my being. I don't want you to go in there."

"Okay," I said.

He looked at me long. His eyes watery, searching.

"Don't you want to know more?"

"No," I said.

"You know, I was almost married before," he said, lifting his bell. Tendrils of steam curled to the ceiling.

"I did not know."

"And she left me," he said.

I raised and lowered my glass bell, too. It clinked like crystal on the tabletop. "You've never told me. Did you love her?"

"We've only known each other a few weeks, you know," he said, not unkindly. He rested a hand on mine. "There is a lot you don't know about me. I did love her, yes."

"I will love learning," I said, clasping his hand.

"I just—I just don't want you to go in the room," he said. "The room off the guest room."

"I understand," I said.

"This is the key for it," he said, jingling the blue.

"I won't use it," I said.

The next morning, he went to work, in his finely threaded suit, with cuff links and shoes from Italy that he slipped on with a shoehorn made of hammered gold. It was the first real day of my tenancy, of my wifehood. "Enjoy the castle, my maiden, " he said, kissing me deeply. "I will be late today. There are numerous meetings." Off he went, and as I had quit my job, which I had despised, working the phones at a health insurance question and complaint line, I spent the day rearranging the master bedroom, as he had encouraged: "Make it your own," he'd urged, and I tried four different angles until I ended up putting everything back as it was originally. He had such an eye for placement. I made a watercolor of a lily in the painting room, and took a bath. I slept, then read, then slept. I found a delicious lunch in the refrigerator with my name on it and ate it at the table, and then stood over the kitchen sink and finished the last bites off the bones of the pheasant leftovers, those tiny delicate leg bones, my nibbling teeth.

When he came home, his face was lined with weariness, and I served him a winter root soup he had made at some point, I did not know when, that he had requested via text that I heat, and he complimented my warming technique, which made me laugh. Were his expectations so low? As had been mine. While we sat facing each other, sipping, his face changed, and he looked at me with a grave intensity, and his voice wavered, and he asked to see the key ring.

"My key ring?"

"Please," he said.

"You mean now?"

"Please," he said, gruff. "Now."

I went to my purse and found it. I had hardly used any of the keys at all, as I had stayed home all day.

When I brought him the ring, he took his time thumbing through all the colors, touching each one with great attention and care, until his fingers came to rest on the blue. He held that key for a long moment, staring at its glinty metallic coating, turning it over and over in his palm, and I could not attempt to describe the look on his face, not adequately. His mouth tightened, and his eyes seemed to grow sharper, boring into the key like a drill. What was so very precious about that room? I allowed myself a fleeting moment of wondering—illegal tech equipment? porn?—but really, it didn't concern me. A person is entitled to privacy.

> What was so very precious about that room?

"That lunch was delicious," I said, to lighten the mood. "When did you possibly make it?"

"I don't sleep much," he said. He looked up, eyes wide.

"Well," I said. "My goodness. Lamb kabobs? Thank you. And this soup?"

"I enjoy cooking," he said. "It relaxes me." He put down the key ring. His face softened. "Tell me about your day. Did you explore?"

"I painted a bit," I said. "I took a nap in the room with the mattress, just thinking of you."

He dabbed at his mouth with a napkin. "Oh, really?" He stood and took me by the hand, led me back inside.

He had a habit, sometimes, of pretending to be a murderer when we were in there. It was such a sacred space, our half-door room, so it did not frighten me, though it was not my favorite game. Still, I wanted him to feel free to be himself. He would want to kill me, and I would lie there and he would pretend to, chopping at my hands and feet. It seemed to arouse him, and he would still manage to attend to me; it all had a cartoony feeling more than anything, a ridiculousness, but I would have never dared laugh. After, when he was done, and I was done, and he was almost sleeping, and I felt sure he'd fully enacted what he'd needed, I'd spring up, and say, "Alive!" and he would chuckle through closed eyes and pull me to him, hold me close. During the day, at work, he began texting me about packages arriving, asking me to dress up, so sometimes I'd open the door for him in pajamas of silver silk, and other times as a nurse, or his overweight bus driver, or wearing the exact miniskirt outfit worn by the victim in the *Law & Order SVU* episode we'd watched the night before, and then he asked me to get him to dress up and so he came home as a pirate, once, which was dreamy, or I suggested that he wear his business clothes into the room, as I liked them very much, especially the shoes. "Who else do you want me to be?" he texted, but I found it difficult to say. "Just you," I wrote back. "You tell me." The anticipation was tremendous. Usually around 3:00 PM the UPS fellow would trot up the brick walkway with a package, and I would sign for it with my heart rate quickening, and open it in the sex room as a preparatory gesture and then spend the remaining hours before his arrival getting ready. I had been a theater minor in college, and it was terrific fun for me. The wigs! Pink, long and red, black curls, even bald. Desires for accents, for backstories, for women angry, women crying, women giddy, women strong. The occasional stoic man. I relished them all.

> "Who else do you want me to be?" he texted, but I found it difficult to say.

Still, despite our growing closeness, every evening, upon coming home, sitting down to a soup I had warmed and that he had made sometime in the middle of the night, he would ask me to bring him the key ring.

I grew so used to the request that one night I just brought it early to the dinner table, using it, as a little joke, instead of the usual silver napkin ring that held the linen.

"No!" he said, the minute we readied our napkins for our laps. His face grew paler. It was the most upset I'd ever seen him. "You must bring it to me when I ask, no! Hide it!"

So I hid it. I apologized several times, and he ate his soup quietly, and sipped his wine, and when he was calmer, he did ask for it and I brought it and laid it by his side. As every day, he looked at it so carefully, key after key, like reading a key book, finally lingering on the blue. He turned it over in his fingers, tapping on the ridges.

"Tell me," he said, that Saturday, after a lazy lunch and tryst, when he had the afternoon off work. "Why aren't you curious?"

"About what?" We were in the sex room, lying wrapped around each other. In the distance, the sound of slamming doors, which he had turned down but not off. Slam, slam, slam. So many angry people in the world.

"About the room off the guest room," he said.

I shrugged. "It's yours," I said. "You've given me so much. I don't need to go in there."

"But you barely know me," he said. "We've known each other just over two months now. There could be dead bodies in there for all you know!"

I turned my head to look at him. His sunken eyes. His sallow skin. That beard. The too soft nose. The way he had just pushed his body into mine and told me I was dead, that I was dying, and to please close my eyes and lie still as he came.

"I killed all my exes," I said.

He pulled himself up on an elbow.

"Slow death," I said. "Like I was killing them by listening to their stories or something. I don't know. I encouraged their weakest selves. They all perked up without me."

"What are you talking about?"

I pulled the pink satin pig mask back over my eyes. "Never mind," I said.

"Are they alive?"

"They are alive," I sighed. "Don't worry. I mean, I'm talking figuratively, okay? They were the wrong matches, right? Not like you. Nothing like you. They just all seemed kind of dead around me."

He made some kind of grunt, and grew occupied with pulling at a string hanging off the mattress. After he left the room, a little jitter picked up inside me, a worry that I'd said too much, so I stayed there for a while, listening to the slamming of those doors. First my father slammed, then my mother, then later my brother, too. No one could stay in a conversation in my family. Long ago, I told my first love that I thought of it like music after a while: voices regular, voices raised, crescendo, leading to: door! I had laughed. He had looked at me, hard. "That is a weird way of talking about something that sounds really painful," he said. He and I eventually stopped talking too, though instead with that slow petering out, when sentences trail off into nothingness, doors ajar, which quite possibly was worse.

B. was remote with me that evening, and did not want to return to the sex room the following day, even when I offered to wear the red wig and the nurse outfit, and to give him shots, real shots, which he usually enjoyed.

"I'm tired," he said, which he had never said before.

I asked him if what I had said about my exes had frightened him.

"No," he said. But he tightened his watchband, and looked out the window.

"Do you want me to go in the blue key room?"

"No," he said, turning back to me. "Please. Never go in the blue key room. Did you go?" He stared at me, then, and his face trembled a little with what looked like excitement as he asked me to please bring him the key ring, to bring it now, right now. Please! I did as told. I was so relieved to see him energized. He tore through it this time, none of that false theatrical looking at every other key like he'd never seen a key before, and just racing to the blue, but when he saw it his eyes glazed over with something deep and important I could not possibly identify. He grabbed my hand, and put the key ring back in it, and led me right to the door in the guest room. He picked the blue key off the ring and held it at the lock. He let go of my hand and let it hover there, with the key, at the lock. One push and I'd be in.

"Do not go in," he said, but his face was pleading. "That's me in there," he said. "That's the essence of me. Don't you go in there."

We stood there for a while together. What was I to do? I have been taught to respect a person's wishes.

"Why not go in?" I said. "If it's the essence of you?"

"Just don't do it," he said, beginning to cry.

I had never seen him cry before—nothing even close. "I won't," I said, alarmed, "I won't, my love," and I put down the key ring and held him, and he shook and wept in my arms.

The next week, the packages stopped. When I asked him to go into the artist's room with me, to paint with me as a way to rekindle, he said no. That he was no longer attracted to me. "I'm sorry," he said. "Desire is elusive, and I seem to have lost mine." I painted in the painting room by myself. I began to paint women with outlines as bodies, women missing heads. I taped them up in the sex room for him, decorating the walls, but he never commented. Perhaps he did not go in there at all anymore. He spent longer days at work.

After a few more weeks, he told me he had met someone else, a journalist in the publicity department; that he was so sorry, but I had to move out. That he would help me find a new apartment, and he would give me a very fine settlement in the divorce, and that he had cherished our time together.

"Why?" I asked, crying. "Why? We were so happy!"

He said the heart was not easy to track, but that she made him feel . . .

He looked away, but I saw the gratitude on his face, and we both knew the missing word.

The day I was supposed to be packing up my things, which took about five minutes, as I was not going to take any of his gifts with me, tainted as they were now with heartbreak, I took the blue key and brought it again to the door off the guest room. What else was there to do? Something had to be completed. When I turned it in the lock, the metal must've triggered a chemical reaction, because the blue color coating lit as if on fire, and the key turned a charred black. It did not warm under my fingers, though, and I saw no ash or residue. Just a black key that had once been blue. Somehow I knew right then that the room would be empty, and as I pushed open the door, hand trembling, there it was, beige carpet, white walls, simple light fixture, two outlets, just a way station for something, charged with its vacancy. The black key in my hand the only proof of a breach I had been unable and unwilling to commit. 🏮

Jerry Williams

MY LITTLE PROBLEM

Crushed up pills decorate my family tree.

Crushed up pills like gold flakes in the rivers of the Rust Belt.

Crushed up pills cure the disease of nostalgia.

The dust of crushed up pills lie thick upon a Triumph Bonneville.

Crushed up pills swoop down and christen my morning coffee.

Bring on a shovelful of crushed up pills and bodega scratch off shavings.

Crushed up pills float like plankton in a trough of holy water.

Crushed up pills erase manifestoes.

Crushed up pills speckle the parapets of the debtors' prison.

Crushed up pills blur the cut of my father's ashes.

Three of my four diplomas on crushed up pills.

The bathroom between classes imparts a pedagogy of crushed up pills.

Crushed up pills in memoriam to my Caribbean nuptials.

Crushed up pills freckle my mother's arms.

Crushed up pills leave cantankerous suicide notes.

Like cosmic microwaves harmonizing with the Milky Way, crushed up pills last forever.

Crushed up pills stick to the bleeding edge of the technology of bones.

Crushed up pills gravity assist divorce.

Crushed up pills *über alles*.

No acid in the world dissolves crushed up pills.

Crushed up pills *walk through the valley of the shadow of death* and *fear no evil*.

The point of no return prescribes crushed up pills for the twilight years.

Crushed up pills make a slurry of forgotten genitals.

Crushed up pills encrypt the senses.

Crushed up pills lock down the last breath on earth.

METHODS

Meehan Crist

A history of pain

I. THE FALL

Imagine a frog. One of those lime-green tree frogs that cling to slim branches and stare out with dinner-plate eyes. Now imagine the frog is red. Bright red, like a stop sign. Give it wings. Watch the frog let go of the branch and fly away, red legs dangling. Some experts argue that other animals can't imagine like this, piecing together information into something that does not exist. Perhaps this, they say, is what separates *us* from *them*. This and the

ability to plan for a distant future, to envision a reality that does not yet exist and make steps toward it. They say nothing, however, of a future that presents itself in spite of the plans we lay out.

I didn't see her fall. Or don't think I did. I remember a forest of evergreens silhouetted black against the moonlit sky. My breath hung in the air, white against the trees. I was eleven years old, a stork of a girl well into braces and bony knees, and a few moments before, my mother had held my

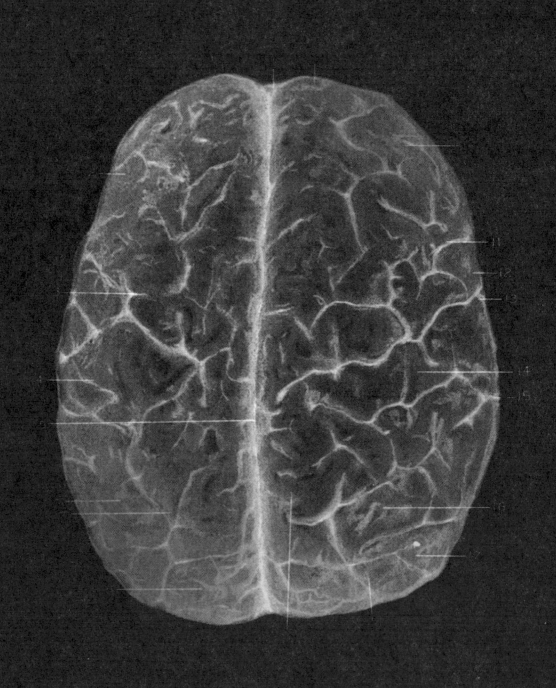

gloved hand in hers while we skated side by side. I leaned into the anchor of her grip and tested my legs; she matched her strides to mine. I let go of her hand and set off on my own. Skaters zipped by with scarves flapping and cheeks ruddy with cold. The outdoor rink, which had been erected on a frozen lake, was a tiny circus ring in the middle of a vast wilderness. The pocket of light was filled with tinkling laughter and the clean slice of metal across ice. Gradually, I lost track of my mother.

I'm not sure what happened. There was just a moment when I noticed, while gliding around the curve at one end of the rink, that skaters at the opposite end were slowing around someone lying on the ice. I drifted toward them, the skates heavy at the ends of my legs. Halfway there I saw the person on the ice was my mother.

As my father led her off the lake to sit down, she said she felt dizzy. She seemed confused and uncertain, shutting her eyes against the glare of the artificial lights. But no one called a doctor. Certainly not an ambulance. It was just a slip and a bump on the head.

I have begun to think that the human head is not the safest place to house the human brain, the organ that allows us to taste our favorite foods and wonder about the breadth of the cosmos; that fosters the euphoria of new love and sustains the ache of lost love; that enables our awareness of the body moving through space and the whole art and architecture of the self. The head perches on the pliable stem of the neck, far above the whole upright, two-legged balancing act of the body. It's prone to snapping back and forth, is exposed to falling objects, and is likely to hit the ground—or things along the way—when we have trouble with balance.

Despite its myriad powers, most of us take the brain for granted until it breaks down.

The tissue of a living brain is soft, like custard. Put a finger to it and it gives. Blast a bullet through it and it splatters. Removed fresh from the skull, a human brain will quickly succumb to the pull of its own weight, slumping out of shape like warm Jell-O. This fragile mass is protected from the outside world by only a few millimeters of skull. Anything that meets the head with enough force can be devastating: shock waves, a car windshield, concrete, ice.

Despite its myriad powers, most of us take the brain for granted until it breaks down, noticing normal function only in its absence.

Looking at family pictures taken over the holidays after she fell, I can see that my mother's face is swollen—it looks as if she might have been punched in the jaw. She doesn't look well, but it's hard to name what might be wrong. "Seasick" is the best I can do. She looks seasick. At the time, it didn't occur to me that there might be something wrong with her brain.

The living brain is a lucent pink, not the gray of those lifeless oddities floating in glass jars. Living tissue is marbled with the blue of blood vessels that wind along blushing folds of cortex like rivers along canyons. Underneath lies a jigsaw of sub-cortical structures whose names ring with the confidence of scientific precision—*thalamus, basal ganglia, substantia nigra*. The threads of individual nerve fibers are bundled into ropy tracts woven throughout the brain, passing information from one brain area to another, from the spinal cord out into the body, from the body back up to the brain. The whole organ is awash in a churning soup of hormones and neurotransmitters, electrical and chemical activity shifting through it like fast-motion weather patterns.

Researchers are still chasing the brain's patterns of architecture and activity with the imperfect tools of modern science: theory, experiment, data. But the mystery remains: How do sensation, thought, emotion, memory—*a self*—arise from a few pounds of tissue? The history of our attempts to answer this question is the story of our desire to understand what it means to be human.

At first there are photographs, and in every one my mother wears the same strange expression. It's the look of a puppy given too many commands at once. Her smile is wide but her eyes are uncertain.

Then she stopped letting people take photographs of her. She would bow her head and step out of the frame, away from the eye of the camera.

What no one could see as the back of her head slammed against the ice was the force of the fall rippling through her brain. The sudden deceleration compressed precious brain tissue toward the back of her skull, rotating and distorting her brain, then smashing it against the curved back wall of bone, which may have dented inward like a rubber ball bounced against pavement. In an instant, an unknowable number of brain cells was crushed, and others were stretched or torn. While a more shock-absorbent surface—a foam mat or field with long grasses—might have mitigated the force of the fall, the ice was unyielding. After that first impact, her head bounced up off the ice and pressure waves ricocheted forward through her brain, rotating and distorting it once more, compressing neural tissue toward her forehead, where the front of her brain crushed up against her skull roughly opposite the first point of impact. This injury is known as coup-contrecoup, *blow-counterblow*, and the damage it describes is not limited to two bruised

You're in a crowded public hall in imperial Rome around the year 161 AD.

patches of cortex. Powerful rotational and shearing forces can injure areas throughout the brain. As the whole organ shudders like Jell-O in the cranial cavity, the long strands of nerve fibers that wind through it like millions of microscopic strings get twisted and pulled. Some are strained; others snap. A cruel oversight of evolution has left the floor of the human skull just above the eye sockets ridged rather than smooth. When the brain is forcefully moved inside the skull, the underside of the frontal lobes can grate across this uneven field of bone, causing additional damage.

But the injury does not end at the moment of impact. The event triggers a cascade of chemical and electrical activity that continues to damage the brain for days, weeks, and even months afterward. Waves of disturbance persist on the microscopic level, leading some scientists to suggest that we think of brain injury as a disease—a process that unfolds over time. I have begun to think of it this way, as expanding across time and space, silently coursing through the brain and beyond.

My mother's green eyes, which had clenched shut upon impact, remained closed as skaters slowed around her.

Her eyes opened. She looked up at the ring of worried faces.

Rising on slippery feet, she told my father she was fine. Just dizzy, she said, as he helped her off the ice to a wooden bench where she could untie her skates. Sitting in the cold, she leaned her head forward for a moment and held it in her hands.

2. METHODS

Use your imagination to get your bearings: You're in a crowded public hall in imperial Rome around the year 161 AD. Men draped in the empire's finest fabrics mill and greet each other in voices edged with excitement. Light glints off rings and epaulets. The air is fragrant with perfumed oils and men's sweat and something more feral—pig excrement. Heads jockey for an unobstructed view of Galen of Pergamum, the anatomist and physician who stands on a dais gesturing over an unfortunate pig lashed to a wooden board, its teat-lined belly exposed and all four legs secured with ropes cinched tight. The top of the pig's head is pressed against the board and the flesh of its throat is exposed to the expectant crowd. The squealing is ferocious, piercing—just as Galen intended.

Galen stands in front of his audience and declares his intention to show that the voice does not originate from the heart, as commonly believed, but from the brain. Hackles rise throughout the hall. The city's most influential politicians, scholars, and surgeons are gathered here, many of whom are Aristotelians who believe that thought, and therefore the voice, emanates from the heart. The heat of the human body, Aristotle argued, is stoked by the fire of the beating heart, whose feverish "spirits" pass through the nerves up through the neck and into the brain, where the organ's hollow blood vessels make it the perfect cooling apparatus.

Many creatures have a brain, of course. Aristotle saw them moist and rotting with his own eyes. Octopus. Elephant. Ape. He dismantled the corpses of at least forty-nine different species and observed that the human brain is larger, in relation to body size, than the brains of animals. Holding humans apart, he did not think "other animals." And he did not know that in the human brain the neural systems responsible for "reason" and "emotion" are as interwoven as the mythical fabric of the Fates. According to the times, the two were separate faculties, and according to Aristotle our relatively larger brains could better temper the "heat and seething" of the human heart, cooling emotion and leaving us the most rational of all creatures. In other words, the heart was the organ of the mind and the brain was a fancy utensil.

But experience has taught Galen otherwise.

When he was only twenty-eight years old, Galen was the youngest physician ever to be appointed to care for the gladiators at Pergamum. He treated men who suffered terrible wounds inflicted by sword and mace and half-starved beasts, which offered him an otherwise impossible access to the inner workings of the human body. He treated head injuries inflicted by clubs, claws, and metal spikes of all ominous shapes and sizes. He watched the wounded men recover, or not. And what he saw taught him to believe, like Hippocrates before him, that the brain, not the heart, is the organ of the mind.

Galen knows his audience is riled. Prickly and antagonistic, he delights in using public experiments to show other physicians to be fools. A well-known Aristotelian philosopher by the name of Alexander Damascenus interrupts Galen's brazen introduction to raise the objection foremost in many minds: "But should we concede that the evidence of the senses is to be trusted?" The eyes can be deceived. The mind led astray. One should rely on the abstract logic of philosophy alone to reason one's way to knowledge of the natural world. At issue is more than just the brain-heart debate; this is a debate about Truth, and the methods by which it might be known.

I have been wondering when the silence began. Maybe it started when I was trying so hard to stay quiet so she could get better.

Or maybe it came later, when I had tired of getting "I don't know" as an answer and stopped asking questions.

Then again, maybe I didn't ask much in the first place. Perhaps I was too shy to intrude on the adult world of illness and recovery, or too wrapped up in my own world to notice the silence stealing around me and settling into place.

I have been trying to remember what she was like before, testing for gradations of difference. I keep thinking about the day we went to the National Museum of Natural History, where the collection we wanted to visit was closed to the public and closed to children. I must have been nine or ten years old, but she took me looking for it anyway. There were no crowds in the basement of the museum, no children with sticky fingers pressed up against brass railings or distracted grown-ups with fanny packs and cameras searching for a sign pointing the way to the Jurassic Period, just the sound of my mother's sandals ticking confidently through empty white corridors. I tripped along next to her in dirty white Keds, goose bumps rising along my arms every time we passed a vent blowing cool air. When we finally found the door to the National Bird Collection, a woman in wire-rimmed spectacles discreetly blocked our entrance, insisting we could not visit this particular collection. We were not scientists. Not experts. We had no business there.

My mother talked to her, warm and earnest, about how much I would enjoy it. We won't touch anything, she promised, holding up her manicured hands with scout's-honor palms facing out. She was a good talker, not like a used car salesman trying to be your best friend, more like your actual best friend. The skeptical guardian of the bird collection eventually agreed we could come in for one hour.

The massive warehouse was clean and quiet, divided into aisles by archival drawers like those that hold unframed paintings or blueprints. I remember feeling as though we were a million miles underground. We tried a drawer at random, and it slid open to reveal six huge parrots lying belly-up. This was almost too good to be true. I was a child of minor obsessions,

I have been trying to remember what she was like before, testing for gradations of difference.

and my interest in dinosaurs had recently turned, in a Darwinian way, to birds. I daydreamed over James Audubon's field drawings and the language of avian anatomy. *Pinfeather, ulna, alula.* The words promised a precision I found irresistible. The parrots had been arranged in two rows of three, their green plumage brilliant against the white lining of the drawer. Six pairs of leathery feet curled up toward the ceiling, one foot of each pair tagged like evidence. The slim anklet announced the dead animal to be proof that others like it lived.

"Is there one of everything here?" I asked the woman in spectacles.

"No," she smiled, "the collection isn't complete."

I couldn't decipher the coded tags, but wondered if they recorded where the parrots came from and who had brought them here. Even now, I can't help imagining a bearded naturalist in khaki safari gear, a machete for hacking jungle trails in one hand and a clutch of dead birds swaying from the other; men sweating in a long line behind him, balancing trunks full of tea, notebooks, and feathered bodies. It's hard to unlearn the idea that science is about white men and their adventures. Leaning closer, I angled my head to examine the electric-blue markings around the eyes of the nearest bird. Close up, it smelled dry and slightly stale, like a library book. It rested inches from my face, within reach of my hands, so much better than the Hope Diamond upstairs.

My mother said, "If only we had a ladder . . ." and I turned to see her standing with her hands on her hips, looking up. This image remains: a tiny woman with golden curls in a sea of drawers, looking up.

Those drawers held thousands of birds, nests, eggs, and skeletons—the tiny bones linked up in patterns reminiscent of a symphony, the parts humming together into something new and irreducible. But the skulls were my favorite. I lingered over the depressions where avian eyes once rested, the bone smooth and graceful with its hollow curve and then, behind, nothing. I was mesmerized by the idea that this was the place from which the bird would have looked out at the world.

"I think she really likes this," my mother told the woman in spectacles as we left. They were on a comfortable first-name basis by then, and we were invited back anytime the following day.

After she fell, my mother changed. She did not become a different person, she became different. I don't know how else to say this.

Galen's demonstration takes an unexpected turn, his response to Damascenus pitched to maximize dramatic effect: "I was mistaken in not realizing that I was coming to meet boorish skept-hicks, otherwise I should not have come." Leaving the squealing pig untouched, he steps down from the dais and sweeps out of the hall, which has erupted in a din of discussion and disagreement. If the crowd was hungry for Galen's performance before, it is ravenous now.

Over the next few days, he is begged to return, and when he finally steps up to the dais once more, his audience has swelled—his is now the hottest show in all of Rome. A pig lies lashed to the board, as before. This time, Galen slices through the tough skin of the pig's throat, laying bare the thorax. He fishes in the bloody riot of exposed flesh for the pig's intercostal nerves, which are known to be connected to the brain—not the heart—and which we now know include the laryngeal nerves. Finding what he wants, Galen deftly loops threads around the slippery strands. Leaving the threads loose, he strikes the animal to make it cry out.

Perhaps Galen lingers a moment and lets his audience listen to the pig's shrieking porcine voice. Then he tightens the threads around the exposed nerves and strikes the animal again. This time, though the pig flinches and struggles, there is no sound. One can almost see startled observers raise hands to throats. The crowd marvels at the silence.

They marvel yet again when Galen unties the threads, strikes the animal a

Ask a question. Form a hypothesis. Test it. Make conclusions based on evidence.

third time, and produces a resounding squeal. The voice, if beholden to these nerves, must be beholden to the brain. This is the first time an experiment has shown a causal relationship between brain and behavior. What a miracle to suddenly see a fact of physiology with such clarity—the mystery of the voice made, by one deft twitch of the surgeon's hand, less mysterious.

Galen's demonstration with the squealing pig marks the dawn of experimental brain science and his legacy will stretch across centuries, continents, and cultures. His most influential work, *De usu partium corporis humani*, will define the practice of Western medicine for fifteen centuries, well into the European Renaissance, but perhaps his most significant achievement was to unite the logic of philosophy with experimental observations of the natural world. This union paved the way for the scientific method, that elegant equation of theory, experiment, and data now inscribed on the very heart of modern science.

Ask a question. Form a hypothesis. Test it. Make conclusions based on evidence. This logic is repeated in every scientific paper published today, in which you will also find a "methods" section, where the researchers describe, sometimes in numbing detail, exactly how they did the experiments that gave them the data that led to their conclusions. But how can someone who is not a scientist, who does not have the controlled setting of a lab and the precision of finely tuned instruments, come to any sort of reliable knowledge about the world through which she moves?

To say that my mother became "different" does not satisfy. There is always more than one way to say a thing, and language is always privately polyvalent—I say "red" and you see a color and also apples and anger and the swish of a matador's cape, the ribbon tied around a gift given by a man you loved and never saw again, which reminds you that sea horses mate for life. You know, "red." So let me try again.

After she slipped on that frozen lake in Yosemite National Park, my mother became quiet and tender, sensitive to the world in unexpected ways. I remember riding in the back seat as my father drove us home to the California coast a few days later, leaning my temple against cold glass and watching her hand grip the passenger door handle. She gripped the door handle, her whole body tensed against the back-and-forth of the car. As the trees thinned out along the dizzying route of switchbacks that ribbon across the Sierra Nevada, the car wound to higher altitudes and she said my father's driving was making her nauseous. He slowed and tried to take the turns more gently, but still she felt queasy. This was not like her. Usually I was the one to get carsick. When we arrived home, just north of San Francisco, she complained of dizziness and exhaustion and disappeared into her bedroom. I think I'm falling back, here, on the conditional language of the medical literature—"the patient complains of"—as if the facts of her particular suffering have yet to be established. I will try to do better.

A few days later, my older sister flew home from college for the winter holidays and we slept stacked in the bunk beds we'd shared until she left. Our parents stayed up late on Christmas Eve, arranging presents even though we were far too old to believe in Santa Claus. My mother crafted bows out of ribbons lovingly recycled year to year, then made sure all the packages were visible from the living room doorway, where we gathered in the morning and waited until everyone was ready before anyone could take a step into Christmas Day. We spent the whole day in our pajamas, opening one gift at a time, meals forgotten in the wake of hot chocolate and leftover pumpkin pie. In the evening, my father cooked a turkey and we made the obligatory visit to church, where my sister and I knelt close, poking each other and jostling elbows across wooden pew backs. But that year, my mother suffered from headaches, dizziness, and fatigue. She seemed sensitive to light and sound, and she spent long hours in the bedroom with the blinds pulled and the door closed. Eventually she would emerge, rejuvenated. She would laugh and eat pie. After a few hours she would retreat to the bedroom again, looking pale and confused. The holiday cards, which she usually opened with such fanfare, sat piled in bright stacks on the hall table.

"I'm tired," she said.

"She just needs to rest," my father said.

In those first few weeks, I didn't feel alarm, or even great interest. I wanted her to feel better the same way you want someone to feel better when they have the flu.

It must have been January before I noticed that the changes in my mother's behavior didn't seem to be going away. She forgot appointments, her wallet, to put mascara on one eye. Her speech had slowed down, her voice crawling over elongated vowels as if she were speaking underwater. Words escaped her, the things she wanted to say just out of reach. My purse. Stuck. Blooming. She would put a hand to her forehead and sigh, heavily, as if what was being asked of her was simply too much. I got into the habit of guessing what she wanted to say, finishing her stalled sentences, often incorrectly, just to help them end.

I remember slipping quietly into my parents' bedroom one afternoon while she was resting—there must have been a reason, a permission slip to be signed or a message to deliver, because when that door was closed it was not to be opened. Sunlight seeped through the white curtains and cut a pale rectangle across the foot of the bed. I don't remember what I said, but I can still see how she shut her eyes when I spoke. She pinched up her forehead as if I were hurling words into her face and she had to duck to avoid getting hurt. When they weren't closed, her eyes ran across her bedside table and her blankets, flitting from alarm clock to bedposts to my face to the wall beyond like a pair of restless birds looking for a place to land. It scared me.

She was a ship taking water, the currents changed and changing, the wind no longer at her back. She was routinely exhausted by the pace of daily life, her mind unable to keep up with demands it once met so flawlessly.

But then, she had good days. On good days my mother was lucid and charming, just like her old self. Once, she packed a beer in my school lunch, but most afternoons, when I opened my brown bag in the concrete middle school courtyard, I would find a sandwich and a drink as normal as those my classmates pulled from theirs. Or at least as normal as could be expected from a household where chips, candy, and soda were forbidden. My parents leaned, though not as far as some California transplants, towards the hippie side of the cultural spectrum. At least one piece of furniture was upholstered in striped velour, and I distinctly remember a macramé lamp. On good days, my mother whirled around us as she always had, and my fear was lifted and forgotten in her wake.

This backsliding scale of wellness confused the whole family. She seemed fine one day, addled the next. So was she sick, or not? As a child, I didn't understand what was happening to her, but I assumed whatever was wrong was an adult problem that would have adult solutions. I figured they were handling it.

Did my mother have a "concussion" or a "traumatic brain injury"? What was the difference?

"Be quiet, your mom's resting."
But not getting better.

There is much I don't remember, but much I never knew to begin with. In the same way a body doubles over in response to a punch in the gut, our lives contracted around my mother's injury, curling over to hide and protect it. We didn't talk about what was happening to her, or to us. Silence became habit, and it's only as an adult that I've begun to see the damage it can do.

By the time I left home for college the silence had become so routine as to be indistinguishable from the noise of daily life. Eventually I turned to the Internet, where I found hundreds of websites riddled with unfamiliar terms like *closed head injury*, *post-concussive syndrome*, and *traumatic brain injury*. There were acronyms—LOC, PCS, TBI— and jargon—*lesion*, *sequelae*—written in a language I didn't speak. Did my mother have a "concussion" or a "traumatic brain injury"? What was the difference? I had no idea. This was before TBI had become a household term because of stories told by professional athletes and veterans of the wars in Iraq and Afghanistan. At the time, I had never heard of TBI.

Though overwhelming, the Internet provided a few basic facts. It's a common misconception that "head injury" and "brain injury" refer to the same thing.

Head injury: any injury to the head, including broken cheekbones and a lacerated scalp. Brain injury: any injury that affects the brain itself, sometimes with no external injury to the head. The latter includes everything from shaken baby syndrome to blast injuries to a bullet lodged in the brain. (It took me an embarrassingly long while to figure out that "acquired brain injury" simply means damage that occurs after birth, as in acquired vs. congenital.) These terms are often confused in the scientific literature, adding to uncertainty about the prevalence of brain injury and fueling debates about diagnosis and treatment. Confusion reigned at every level, from how to diagnose the severity of an injury to what might be the most effective treatments. From the outside looking in, the field of brain injury research seemed to be a bit of a mess.

Or maybe I was looking in the wrong place. I needed a field guide, so I ordered a slim green paperback with the promising title *Head Injury: The Facts*. It was simple and forthright. It promised answers.

The first few paragraphs are written in a reassuring, expert tone: "Until recently the psychological ramifications of head trauma had been largely overlooked, and they were therefore unknown to almost everybody including the patient and the people close to them." This sounded familiar. "Most people suffering a residual

> Our silence and inaction were not, in fact, a mystery, and my family was just one among many.

compromise of mental efficiency following an accident with minimal or no loss of consciousness attributed their problems to psychological causes: their physicians often dismissed these patients as neurotics, compensation seekers, or both." This was getting uncomfortable. I had sometimes wondered whether my mother's problems weren't more psychological than physical. I thought of those categories as somehow separable. It was hard to imagine that such a seemingly minor fall could leave such a bizarre constellation of symptoms in its wake. But my feeling of concern was warped over time by frustration that she wasn't getting better, as if this were a test she was somehow failing. It didn't occur to me that lack of empathy might be a failure of imagination.

The book goes on to suggest that people with cognitive and psychological problems resulting from a brain injury not accompanied by any obvious physical injuries are likely to have those problems overlooked: "Only patients with obvious crippling or other physical alteration were likely to have the permanent neuropsychological residuals of their brain injuries recognized, although even then higher mental functions were either ignored or misinterpreted."

The *Oxford English Dictionary* defines *neuropsychological* as "the study of the relationship between behavior, emotion, and cognition on the one hand, and brain function on the other." My mother certainly seemed to think and act more slowly, to "suffer a residual compromise of mental efficiency," but she wasn't an invalid. She didn't need a wheelchair or a cane or help washing and dressing and eating. She didn't need nurses and trays of sterile white plastic—the care an institution can provide. But she was not well. This left her, according to these authors, in a group that was not "likely to have the permanent neuropsychological residuals [of the injury] recognized." She was someone whose difficulties with "higher mental functions" like memory and attention were both "ignored and misinterpreted" by those around her. By me, at the very least.

The last paragraph on the first page stopped me cold. That page is now marked in faded green highlighter and has been read so many times the book's binding has begun to crack. This paragraph articulated my experience so clearly I couldn't believe the words were written by someone who didn't know my family:

> As the misdiagnosed patients have suffered from neglect, bewilderment, and despair, families lacking knowledge about their head-injured patient have suffered too. Many families have gone through a progression of torments that begins with puzzlement and then confusion as the patient no longer responds in familiar and appropriate ways. Frustration and

anxiety arise as the uninformed family members discover that their efforts are ineffective, and may even make the situation worse. Many family members feel shame and guilt at what they believe are their failures to cope with the patient's problem behaviors. Depression is almost inevitable. Disruption of once solid family relationships is not an infrequent occurrence, which further compounds their misery.

"Misery" seemed a bit melodramatic, but basically this book had us nailed. I'd always thought that no one, not even her doctors, knew what was wrong with her. I'd always reasoned this was why we ignored her behavior, for the most part, and waited for her to get better, as if it were something she was doing, and had to do, on her own. But someone knew. These authors, certainly. Our silence and inaction were not, in fact, a mystery, and my family was just one among many.

When I finally asked my mother if she would talk with me about her brain injury, I was home for the holidays and we were passing each other in the downstairs hallway of the house where I grew up. Her arms were full of folded sheets.

She paused and said, "I'll think about it."

For the next three days, we pretended this conversation had not taken place. We shared meals, walked my parents' dogs, went to a movie, and the subject very purposefully did not arise.

On the third day she said, "Do you know you're the only one in the family who's asked me about this in fifteen years?" She said it quietly, without anger or reproach, but it broke my heart.

Method, from the Greek *methodos*: pursuit of knowledge.

At first, I wanted to know which areas of my mother's brain were damaged and how that damage could explain how she changed. I assumed that what I learned could be organized into neat columns in my notebook: brain area, function, deficit. This seemed like an achievable task—a logical road of inquiry. At the end would lie the answers, facts to be picked up and held in my hand like pebbles, each one hard and round and certain, ready to be placed safely in my pocket as I turned to head for home.

RELIQUARY (AUGUST)

In the sweet pit of summer there's a boy
waiting to be

exposed
though all he has done

is pray
the barn away—

the barn where he was a boy
and a man

laid where the horses turned
the hay blue & holy

with their unapologetic
shadows   some nights

the sky remains
sheathed in its own skin

and that's all a queer boy
can hope for   isn't it

when all he can see
is the gun in the hand

of his father's reflection
when the only light in the barn

is fire   and he doesn't have to look
because he knows   what rises

falls & what had risen was the moon

APHELION

Orlando

They are the boys I could've been
had my body slimmed & dropped
like a comet into the barrel of the gun—

though even in the face of smoke
they don't apologize for being queer. By dawn
the club is taxidermied—preserved

in memory, despite the trace of a pulse.
In his dream, a dying boy is locked
in the unlit cellar of his childhood home

with no candle & no mouth. Once a queer body
is the only bullet in the gun, the man
reloads & watches his warped face

in each gold cylinder. Meanwhile, God
drops the moon into a foxhole, fingers
laced together as the bleeding boys

reach for each other in his hands. Regret
is something these men do not possess.
How queer & red God's stained hands turn.

Karaoke

I sang karaoke every Thursday night for some years at a place called Tee-Tee's. I'd meet my girlfriends at six thirty and we'd order the half chicken for four dollars, eat it fast, then be the first people downstairs when the mics were turned on at seven. We all shared an extreme need to walk on stage and out of our actual lives.

No one knew very much about anyone else, apart from the fact that we'd all had too many jobs and too many boyfriends. The night I told Sandra I'd begun taking antipsychotics, she replied that she'd been having an affair. She wasn't the only one. When Dora's husband found out about her affair, we all met at Sandra's house, hungover, wondering what to do. Her husband had once tended bar at a place in Idaho and let people drink for free if they let him keep their AA chips.

Occasionally someone brought a boyfriend, but never two weeks in a row. Everything was already too easy, the endless glasses of bourbon, the weird appetizers no one could ever remember ordering, the grand tips we left for our favorite waitresses. We preferred to wake up alone and hoarse.

Tee-Tee's was a good place to hear people before they got record contracts. Also occasionally after they got them. It was better than *American*

Sarah Manguso

Idol, that much is true. I'd had twelve years at conservatory and five years in a professional church choir, so I believe my judgment fair.

A city alderman showed up with bodyguards one night, asked for a mic, and crooned an Ellington tune a cappella after dedicating it to his wife. It was their anniversary. She'd been dead a long time. It was the most dignified thing I ever saw anyone do there.

I was never interested in those K-Box places in Koreatown where you could rent a room with friends. I was interested in the places where you had to stand on stage or where you could walk around like a lounge singer. A place where you had to preach to strangers.

One night we met a bunch of Hells Angels out with their buddy who'd just gotten out of prison. It wasn't for a nonviolent crime. "I know karate," I said at one point, having had exactly one lesson at the Center for Nonviolent Education. "I know Smith and Wesson," he replied, showing me his gun.

Norman ran the karaoke machine. He had three teenaged daughters and a lot of brothers, all of whom were in the Dirty Ones, a Bushwick biker gang. He said he was the only straight one in his family.

Halina, the cocktail waitress, worked as a bond trader on the floor of a big Wall Street bank. She had a teenaged son to support. I am quite sure she had two different wardrobes and personalities for her two jobs. Probably two names, too.

There were plenty of regulars, and we knew them all. We had a fondness for the Polish guy who sang only the Doors in extremely accented English, occasionally on key. The bartender, Dave, who looked like he'd done hard time, stood with tears in his eyes when Sandra sang "Along the Yellow Brick Road." "You gonna sing Judy Collins tonight?" he'd whisper-croak desperately as she and I walked past the bar to pick up two copies of the songbook.

We'd stay until one, two, sometimes after two. We were all either middle-aged party girls or precocious alcoholics. One night a girl stuffed a hundred-dollar bill down Annie's pants after she sang "Proud Mary."

We were all trying to be playwrights or poets or journalists or photographers. We'd listen to each other and suggest songs that worked with each other's ranges. Several of us included "Rock 'n' Roll Suicide" in our repertoire, and sometimes it played several times in a night. I wasn't the only one who practiced at home. It eventually became my signature song. I mean, if you'd asked me what my signature song was, that's what I'd have said even though Dora sang it better.

I hadn't had a Bowie phase in middle school or high school, so the song was for me an island of Bowie, a free-floating craft of genius in an ocean of the unknown. I hadn't heard *Hunky Dory* or even *Ziggy Stardust* all the way through, but I knew every deliberate crack of his voice in "Suicide," and I copied them dutifully.

When I sang that song, his song, I felt genderless, bodiless. By the end I was screaming, *you're not alone, you're wonderful!* and I was all voice, just a living embodiment of the great voice.

It started changing around the time that a few of us got sober or divorced—becoming a place where small groups sang to and for only themselves and barely listened to the others. It was no longer a church of lonely souls, no longer a place where a stranger would shed tears while my friend sang "Dear Prudence" into the basement murk.

I walked past Tee-Tee's a few years ago, after we'd stopped singing, and saw that the board of health had shut it down. Several of us had left town by then, and anyway, I didn't know anyone who sang there anymore.

But now one of my favorite things to do is go out alone to a bar I've never been to and sing. This sort of karaoke, during which no one knows you, during which you might become free of self-consciousness, unaware, for the length of a song, even of your own body—you can just walk onto a lit stage and disappear.

THE CAR WASH OF THE DEAD

Amy Bloom

The dark magic of memory

Not every dead person goes through the car wash. Not everyone needs to. Two of my best friends were superb and flawed in life and are superb and flawed in my memory. My grandparents haven't been through the car wash, either. They remain as bright or as dark as they were: one beloved, and the others—not bad. Memory keeps them in the same place.

But my late parents have gone through the Triple Foam Shine car wash of the afterlife.

When I remember my lovely, loving, kindhearted, conflict-avoidant, largely useless-for-big-moments mother, I *think* I am remembering her clearly but I know I am not, because I cannot summon the anger (justifiable, I believe, and white-hot, I know) that I used to feel toward her, at times. When I was fourteen my first therapist asked me if I was very angry at my distant father. I said that if I wasn't so busy wanting to kill my mother, I certainly would be. She didn't like to upset others, but more, she didn't like to be upset by unpleasant reality, of any kind.

Decades later, I have no trouble enumerating her faults and foibles. Highlights

from the reel: 1. Neighbor boys broke my arm and her wish not to cause trouble made her keep me home, while insisting that I was malingering, for three days, before she took me to the doctor. 2. My mother's attitude toward her wealthy friends was horribly Uriah Heep-ish. If a woman with a bouffant could be said to tug at her forelock, she did. 3. When I was getting divorced, my mother expressed tearful concern for my children, for my soon-to-be-ex-husband, and for herself. When I muttered that I had not been mentioned, she said, "You're so strong." I screamed so hard, I almost passed out. 4. Soon after that chat, my mother said to me, memorably—and by memorably I mean, seared into my cerebellum—"I like the roses of intimacy, honey, I do. But I don't like the thorns."

Clearly, I do remember. But the celestial car wash has left me fondly admiring her self-awareness and honesty (many people feel about intimacy the way she did, I find; most people—especially female people— won't tell you so) and when I think of the ways in which she disappointed me, what I feel most is that it was too bad, for me and even more so for her, that she couldn't stand up for herself or me, that she found the world so scary, that she had to settle for a bunch of rubber roses. And I miss her, all the time. I pick up the phone to call her on the way home from the airport,

> He looked down on a lot of people. He enjoyed looking down on people.

with news of my life, of her grandchildren's lives, wanting to say the very things that might (sometimes did) result in my bitter disappointment or screaming rage, and all I feel is loss and love. I can see her in one of her many housecoats, hair ash-blonde rather than gray, with a lousy cup of instant coffee in front of her. But I prefer to see her, before I was born, in her big black cartwheel straw hat and nipped-in black suit, holding her gold cigarette holder, taking notes at the 21 Club for her gossip column. I adore that woman. We are best friends.

That is some fucking car wash. And it's nothing compared to the one I've put my father through.

My parents were married for sixty years. I keep their urns on opposite sides of my living room, out of respect for the unhappiness of their union. My mother's is navy cloisonné, a word I would not know if she weren't my mother. The urn is decorated with a picture of my mother in high school, all black curls and snug sweater, and by a necklace that my daughters call Boca Bohemian. I should keep a bottle of Ma Griffe by Carven next to it. My mother referred to my father, sometimes, as Mr. Belittle. He wasn't given to admiration, exceptions made for John O'Hara, Christina Stead, and Franklin D. Roosevelt. He looked down on a lot of people. He enjoyed looking down on people. Belittling was a pleasurable expression of his guiding principles:

Never be taken in, suckered, or impressed. Do not be taken in by modern-day injustice, especially when suffered by other people. (He was openly deprived of jobs and awards in the 1930s because he was Jewish. He wasn't even moved by injustices done to *him*.) Do not be snookered by artists, by contemporary fiction, by contemporary poetry, by politicians, by pomposity, and do not be moved by tears or the opinions of others. I never saw him give in to my mother's tears or mine, or my sister's. I never saw him cry.

He felt that being Murray Teigh Bloom was, pretty much, a great way to be and it was tough nuts for anyone who didn't agree and more of that for everyone who was not MTB.

For most of my life, from ten to fifty, I found Murray Teigh Bloom to be a deeply unsatisfactory father. I chose people (People! Not just one person!) because, whatever their faults, they were not like my father. They were nice. They felt that niceness was a signal virtue. They were not fearless, self-centered, and cheered by the prospect of a good fight. Over thirty years, I wrote him two scorching letters about his blunt selfishness. "You'll die alone," I wrote. He didn't. He died well cared for by me, my sister, and a devoted aide, and I'm glad. My father, distant, disappointing, relentlessly self-involved, and as immovable as Stonehenge, is the true poster child for the Great Car Wash.

Here's what it's given me:

Complete recall of every moment of the days before he died, when I'd walk into the room and his face, which I'd so often found distressingly neutral, his eyes focused on a page and away from me, now lit up. He'd turn to my husband and say, "My boy, it's good to have daughters!"

In *Persuasion* (my father reminded me, pointing out how shitty most advice is) Anne Elliot says to Lady Russell, who has often offered advice and prides herself on it, something like: We only know that advice has been good after we judge the outcome. We can't call it good advice if it leads to a bad outcome.

By that measure, my father never gave me bad advice.

When I was senior in high school, I told my parents I wasn't going to college. My mother was upset. My father was a little surprised but refused to get drawn into a discussion. It was my life, he said. Also, my money, as he was not funding thirty seconds of self-discovery. A few weeks later, I told my parents I was going off with my boyfriend, a college junior, for at least six months of travel, for which the boyfriend had received a National Science Foundation grant to study organic agriculture throughout the Southwest. (Most memorably, Texas. We pretended to be married and I learned how to pick peanuts in Deaf Smith County.)

He didn't praise the book. I'm not sure he even *read* it.

"And you," my father said, red-faced with disappointment, "what will you be doing? What project did you design? What grant did you get?"

Good point. (My father would not have described himself as a feminist. He wasn't *against* equal pay for equal work, but he didn't care much. On the other hand, he knew Betty Friedan and liked her. He said that her husband, Carl, was a bully and a blowhard and the kind of man who could make a feminist out of Zsa Zsa Gabor. When he died, I got condolence notes from women writers all over the country, telling me that my father was a mentor and a coach and a source of encouragement. Who knew?)

I was not a woman writer he mentored. My first book was not the collection of short stories I published in 1993. My first book was a mystery novel. It was called "Them There Eyes" and I wrote it late at night, after work, while my children slept. I hadn't planned to share it with my parents, because it wasn't finished, because my hero was having the kind of torrid sex that I was not, because I was embarrassed to have written so many pages when there was no reason to think anyone would publish it, because my father had so thoroughly red-slashed my middle-school short stories. But I lugged the pages with me everywhere, to make revisions, to remind myself that it existed, and when my mother unpacked my bag while I sorted the kids, she found the pages. She found that I'd named my hero Dell Chandler, which was my mother's pen name,

back when she was a syndicated gossip columnist and nobody was going to carry a glamorous Manhattan gossip column written by a Jewish girl with the Jewish name Sydelle Cohen.

My mother loved everything about those badly written pages. She asked me if she could show my father and I refused because . . . those pages in seventh grade. She showed him the pages anyway.

After he read them he found me in the kitchen. He didn't praise the book. I'm not sure he even *read* it. He said, "Fix the typos and send me a copy. I'll send it to my agent, see what he thinks." He sent it to Julian, his own long-retired, nearly *dead* agent and asked him to help me. My father reported two weeks later that Julian was truly out of the business and he, Julian, wished me luck. I feel sure that this was the nicest possible rephrasing of what Julian actually said, but this was Murray Teigh Bloom, so how could that be?

When my story collection was published, some journalists noticed that I had a father who also wrote, although books of a different kind (nonfiction: finance, legal issues, counterfeiting, white-collar crime). When asked, he explicitly disavowed all influence and, it seemed to me at the time, all interest. *Fiction, pah.* Courtesy of the car wash, I see that he was making sure that anyone interested in my work would know that he laid no claim to my talent or style. He made clear that he had never helped me with a sentence, inspired a story, or edited a page. Now that I have a daughter who's a novelist, I get it. He gave no one credit for his success and he was taking none for mine. He believed, as he said to me a thousand times, you make your own way in this world.

I find I have a watered-down version of his remarkable work ethic (Never quit.) and, considering what I do for a living, a reasonable amount of confidence in my ability. He also made it clear, every day, that anyone who'd done their best and was cowed or shaped by the opinion of others should be ashamed of themselves. So I don't read my reviews. Well done, Pop.

The car wash has stripped him of his frayed black Ban-Lon polo shirt, spattered gray trousers, and worn black loafers. It has rinsed him off, buffed and polished him, changed him from someone complacent, smug, and impenetrable who so infuriated me that I could hardly speak to him for more than a few minutes, and given me back an attractive, amusing, beloved spectral presence, now in his favorite gray and moth-eaten cardigan (I have one too), pipe in hand, crystal ashtray on the side table, next to a pile of books, all written before 1950. This version is somewhere between Rex Harrison and the guy from *Masterpiece Theatre*. Thanks to the car wash, his voice is in my ear, his no-fucks-to-give runs in my bloodstream, and his remarks pepper the pages I write.

When I was twenty-one, my father, who had written me three letters in my life, despite many long summers apart, wrote me an extraordinary letter, assuring me that there was nothing I couldn't accomplish, telling me not to be afraid of hating, not to be afraid of making judgments, and to trust my own instincts more than anyone else's opinion. I moved and couldn't find the letter. After thirty years, it resurfaced. Car wash works in mysterious ways.

Maybe the car wash of the dead is for rehabilitating the dead. Or maybe it's to wash pointless grievances and childish expectations out of the living. It makes no difference to me.

Triple Foam Shine, please. 🔱

Marie Howe

FRAGMENT: HOLY SATURDAY

everything moving underneath

half alive half awake

What tunnels through the loam?

What rises from the sheath of leaves?

MAGDALENE: AT THE GRAVE

That long-gone year, that late summer afternoon

driving toward the cemetery

and when the rain started falling hard—and then harder

turning back toward home

and then—as if something were pulling me—

pulling into a driveway and back again toward the grave.

Ridiculous as it was to park and kneel where he'd been buried

—to kneel in the rain—I laughed out loud!

After a few minutes, I looked up and saw the other car idling,

the driver's window rolled down.

The tears I wept then were not tears of grief.

How many times must it happen before I believe?

THIS TOO SHALL PASS

ON JOHN BERRYMAN'S

Recovery

ADAM WILSON

John Berryman is best known for two things: *The Dream Songs*—a series of 385 poems, published in two editions, for which he won, respectively, the Pulitzer Prize and the National Book Award—and his suicide.

In 1972, Berryman jumped off the Washington Avenue Bridge in Minneapolis onto the bank of the Mississippi River.

Despite critical adoration, Berryman wasn't canonized to the same extent as Robert Lowell and Sylvia Plath, his co-pioneers in what came to be called Confessional Poetry. Berryman despised the term, and *The Dream Songs*—which shifts between first and third person, and which follows a character called Henry, who, according to Berryman, both "is and is not" a stand-in for himself—never quite fit under its rubric. With its freewheeling meter and idiomatic diction, Berryman's work is less rarefied than Lowell's and less accessible than Plath's. So it makes sense that he achieved cult status rather than canonization, the kind of poet who isn't taught in AP English, but does appear in songs by Nick Cave, Okkervil River, and the Hold Steady.

In 2014, to mark the author's centennial birthday, FSG reissued *Berryman's*

Sonnets, 77 Dream Songs, and *The* [Complete] *Dream Songs*, as well as a *New Selected Poems*. Notably absent from this reissue, however, is any of Berryman's prose, which includes a critical biography of Stephen Crane, a collection of Berryman's assorted essays and stories, and *Recovery*, his posthumously published, unfinished, autobiographical novel based on his experiences in treatment facilities for alcoholism.

My edition of *Recovery* (Thunder's Mouth Press, 1993)—found deep in the bowels of the Strand and featuring on its cover a photo of a God-bearded Berryman staring glass-eyed into the camera—includes a foreword by Saul Bellow and an introduction by Philip Levine. Interestingly, neither writer's remarks contain much comment, if any, on the book they purport to present. Levine even goes out of his way to offer a kind of counter-Berryman to the one we might project onto the author of *Recovery*. The vibrant and life-loving Berryman he describes would seem to have little in common with the Berryman who wrote, and failed to complete, this grim book.

What is it about *Recovery* that's so scary? And why, in our voyeuristic culture, where buzzwords like *suicide* and *addiction* spell entry into Oprah's Book Club and tortured genius is the stuff of Best Adapted Screenplays, is no one reading this novel?

For starters, *Recovery* provides little in the way of voyeuristic satisfaction. If Berryman's suicide was romantic (according to one bystander he waved goodbye on his way down), his attempted recovery—or at least the fictionalized version of it we get in *Recovery*—was decidedly not. Berryman has little interest in the highs and lows of the drinking life, or even the anguish of detox. Instead, he captures, in all its claustral and quotidian boredom, the day in, day out struggles of adapting to sobriety in a hospital ward.

The novel follows Dr. Alan Severance through two months of inpatient treatment, mostly spent agonizing over the first of the twelve steps of recovery: *We admitted we were powerless over alcohol—that our lives had become unmanageable*. Severance, only recently released from a previous stint at a different facility, blames his relapse on his failure to fully accept that first step. It's not the admission that gives him trouble, but his anxiety about his sincerity in making it. How can we ever know when we're being honest with ourselves? These are the kinds of gray area questions that the black-and-white dogma of AA attempts, out of functional necessity, to mute. If nothing else, *Recovery* offers testament to the difficulty in embracing such rigid doctrine, even when that doctrine might be lifesaving.

"I have a memory like a steel trap," Severance later explains, "except of course for alcoholic distortion and brain damage." He's the opposite of your typical unreliable narrator because he's aware of his own unreliability. He doesn't trust himself, and that mistrust leads to a vicious cycle of doubt and anxiety. One thinks of another AA aphorism: "Let go and let God." For Severance, a believer, it's the letting go that's hard.

Like Henry in *The Dream Songs*, Severance both is and is not Berryman, though

I'd venture to guess that, here, he more is than isn't. Both are Pulitzer Prize winners who remain haunted by their fathers' suicides. Severance's field is biology, but this fact seems forgotten by the fifty-page mark, after which Severance rarely mentions science, though he does speak with depth on various literary matters. But while the fictional scrim may be thin, the distinction is important in a book so caught up in questions of identity. "Jack-Who-Drinks has got to alter into Jack-Who-Does-*Not*-Drink-*And*-Likes-It," explains one of the facility's counselors. Anyone who's ever attempted to give up a defining behavior (for me: smoking) understands that this is easier said than done. Severance is a purposefully loaded name. To sever, to be severe, is to persevere.

Until, of course, one can't. *Recovery* doesn't end so much as stop, which frankly causes more relief than disappointment in the reader. *Recovery*'s early pages brim with the bright and inimitable music Berryman brought to his *Dream Songs*, and the vitality of the prose offsets its gloomy content. At times, there's even humor, such as Severance's fantasy of converting to Judaism (among reasons listed: "Unique horror of anti-Semitism") or his frustration with the Lord's Prayer ("what the *hell* was the point of reminding the Lord of the Lord's power[?]") But *Recovery* quickly stalls, and in its attempt to chronicle the boredom and redundancy of rehab, it can't help but succumb to those qualities itself. Even the manic prosody of the early pages gives way to a kind of barbiturated flatness.

Still *Recovery*'s messiness dignifies the messiness of its subject. I first read it around the time of the James Frey fiasco, and in many ways it felt like a necessary corrective to books like Frey's, which arc from humble-brag degradation to self-righteous redemption. One tenet of AA is that there are no recovered addicts, only recovering ones, but in the neatness of their narrative schematics, these books tell a different, more comforting story. In *Recovery*, by contrast, there are no answers, only desperation punctuated by giving up. The takeaway is truly demoralizing: the futility of art to actually save a life. It's not an easy book to read, or a pleasant one.

Ultimately, I feel much the way Berryman felt about one of his own idols, W. H. Auden: "My love for that odd man has never altered / thro' some of his facile bodiless later books." *Recovery* is not remotely facile, but a certain blind love for anything Berryman helps push past its roadblocks.

In graduate school I once spent a long Christmas break reading Berryman alone in my studio apartment while composing what would become, after another half decade of drafts and disappointments, my first novel. I had decided to isolate myself during this period, interacting only with the bodega owner who sold me cigarettes and the takeout guy who brought my Thai food. This was ostensibly so I could buckle down and finish my book, but also, in retrospect, because I was depressed. My window overlooked a large McDonald's, and I'd often climb onto the fire escape with a cigarette and *The Dream Songs*. In my memory, snow swirls around me, though I doubt this was the case; I would have been anxious about slipping off the fire escape. This is the power of *The Dream Songs*: it makes weather. These poems didn't just capture the despair I was feeling, but did so with such beauty and contour as to render it transformative. The result is not despair but something like its opposite: a hard pulse, a deeply human hum.

Recovery is a different book, by a different Berryman, and one that doesn't end on the side of life. It doesn't end at all. David Foster Wallace, another tragic suicide, thought that great literature makes us feel less alone. Berryman put it differently: "Any writer's, or even scientist's permanent message perhaps is really just this: *come and share my delusion*, and we will be happy or miserable *together*."

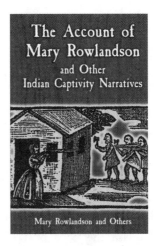

ON MARY ROWLANDSON'S

A Narrative of the Captivity and Restoration of Mrs. Mary Rowlandson

MICAH PERKS

Hemingway famously wrote that "all modern American literature comes from one book by Mark Twain called *Huckleberry Finn*." A charming idea: American literature miraculously born out of the head of a colorblind trickster who is always "light[ing] out for the territory ahead of the rest." But about ten years ago I read a pamphlet-sized book by Mary Rowlandson. I felt like I'd been slapped. Like, you can't float on that raft forever, Huck. Like, Huck, time to grow the fuck up. This is where you came from.

(This "you" includes Huck, Hemingway, Mary Rowlandson, I don't know about you, but definitely me. I'm talking about the uncomfortable truth about where our

American story begins, the white you singing, *This land is your land, it was made for you*.)

A Narrative of the Captivity and Restoration of Mrs. Mary Rowlandson is the first book of prose by a woman published in the Americas, in 1682 about Rowlandson's three-month captivity with Algonquian native people during Metacomet's (or King Philip's) War. This book was the beginning of the captivity narrative genre, a literary genre indigenous to the Americas.

It all begins in Lancaster, a farming community on the edge of the known world, on February 10, 1676, "about sunrising." You're holed up in your garrison with your neighbors, your relatives, your three children, and six cowering dogs—and without your minister husband. He is in Boston begging for more troops to protect Lancaster, perhaps because he knows about the Great Swamp Massacre. Just that past December, the colonial militia murdered hundreds of Narragansett women and children. Maybe Reverend Joseph Rowlandson knows to expect retaliation.

Later, remembering that cold, breath-smoking winter sunrise when it all began, you write:

> Now is that dreadful hour come, that
> I have often heard of (in time of War,
> as it was the case of others) but now
> mine eyes see it. Some in our house
> were fighting for their lives, others
> wallowing in their blood, the House
> on fire over our head, and the bloody
> Heathen ready to knock us on the

head, if we stirred out. Now might we hear Mothers and Children crying out for themselves, and one another, Lord, What shall we do?

Choking on smoke, you heave your six-year-old daughter, Sarah, onto your hip, and you gather your ten-year-old daughter and thirteen-year-old son, and with your sister and her children, you burst out of the low door into chaos under gray February sky, no walls anywhere. Along with others, your nephew William is clubbed to death. His mother says, "Lord let me die with them." She is shot in the head and falls on your doorstep. Then a bullet goes through your side. The same bullet enters Sarah's hand and stomach. There must have been an intense heat, boiling between you and your little girl.

You always thought that if there was an Indian attack you would rather die than be taken. But now your mind changes. Separated from your older children, carrying your wounded child, wounded yourself, you choose "rather to go along" with them into the wilderness. You choose to try not to die.

You organized your book into removes rather than chapters, each remove pulling you farther into the wilderness, farther away from everything you know.

Your story is about surviving, about walking miles through the woods in a New England February winter, a bullet wound in your side, carrying your wounded child. It's about your child dying in your arms ten days later. It's about starving, about what you're willing to eat to survive: "As we went along, they killed a Deer, with a young one in her, they gave me a piece of the Fawn, and it was so young and tender that one might eat the bones as well as the flesh, and yet I thought it very good."

It's about insisting that it's other people who are "wolves and bears" even as you take a horsehoof out of a little girl's mouth and crunch it in yours, even as some of those "wolves and bears" invite you into their homes and feed you when they are starving themselves. You learn to sew for your captors, to trade with them, and your wound stinks, but they tell you to put an oak leaf on it, and perhaps it heals like a purple, puckered kiss. One of them, Quinnapin, the one you call "your best friend of an Indian," gives you money for your work and makes sure you're washed. Others hate you for what your people have taken: "Sometimes I met with favour and sometimes with nothing but frowns." You don't understand why. This is a story about not understanding who has what kind of power. And it's about God, about a terror that God has forsaken you. Why did you smoke all that tobacco and not go to church? Is that why this is happening to you? Or maybe this is a test, you're actually the chosen one, maybe He loves you more than all others. But then why is no one saving you?

Susan Howe writes, "Mary Rowlandson saw what she did not see, said what she did not say." You see and don't see Weetamoo, your "mistress." You call her a "proud strumpet" because you don't see that she's a great warrior queen. Weetamoo: ignored by history because she's no helper of white people like Sacagawea or Pocahontas. You hate her, you don't understand her, and yet your description of her is so vivid, so precise, as if you are recording forever what you'll never forget:

She has a jersey coat, and covered with girdles of wampum from the loins upward; her arms from her elbows to her hands were covered with bracelets; there were handfuls of necklaces about her neck and several sorts of jewels in her ears. She had fine red stockings and white shoes, her hair powdered and her face painted red.

This is also the story of your fierce voice, the one that reaches out over three hundred years with that slap upside the head. Your words are hemmed in on one side by an introduction almost certainly from Increase Mather, who begs pardon for the great outrage that you, a woman, dared to write a book—Increase Mather, whose writing is like this: "But it is not my business to dilate on these things, but only in few words introductively to preface to the following script, which is a Narrative of the wonderfully awfull, wise, holy, powerfull, and gracious providence of God." There are fifty-seven more words in this one sentence, so the writer is not actually a man of few words, after all. You're hemmed in on the other side by your husband's sermon, a jeremiad warning us to repent:

"Gods forsaking of such as he hath been near to, is a thing of such weight and solemnity, and hath such bitter effects, that it is a meet subject, (especially in a dark and mourning day) for Ministers to speak to." It's easy for a contemporary reader to think, *Oh, that's just what those old folks sounded like,* but you don't sound like that. Even pressed between these onslaughts of words, here's your surgical voice, a voice of brutal accounting: "That night we had a mess of wheat for our supper" or "I have seen the extreme vanity of this world. One hour I have been in health, and wealth, wanting nothing, but the next hour in sickness, and wounds, and death."

You were eventually ransomed, restored, returned. Not everyone was restored. Weetamoo drowned trying to escape soldiers. They put her head on a pole in Taunton, Massachusetts. When you heard that they had hung "your best friend of an Indian" Quinnapin, did something shiver over your face like lightning? Something too complicated to record?

You moved to Wethersfield, Connecticut, then known as Oniontown, because of its famed red onion production. Is that where you wrote your book, between cutting and eating onions? Did you finally get enough to eat? Were there always tears streaming down your face?

And perhaps it's there where American literature originates, between the many-petaled onion and the tears. There you narrated a tale of whiteness, a whiteness defined by hostility to others and the constant threat of the hostile other. A whiteness that believed itself chosen by God. At the same time, it's also the story of a female other struggling to describe hunger and grief between the thick voices of white men trying to control all meaning. Your story is complex and uncomfortable, a clash of voices, and maybe that's a good place to start.

ON KERI HULME'S
The Bone People

LAURA BOGART

When I was young, my father was the love of my life. When I huffed because I couldn't wear my Ninja Turtle Halloween costume to school in January, he took me with him to the grocery store (much to my mother's chagrin) dressed as Raphael. When I feared that my closet held a portal to some savage realm where monsters dwelled, he was the monster slayer who slept on the floor by my bed. His presence alone was enough to console me. My father's hands could fend off any beast my imagination could conjure.

But my father's hands could also snap my heart in two. Every time the black lightning of rage crackled through his mind, gathering heat as it got closer to the part of him that would have to decide how he'd handle the C- in math, or the backyard fence that had been painted with flowers and turtle heads, he'd take off his belt, or forget to take off his rings. On a good day, he'd hit me once, maybe twice, just enough for me to learn a lesson. On a bad day, standing up again, ever again, felt like a triumph.

My memories of my father reaching up from my bedroom floor, stroking my hair, and telling me to sleep now, that I was safe, are still a part of me, as present and potent as the scars on my back.

Understanding this dichotomy is the great knot of my life. I try to untie it on the page; I feel the sting of rope burn on my fingers. I've sought answers in art, but the cultural narratives around domestic violence don't speak to my history. Those narratives say that the batterer is a bad man who needs to be taught—usually by a hero's fist—to pick on someone his own size, and the only way that his victims can truly survive him is to make like Stella at the end of (the film version of) *A Streetcar Named Desire* and bolt for freedom. As if her attachment to Stanley were the darkness in a room, gone with a simple flick of a switch.

Then I found Keri Hulme's novel, *The Bone People*. The paperback copy I bought is a doorstopping 553 pages (including the glossary of Maori phrases), yet I read it in a weekend because, in Hulme, I had finally discovered a writer who spoke to my uncomfortable, inconvenient truth. The heart of the book, ticking through Joycean prose, is the great ache of hurting someone you love—and loving the one who hurts you.

The novel, which was published in 1984, is the story of three unlikely friends—a father, his son, and a woman hermit—who are each unmoored by the loss of their families through death and estrangement and how they swim together through the cold, heavy waters of their grief. However, their union is complicated by the father's bullish temper and his repeated, and increasingly vicious, assaults on his child. The self-proclaimed "heavy father" of *The Bone People* is Maori laborer Joseph Gillayley. Joe remains devastated by the sudden deaths of his wife and infant son. He's ill-equipped to care for his wildling of a foster son, Simon—a seven-year-old boy struck mute and sparked wild by the trauma of surviving a shipwreck. The Gillayleys cycle through belt whippings and tender reconciliations, even when they befriend Kerewin Holmes, the wealthy and reclusive artist who tries to broker a measure of peace between them and when that doesn't work, deploys her martial arts training on Joe. Kerewin serves as audience surrogate as she speaks with shock and disgust at discovering the full extent of Joe's violence on Simon's scarred, bruised-up body: "Joe, you good kind patient sweet natured gentlefingered everloving BASTARD . . . what on earth possessed you to beat up Simon?"

And yet, inside Kerewin's expression of rage, there is an understanding that Joe is not a movie monster, all wicked cackle and fang. He is the same man who soothes Simon's screaming nightmares ("cajoling and pleading in English and Maori and begging . . . beyond language, to reach the child"); who takes on the Sisyphean tasks of creating the normalcy of enforced school attendance and regular bedtimes; who literally breathed life back into the half-drowned boy he's found on the beach. Kerewin's reluctance to call child welfare isn't rooted in any belief that Joe's punishments of his son are at all appropriate—and Hulme's graphic descriptions of Simon's "eyelids . . . swollen, buddha-like, and purple" and his clothes stuck to the open weals on his back suggest that Hulme agrees. Character and author alike hold, in one hand, the unstoppable force of Joe's violence and, in the other hand, the immovable object of his love.

Hulme's work is a remarkable immersion into the hellscape of rage and shame inside the batterer's mind. Joe's cruelty isn't calculated; it's the opposing current in the same circuit that contains his capacity for love (which only makes it more tragic):

> At the moment, he'd rather cut his
> throat than hurt his son, but he
> knows . . . that come morning if the
> child is sulky or rude . . . he'll welt him
> with a cold and righteous intent . . .
> do I hate him then? . . . I love him . . .
> it doesn't even seem like him I'm hit-
> ting. His disobedience or something.

Joe grapples openly, often tearfully, with how naturally that "cold and righteous intent" seizes his heart and freezes out the "gentle-fingered" "ever-loving" parts of him, the parts that marvel that his child should still care for him, still crave his affections—and Simon does, as I did for my own good, kind, bitter-hearted father.

Even after the final, near-fatal beating that separates the threesome (until the novel's epilogue), Simon's first concern upon waking in the hospital is Joe. This devotion may strike the blissfully uninitiated reader as desperate and pathetic. Maybe it is, but it is what it is—and in legitimating Simon's grief over losing his father to prison, Hulme demonstrates her keen understanding that the "family" is the most devastating part of "family violence." Simon leaves the boys' home where he is being cared for and staggers back to the house he shared with Joe, haunted by memories of shattered dishes and goodnight kisses. Hulme treats Joe's incarceration as a necessary palliative, the crucible he must pass through in order to be worthy of his son's devotion.

I read this book every year around Father's Day, and every time, I cry at Joe and Simon's reunion. Hulme's description of Joe, "stooping, weeping, cupping both hands around the small face, framing it, fingers spread in a protective flange for the thin bone cradle of the skull," is menace twinned with tenderness. In it, I see my own father, carrying me up to bed, yelling, "It's a bird, it's a plane, it's Supergirl," before dropping me on the mattress. I am so thrilled to be held up high in my father's strong hands that when I land on my sore, bruised spots, I barely feel the pain. For a moment, at least.

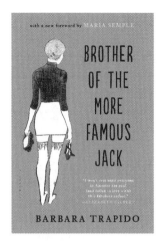

ON BARBARA TRAPIDO'S

Brother of the More Famous Jack

ALIX OHLIN

Last winter, I found myself deep in gloom, mired in some combination of stress and exhaustion and crappy weather that added up to a vague but intractable sadness, the worst symptom of which was that I stopped reading for pleasure. I never stopped reading completely—for a writer and teacher of writing, that's not possible—but my reading was mechanical and professionalized and rote. It was a terrible feeling. I'd always been able to lose myself in books, a loss that paradoxically gave me back myself, and without that ability the world grew a little grayer each day. Sometimes I sat and concentrated on a beautiful sentence by a writer I loved, and I could see the beauty but not feel the pleasure, the kind of palpable, almost bodily enjoyment that had made books so important to me in the first place.

Instead of reading—look, I'm not proud of this—I watched hours of sitcoms, usually sitcoms I had already seen. They didn't even make me laugh. I mainly wanted to be reassured that someone, somewhere, was laughing regularly, at thirty-second intervals, even if it wasn't me. And there was something comforting, of course, about the familiarity of the sitcom structure itself, its dependable resolutions and repetitions, everything wrapped up in twenty-two minutes, only to begin again in the next episode.

In this dreary state I came upon Barbara Trapido's *Brother of the More Famous Jack*, originally published in 1982 and recently reissued by Bloomsbury. I flipped to the first page and, to my surprise, sank into it with unselfconscious enjoyment. I read the first chapter almost without breathing, not wanting to disrupt the spell, and then the whole book. When I finished it, I was a person who loved reading again.

How did she do it? Trapido's sentences are pleasure palaces, meaning they are both intensely pleasurable to read and are *about* pleasure of many kinds: sexual, intellectual, aesthetic. *Brother of the More Famous Jack* is narrated by Katherine, a beautiful, artsy girl from the suburbs who likes to make her own clothes ("I can knit prodigious landscapes into my jerseys"). As she begins university, she falls under the thrall of her philosophy professor, Jacob Goldman, and his large bohemian family.

"'I'll be frank with you,'" Jacob says to Katherine on their first meeting. "'I had you up here because your Head's report on you is so unfavourable, it leads me to suspect that you may be somewhat brighter than the Head. You may of course be no more than an opinionated trouble-maker. Which do you think you are?' He fixed me under his black horsehair eyebrows with what I took to be smouldering animosity."

Scene after scene unspools with this kind of dialogue, barbed, electric, and energizing. The characters ping-pong against one another, all of their confrontations refracted through Katherine's voice, which is smart without being smart-alecky and vulnerable without being timid. She is also candid and clear-eyed on the subject of sex lives, whether it's her own (losing her virginity to an older, bisexual man) or that of Jacob and his wife (who is about to bear their sixth child).

Though she gets involved with Goldman's son Roger, Katherine also loves and is loved by Jacob, his wife, Jane, and their other children in various and meaningful ways. The novel is a kind of polymorphous romantic comedy whose perversities all resonate. Eventually Katherine leaves the Goldmans behind and goes off to Italy, where some terrible things happen to her. I won't spoil the book by saying what they are, but I will note that Trapido writes about loss and pain, both emotional and physical, with the same blunt concision that she brings to sex and romance, so that the breezy momentum of the book is never disrupted even as the experience of the characters flips from light to dark.

It's a pretty astonishing thing to be able to do. Part of how she's able to achieve it is through Katherine's voice, its insistently propulsive, conversational quality. Trapido honed this style by writing much of the book, which was her first novel, in her head. Born in South Africa, she moved to London in her early twenties, married a man who became an Oxford don, had two children, and came to writing late. In the foreword to *Brother of the More Famous Jack*, Maria Semple describes Trapido working in the middle of the night, often speaking the dialogue out loud, over and over, so that by the time she was ready to type, she had the book almost memorized.

Other parts of Trapido's technique are compression and witty description; one character sends another a cake so large it "appeared to be suffering the effects of hormone treatment." Katherine takes a dislike to someone because he blows his nose too politely and "made a point of carving meat with a formidable show of expertise." The book is always funny even when it's not at all happy, a distinction that becomes shattering when Katherine's pain takes center stage.

I've read my way through all of Trapido's books now—Bloomsbury is in the process of republishing them—and it's clear that she is a scholar of comedic forms. Many of her novels are framed around narrative allusions to classical works, from Shakespeare's festive and romantic plays to Mozart's *The Magic Flute*. What Trapido recognizes is how capacious these forms are, how much darkness they can accommodate; Trapido's own novels take in ovarian cancer, apartheid, sexual abuse, cervical surgery, HIV, and many other angles on estrangement and loss.

In her 2010 novel, *Sex and Stravinsky*, Trapido articulates a sort of manifesto about comic forms, through a character who is devoted to early opera:

> He likes those stagy assignations in moonlit shrubberies and the constant dropping of love letters in regulation privet hedges where the wrong people are always destined to pick them up. He likes precipitous conclusions in which all is resolved by timely revelation. A telling birthmark. An ancient nun with a very long memory . . . Life redeemed through wit and coincidence, heady plot lines and acrobatic dexterity.

This is not exactly a description of Trapido's own plot lines, which are shaggy and not always fully resolved, but she does love to bring a cast of characters into orbit and, through acrobatic dexterity, make their intersections matter. Their lives are redeemed but not sanitized; in *Sex and Stravinsky*, the ripple effects of the adults' zany actions are, the ending makes clear, going to be felt by their children for a long time. But Trapido's avowed affection for the comic opera made me think about my own sitcom addiction in a more generous way, both because the rewards of these forms are genuine and because a writer like Trapido can accomplish so much within them.

Since *Brother of the More Famous Jack* brought me back to pleasure reading, I've been pushing it on people with a level of aggression not typical of me. I want other people to share it too, and for Trapido to find a bigger readership in North America. I wonder if Trapido is not better known here because of her particular strain of humor, which is not especially fashionable. It is rich with academic characters and literary allusions, the unabashed Britishness of boarding schools and eccentric intellectuals and young women with precocious vocabularies. Personally, I love all these things and find Trapido's take on them both charmingly familiar and refreshingly modern. If you, like me, grew up reading *Brideshead Revisited* and P. G. Wodehouse but live in the twenty-first century and are a feminist, then Trapido's books are a gift to you, custom-made.

Toward the end of *Brother of the More Famous Jack*, a man sings Katherine a song by Monteverdi in the street, declares his love, and then takes her to bed, where he looms over her and then pauses "like a compassionate executioner." The whole sequence is under four pages long, briskly profane, and delightful; I laughed at the straightforwardness of Trapido's descriptions and at the good-humored sex, one more comic pleasure in a book that's full of them. Katherine cannot speak for joy. It's one of the few moments of silence in a talky book, and it made me cry while reading, which is its own pleasure.

ON LEONARD MICHAELS'S

A Cat

SANTI ELIJAH HOLLEY

I learned about Leonard Michaels sometime during the summer of 2007, when a friend introduced me to his work. In his self-effacing humor, his vacillation between shame and narcissism, and his obsession with sex and guilt, I found Michaels to be something like a role model: an official spokesman of disaffected young literary men with miles-long trails of failed relationships. I was brash and impudent in my midtwenties—everything revolved around me and nothing else mattered. And I sought writers who confirmed this same worldview.

By the end of 2008 I was sure I'd read everything Michaels had written. I thought I'd tracked down every book. And then one day, while scouring the Internet, I noticed an unfamiliar title, one that had been left out of his obituaries, biographies, and most bibliographies. The book was titled, simply, *A Cat*. It was advertised, by *Library Journal*, as a "delightful celebration of the cat." This had to be a joke. "The cat" had to be a euphemism for something more salacious. It didn't take long for me to find *A Cat*, as the local bookshop had a used copy on hand for $2.95.

A Cat was, on first blush, the kind of book you might find in the discount bin at Walmart. It was a book you would give to your lonely aunt for Christmas or Rosh Hashanah. It was a collection of brief, campy aphorisms on cats:

A cat is content to be a cat.

A cat is not owned by anybody.

A cat imagines things about you,
nothing you can know for sure.

What were these sentimental musings, these schmaltzy witticisms? What was with the accompanying doodle-like line drawings by Frances Lerner? Where was the braggadocio, the sexual insecurity, the thinly veiled misogyny? Was this even the same Leonard Michaels? I was embarrassed for him. And angry. Who put him up to this? I placed *A Cat* away on my shelf, accepting it as another book I wouldn't finish.

The first Leonard Michaels book I read was *Sylvia*, his devastating "autobiographical novel" chronicling his brief marriage to Sylvia Bloch in his early twenties. The directness of Michaels's prose, the uninhibited candor of his statements, pulled me in

immediately. In an early scene in the novel, Michaels relates the first meeting between him and his soon-to-be wife: "Then, from behind long black bangs, her eyes moved, looked at me. The question of what to do with my life was resolved for the next four years." Later in the book, when the toxicity and madness of his marriage have become manifest, Michaels writes, "It would have been easy to leave Sylvia. Had it been difficult, I might have done it."

In *Time Out of Mind*—a collection of selected excerpts from his private diaries, extending from 1961 to 1995—Michaels confesses his deepest vulnerabilities, without hiding behind the cloak of fiction. He examines the relationship between the sexes, and makes pronouncements that read like dismal proverbs from a cynical god: "Adultery has less to do with romance and sex," he writes, "than with the discovery of how little we mean to each other." In another passage, reflecting on a romantic interest gone awry, Michaels writes, "They come toward you, anxious to be with you, or anyone but themselves, so they make themselves seductive, offer endless attention, flattery, love, sexual cornucopias. If you desire them as they desire you, they flee." For a young, literary-minded, would-be Casanova—as I saw myself—Michaels's word was gospel.

Time passed. I read and reread Michaels's books. He had died in 2003, leaving behind only a modest body of work, and in the spring of 2009 I was mourning that this was all there was. And then I remembered *A Cat* sitting neglected on my shelf. I decided to give it another read.

Once I got past the ludicrousness of the concept, and the laughably simple line drawings, I began to see that more than a collection of Hallmark platitudes, Michaels offers subtle meditations on the mystery and beauty of life. He explores the same themes as in his other books—pride, arrogance, jealousy, unrequited love—only through the lens of domestic cats.

While some passages are clever, others are enigmatic; others are downright eerie:

> A cat weighs about as much as a baby, and it sleeps most of the day; but if a cat were fifteen pounds heavier, it wouldn't seem cute, and it could tear your throat out.

> If you think long enough about what you see in a cat, you begin to suppose you will understand everything, but its eyes tell you there is nothing to understand, there is only life.

> A cat knows what happens to you after you die.

In the complete works of Leonard Michaels, *A Cat* remains the curiosity, the outlier. Here is another side of Michaels, one he didn't often reveal in his stories and novels. It is difficult to know how Michaels himself felt about this book. In no interview I've read does he mention it, as though it were a late-in-life illegitimate child.

By using its publication date as a point of reference, however, we can make some assumptions. Michaels was sixty-two years old in 1995, when *A Cat* was published. Three years had passed since *Sylvia*. He would publish just two more books while alive: *Time Out of Mind* and a collection of essays. He would live only eight more years. If he wasn't explicitly attempting to rehabilitate his reputation, it seems that he at least wished to go out on a more positive note.

The closing passage of the book is among the longer ones. "When you are packing clothes in a suitcase, a cat will come sit on the clothes," it begins. "It assumes you will include it on your trip. This can seem absurd and funny. You laugh and go out the door. But when you return, your cat acts haughtily, as if it doesn't care that you're home, as if it hardly knows you. In your relation to a cat there is a sweetness that isn't absurd. It is more heartbreaking than funny."

At last, Michaels shows his hand. He unveils, by slow degrees, the book's true message, its hidden meaning. He doesn't wish for us to examine our relationships with house cats. He wishes for us, as he always had, to examine our relationships with ourselves. I imagine this book as his way of communicating directly with me, and others like me, helping us bridge that chasm between conceit and compassion, to make the leap from boyhood to manhood. In this, *A Cat* isn't so much a renunciation of his younger, chauvinistic self; it is a testament to getting past all that, and learning to be still, to watch, and to find truth and beauty in the most unassuming of places. With those six closing words, Michaels sums up not only his body of work but also most of my twenties: "It is more heartbreaking than funny." 🛡

Decor

Rita Bullwinkel

There was a period of my life in which my primary source of income came from being a piece of furniture. I worked for a business that sold sofas that cost over six times what I was paid in a year. The showroom was on the twenty-fourth floor of a beautiful modern building in the Flatiron District of Manhattan. There was no storefront. It was a word-of-mouth business. If you were rich enough, you knew about it. The clients were Saudi princes looking to spend $80,000 on a dining table; creative directors of high-end fashion companies looking to overhaul their runway seating, buy a million or two million dollars' worth of luxury benches; hobbled old Upper East Side women redesigning their Hampton homes, budgets of five million and up just to acquire objects, things to fill the spaces they already owned.

A big floor-to-ceiling stainless-steel door opened from the hallway into the show space. Inside the show space were several interior configurations—dining rooms and living rooms and bedrooms set up on circles of carpet—living quarters that in real life would have been divided but here, in the showroom, were smashed up against each other without any walls. And on the other side of the imaginary rooms, just below the big windows, was me, at a long grand desk, in a pencil skirt. I was a pretty young girl who brought the clients almonds and glasses of wine. I also opened the mail, coordinated the shipping, and did a great deal of filing. But I understood that my primary purpose was my presence. I added to the atmosphere, my employers told me. I added something to the experience of the showroom that my colleagues, all gay men over fifty, couldn't provide.

My colleagues loved having me in the showroom. They said I was beautiful. They said I dressed fashionably. They said my short hair was avant-garde. It is true that I do like beautiful clothing. I feel most at home in prints that are loud. I like objects that startle me when I look at them.

I didn't mind being looked at as much at the beginning. One man, during the early months of my employment, came into the showroom and asked to take photographs of me sitting on the furniture. He said he wanted a human element in the pictures, something that would help him remember the proportions and size. I sat on the chaise lounge and curled my high-heeled feet up under me. I put my hands behind my head and tried to look deadpan. Perfect, said the man. He never bought anything. I would have known if he had because I filed all the orders, knew exactly who bought what and how much money was coming in.

When I opened the mail there were often requests for samples, architects or interior designers wanting to see a swatch of the wood grain or the fabric or the leather used on a particular design. In the morning I made a stack of the letters that requested swatches. In the afternoon I went into the back room, a dingy windowless closet, and found what each person wanted and then sent them the sample. Sometimes people also requested catalogs or lookbooks, big-format photographs of the furniture placed in front of the ocean on a sandy beach, a ridiculous situation akin to a woman in a ball gown on an elephant, which, in fashion magazines, you do often see.

I was a pretty young girl who brought the clients almonds and glasses of wine.

I had been working in the showroom for six months when I got the letter. I didn't immediately know if I was going to show it to my boss. It was a nondescript, cheap business envelope. The showroom address and the return address were written by hand. The return address said *State Correctional Institution—Frackville, Pennsylvania*. Inside the envelope was a piece of paper that appeared to be a photocopy of a letter that had been typed on a typewriter. The paper had the lines and dark spots that come with a sloppily executed photocopy. Stapled to the letter was a note the size of Post-it that said I, the recipient, should be aware that all prison correspondence is read and monitored. The letter itself was short, but alarmingly articulate. The contents were very strange and upsetting. The worst part about it was how overly formal the whole thing was. It said:

Dear Sir or Madam,

You do not know me, and so I understand that it will therefore be difficult to per-suade you to perform the task which I request. My name is Malcolm Danvers and I am currently incarcerated. I spend most of my time in solitary confinement. Alone in this black box I have little joy. Therefore, I have taken to imagining for myself a new home. A new structure that I could build upon my release, a modern structure that I could build in the woods and live in. After being here, in this cell for so long, I no longer believe I am fit for human company. So the only thing I can do, the only thing that keeps me alive, is to imagine a beautiful life for myself, alone, outside this prison. An architecturally stunning feat that brings in lots of light. I have read many books, while imprisoned, on drafting architectural plans and have thus, in the last two years, already estab-lished an achievable blueprint. I am now at the stage where interiors must be considered. I have been made to understand that your pieces are some of the best, some of the most elegant in the busi-ness and that any one of your designs can be cus-tom-made. This aspect of your product is of great interest to me because it allows me an even greater breadth of imagination. Therefore, I have a request of you. If you can, would you be kind enough to send me several cata-logs of your best-selling pieces, and also some samples, so that I might imagine more vividly the furniture in my woods-circled home? Any leather or fabric swatches would be of great value to me. Unfortunately, due to the constraints of my situation, I cannot accept fabric or leather samples bigger than 1" x 1" because of their potential to be used as a weapon. Similarly, I am unable to accept any wood or metal samples because of their violent potential. Thank you, dear sir or madam, for considering this request. I realize that in your office and your life you are, no doubt, a person of extreme impor-tance and already under a great deal of demands as it stands. Any time you could take to send me some samples and catalogs would be greatly appreciated. Perhaps it will give you joy, at least, to picture some of your beautiful furniture in the home of my imagi-nation, looking elegant and stunning in the morning light.

In gratitude,
Mr. Malcolm Danvers

I remember putting the letter down in something of a panic. I feared someone was watching me, as I often feared during the workday. My

> I knew I could probably find out online what this man had done to land himself in prison.

colleagues were very nosy and frequently asked me what I was doing, what I was working on, which task I had at hand. I knew that if I showed the letter to my boss he would be disgusted and make me throw it away. I may have been wrong about this, but I could sense they would not think the letter was of interest. They would probably be primarily concerned with trying to figure out how this man in jail had gotten our name. I couldn't decide what to do so I put the letter in my purse and brought it home with me that evening.

I knew I could probably find out online what this man had done to land himself in prison. But then I thought that this was, maybe, something I didn't want to know. Perhaps if I were a better person I would have looked it up immediately. But I had been made aware, during this time in my life, that I was not as good a person as many of my friends were, specifically when it came to contemplating the death penalty, which it seemed Mr. Malcolm Danvers was not at risk for. But maybe he had narrowly escaped. What I mean is, in the social circles I associated with there were a lot of young liberal-minded people, people who were sexual extremists and in polyamorous relationships and who also were deeply invested in prison reform, despite never having had contact with a prisoner in their entire lives. It was not acceptable to believe in the death penalty, in my social group, and I had been alarmed, at recent evening gatherings and gallery openings, that when the subject of the death penalty came up, I found myself sympathetic. People were bad and they did terrible things. What use was it keeping these bad people alive?

This wasn't an opinion I voiced, ever. It would have been socially unacceptable to say out loud that perhaps some people are meant to die. Also, I usually didn't say much, so it would have been out of character for me to blurt it out. It just seemed to me, as I had experienced in my own life, that true evil did exist and that when it did infect someone it was incurable, and that those people should be killed. I thought of a man from my hometown who broke into fifteen houses and raped fourteen women. This man, I thought, should be dead. I could not conceive of a reason why this man should be alive. What was more, because he had not killed any of the women he would be, after seventeen years, released back out into the world. When I was sixteen and these crimes were being committed, I thought about killing him.

But what I mean to say is that I knew that because of my belief in true evil I could not look up the crimes of Mr. Malcolm Danvers. If I did and it was bad enough, then I would not be able to think about him or contemplate any further his imagined home. I wanted to give Danvers the samples because I wanted the feeling of privilege I'd get from giving another human an object of his wanting. If I looked him up I might not be able to send him any fabric swatches or obtain any possible joy from giving him these things because there would be a possibility that I would want to kill him. If I were another person—a bigger, smarter, more intellectual person—perhaps I could have immediately stomached whatever he had done, but I knew I wasn't, and I still wanted, for a little while longer, to think of him as human, so I did not look him up and the next morning went into the showroom and sent him the samples and the catalogs straightaway.

After I sent him the package I felt good immediately. I sat at my big beautiful desk under those grand twenty-fourth-story windows and basked in the sun. I had signed my return letter with my real name. I told him, Here you are, Mr. Malcolm Danvers, may your home be every bit as beautiful as you have imagined. Yours, Ursula G.

I remember very vividly the rest of that day. Three clients came in and I was exceptionally friendly and sat with them while they drank their wine and talked about the problems they were having training a new dog. I remember specifically Mrs. Sheffield, one of our better Upper East Side old women clients, saying that her poodle refused to pee anywhere but everywhere. I thought of the $100,000 Turkish rug we had sold her the month previous. I hoped that the dog had made a pee river on that rug and really let its bowels run free.

Perhaps getting the letter was a turning point for my time in the showroom. When the letter came I had been there about six months, long enough for the novelty to wear off and for me to figure out exactly what, regarding the purpose of my presence, was going on. I was so grateful for the job when I got it. Before I worked at the showroom I worked for a Chelsea boutique folding $300 T-shirts and steaming silk dresses in a windowless basement after the store closed. My usual work hours had been from 8:00 PM-2:00 AM. I listened to my iPod while I folded and felt very claustrophobic and very depressed. Perhaps a smarter person would have found some way to multitask, some way to use that time more effectively, but all I could feel while I was folding was that I was suffocating in a dark room, which I very well might have been, so when I got the job at the showroom through a friend of a friend, I felt I had landed in a palace on the moon. I mean, there were many things about the showroom that were both moon-like and palace-like. The world that lived in the showroom was completely detached from the world I knew. It was a place where the wealthiest people on the planet could act as if the way they lived their lives was acceptable. And even the furniture, the made-up room configurations, seemed to exist in a space devoid of gravity—free-floating rooms attached to nothing that simply implied life or the way someone might live a life in a home that did not actually contain humans or anything that was alive. And the palatial quality of it all, of being in a space where everything was the finest, made by the finest designers with the finest materials by the finest Italian craftsmen, implied that this was the best man could do: here in the showroom we were at the pinnacle of human creation. The best things money could buy, myself among them. It felt good to be around such fine things.

So at first, as I said, I didn't mind being viewed and being part of the furniture, because it felt good to be considered suitable company for such beautiful objects, and I had, before coming to the showroom, been a ghost that lived only at night, in the basement of a boutique, folding things and wishing I were smart enough to imagine a way out.

There were many things about the showroom that were both moon-like and palace-like.

A month passed before I got another letter from Mr. Malcolm Danvers. It came the same way, in the mail, typed on a typewriter but photocopied, only this time he also sent architectural plans and it was addressed to me, Ms. Ursula G., which obviously caused me a great deal of alarm. I worried someone else in the showroom had seen it. It said:

My Dear Ursula,

Words cannot express the gratitude I feel for you. The leather you sent me is perfect for the low modern sofa I've put in the living room, and I am using several of the fabric samples you provided on lounge chairs throughout the house. Specifically, that dark gray linen has been upholstered on a design I saw and tore out from a feature on Italian innovators in Architectural Digest. *As you can see from the attached blueprints, your signature low sofa is perfect for the space in the left corner of the living room. I cut out the photo of it from the catalog you mailed and have taped it on the wall right next to my bed, where I lay my head to rest at night, along with your fabric*

*and leather samples, so that I see my house, and your beautiful furniture in it, right
before I sleep. I can think of no way to repay you for the gorgeous furniture you have
gifted my imagination. I only wish I could have you over to my home, in its finished
state, to serve you tea and to be able to show you all the magnificent work I have done
and with which you have so graciously aided. Perhaps I can imagine this exchange,
even if it never will, in the world outside this black box, transpire? If you feel gener-
ous, and would like to come to tea, send me a photo of yourself, and I will imagine you
inside my beautiful home sitting on some of your stunningly designed modern furni-
ture, me serving you tea and maybe some fresh biscuits.*

Yours,
Mr. Malcolm Danvers

Was I something they kept around because I looked avant-garde?

I believe I shook slightly as I looked at the architectural plans. I remember sweat-ing a great deal. They were well drawn and very professional looking. I wouldn't have been able to tell they were done by an amateur, let alone by a prisoner. I saw our signature low sofa drawn in miniature in the living room, just as Danvers had noted, and I saw the dark gray linen lounge chair, drawn in acute detail, smaller than the head of an eraser, in a room marked STUDY, and several more notations that communicated other furniture that he must have found from other companies, convinced other people to send to him and to correspond with him. It made me feel a little better that I was not the only one helping him build this home of his imagination. But it also made me feel a little jealous. I had been taken by the idea that I was somehow a unique savior to him, that I alone was helping his dream live on. I mean, I had been taken by the nature of it from the beginning, the idea that someone who lived only in darkness could build for themselves another world to inhabit. It was romantic. And deeply human, this notion that someone would want to construct for themselves a home they could never have, a home they could only ever go to when they closed their eyes.

But Danvers seemed to be somewhat convinced that he might actually get out and that he might actually be able to make his plans a reality. So then I had to reckon with the idea that I could, possibly, be helping him build a hideout, someplace for him to go after he had been released. I was very upset, thinking that this man, a man who probably did do something that would make me wish him dead, wanted to have me over in a room in his imagination.

It was a busy day in the showroom and I had lots to do, so I put the letter and the architectural plans in my purse and got to filing. By the time I got off work my nerves had calmed. That evening I went to a dinner party, a long-standing arrangement where I would meet three friends of mine, some of the friends from the gallery openings, at one of their apartments for a meal. I picked up a bottle of wine on my way. I didn't plan to say anything about Mr. Malcolm Danvers at dinner, but then I had three glasses of wine and it just kind of came out. Marie, the woman whose apartment I was in, asked me about my day at work, and I told her about the letter. Everyone else became very interested in what I was saying and wanted to listen in. Suzanne, Marie's closest friend, said she felt very bad for Danvers, what a horror our prison system was, simple barbarism. Marie asked if I had been able to find out what Mr. Malcolm Danvers had done. No, I admitted, I didn't want to know. You should look it up, said Marie, especially now that he has asked for your picture, don't you want to know what he has done so you can better gauge how to respond to his letter? None of these people could sense my hidden belief that some people deserved to die. They wanted to look Danvers up, right then and there, but I begged them not to. No, I said, please, I don't want to know.

In an attempt to distract them, to change the subject, I pulled out the architectural plans that Danvers had attached to his second letter. I showed them the signature low sofa and the linen lounge chair and they oohed and aahed. Stephen, Marie's boyfriend, who I had forgotten was an architect, examined the plans very intently and said, It's a glass house, these demarcations here on the side mean the paneling should be glass instead of wood. That makes sense to me, I told him. Danvers said he wanted to let all the light in, I guess that's what I would want too if I were trapped indoors. Everyone at the dinner thought this was very beautiful, Mr. Malcolm Danvers's desire for beauty and a home and light, and Suzanne said it was everything she could do to keep from crying.

This angered me slightly. Nobody seemed concerned that Danvers wanted a picture of me to put in his home, that he wanted me to be there with him in the woods in his glass house having a cup of tea. It occurred to me then that in this group of friends, I might also be a piece of furniture. Was I something they kept around because I looked avant-garde? I suppose it was at this dinner party that I first reflected on whether or not the kind of life I was living was lonely. And if the type of life I was living was lonely, what other lives were there? Why did I feel so wholly inanimate? Why did I feel so completely that I was stuffed in a tightly sealed box? I had made great efforts to relieve myself of this boxness. I dressed adventurously. I consumed art. I read widely. So why did the idea that I, like Mr. Malcolm Danvers, might too need an imaginary house to build seem so true?

Stephen got up from the table and went into a bedroom and returned with a laptop. I'm too curious, he said, I'm too interested in the immaculate tragedy of it. I am going to look our incarcerated architect up. *Our* incarcerated architect? I thought. How dare you. I was the one who sent him the samples, I was the one who wrote him a letter, I'm the one who's now being forced to have tea in the house of his mind. He's mine.

Please don't, I said to him, really, I mean it. Marie looked at me playfully and said, Come on now, Ursula, let us have our bit of fun. Everyone huddled around Stephen as he typed in the information. I tried to keep it together as the round circle that signaled the computer search thinking spun around and chased its own tail. Damn, said Stephen, let me restart it.

In this lull I tried, in my drunken state, to get ahold of how I was feeling. My hands were gripped to my knees and no one was looking at me, no one was paying me any heed at all. The conversation had taken off without me and had no need of me. All I had at that moment at that wretched dinner party was my imagined Danvers and what he could, depending on what he had done, mean to me. Danvers's desire to build something of beauty had touched me. I had an image of him in my head, some older man, gently feeling the fabric I sent him, that I couldn't shake off. I was scared of myself, scared to see how I felt about anyone who had done something bad enough to get stuck in a black box, and scared to admit that, in all likelihood, he deserved it. He probably deserved to be dead. I tried to be optimistic. Maybe he had been wrongly accused. Maybe he killed someone, but that someone was a very bad person. He spoke so articulately and had shown me, generously, the depths of his imagination. What types of crimes require imagination? To calm myself I made a list in my head of the worst possible things Danvers could have done: raped a child, raped many children, raped many women, killed many people, raped and killed a young woman who looked like me. Stephen came back to the table and typed MALCOLM DANVERS CRIMINAL RECORD into the search engine and it came up immediately—child pornography ring bust, biggest in Pennsylvania history, creator and distributor Malcolm Danvers put behind bars for only fifteen years because they couldn't find any evidence that he killed them, although eleven of the girls used in his videos (ages eight—thirteen) still couldn't be found.

Mr. Malcolm Danvers, I thought, Mr. Malcolm Danvers you are a murderer and a rapist.

Jesus, said Stephen.

Are you happy? I asked them. Should we go protest for his release?

Calm down, said Marie.

Why don't you write him? I said to her. Why don't you tell him how sorry you are that he has to be in there all alone? Maybe you should go visit him? Pennsylvania isn't that far away, maybe we should all go there together and express our deep regret at the injustice of his internment and the inhumanity of solitary confinement? Maybe we should send his

> He probably deserved to be dead. I tried to be optimistic.

architectural plans to the homes of the girls he raped, to the families of the victims, so they can sleep well knowing that Danvers has a very nice, luxurious home?

Drunk and infuriated, crazed by the fact that I felt I had had my reality violated by this information I so did not want to know, I goaded Stephen to keep going, keep searching, keep digging for more information that would make me want Malcolm Danvers dead. Stephen didn't respond, and only looked at me silently with his brows furrowed, so I took his computer from him. Why don't we search for images? I yelled at him.

Hundreds of photos came up, but they weren't photos of Danvers after his arrest. Rather, they were pictures of him well dressed, beaming, clearly communicating him as a real estate agent for multimillion-dollar homes. One of the photos was surrounded by text in a way that showed it was excerpted from a magazine. Under a photo of Danvers sitting in a living room was the caption PHILADELPHIA REAL ESTATE AGENT MR. MALCOLM DANVERS IN HIS OWN HOME. My god, I thought as I looked at the photo, Mr. Malcolm Danvers, you might use children like furniture, but you have very nice decor. In the photo you could see a great deal of his interiors. There was an Eames chair and a large fine kilim woven rug and expensive mahogany wood floors. On a modern, glass coffee table sat a design book. I could even make out the title—*The French Inspired Home*. I thought back to the man who had taken photos of me in the showroom, the man who had wanted a human element in the photographs of the furniture. What was the human element in this photograph of Mr. Malcolm Danvers? Where was the humanity here?

I looked at Stephen and Marie and Suzanne. What do you think of his taste? I yelled at them. Do you think he chose a nice color for the leather on his Eames chair?

Stephen said he was sorry for looking everything up, that he didn't know how upset it would make me, a terrible half limp of an apology that somehow placed the blame back on my shoulders, back on the fact that I was the one screaming and ruining all that they had enjoyed about their evening, as if without me they'd have had Danvers all to themselves to contemplate and enjoy.

> I needed to send Danvers something that would make him feel less living.

I could feel it then that I had threatened them, threatened their nice cutlery and their beautiful handmade dishware and their abstract, geometric prints that hung on hooks above their sink.

I kept yelling at them, asking them loudly where they got their gorgeous outfits. I complimented everything in the apartment at a deafening volume. I walked into the bathroom and said, These tiles are the most beautiful white. They're perfectly minimalist, I yelled. They do a perfect job at not being noticed.

I could hear Marie and Suzanne at the edges of my awareness, whispering in the living room about what to do with me. Stephen came into the bathroom, where I was rubbing their towels against my hand, and offered me more words that lacked an actual apology, and then asked if I would like it if he called me a cab home.

No, I said. I'll walk out of this apartment. And I did. And then I walked alone under the light-swollen city sky the many miles it took to get to the room where I slept.

. . .

I woke up early the next day, at 4:00 AM, feeling ill and empty. I climbed out of my bedroom window and onto my fire escape, where I sat and watched the sun creep over the adjacent brownstones and thought of what I would send Danvers in return. I could just send him a printout of his conviction summary. A simple message—I know what you've done. But what would that do? It would perhaps incite shame, or just disappointment at being found out. Maybe that was how all his prison correspondence went—generosity and then shame. I do think shame is a useful weapon, but it relies so heavily on the person's own self-hatred, and maybe Danvers didn't really hate himself at all. I wanted to make Danvers feel the worst thing I had ever felt. Make no mistake, if I could have, I would have killed him. People that evil aren't ever cured. It's crazy to me that someone could look at that photograph of Danvers grinning in his luxury home, know what he had done, see his eyes, and ever think that this was a man who should go on living.

I knew that if the gallery opening friends ever heard me talk like this they'd mumble about cruel and unusual punishment and forgiveness for even the worst crimes, some rhetoric that, while true and intelligent, would only prove to me that they had never experienced violence in their own lives.

And then it came to me. I knew what I had to do. I needed to send Danvers something that would make him feel less living.

Earlier that year I had seen an exhibit at the Metropolitan Museum of Art on the furniture of Louis XIV, a fat man who was obsessed with the svelteness of his own legs, who thought he was king of the sun, and who also very much liked furniture that imitated beastliness. His chairs had the legs of deer, his sofas were made from pelts of lions, the hooves of horses were used all over his house to hold up pots or gold urns. It disturbed me when I saw the exhibit, those lion paws holding up Louis's favorite seat. This was perhaps the best way, or the only way, I knew to degrade Mr. Malcolm Danvers.

As soon as the image came to me I felt much more at ease. I could sketch Danvers into a piece of furniture in the style of Louis XIV, make his hairy arms the front legs of a sofa and his toed feet the back. I'd upholster it in a combination of Danvers's skin and that dark linen from his coveted lounge chair.

I went inside and got my notebook. I made an incredibly detailed sketch, and drew Danvers's head mounted at the center of the back of this baroque sofa, right where Louis XIV always put the sun. I drew the back of the sofa scalloped. I drew the arms as intricately carved wood that bent with the curve of the seat.

At 6:00 AM I got dressed and went in to the showroom, several hours before everyone else arrived. I made color photocopies of my drawing. I even shrank down my Danvers sofa to a small enough size that I could fit it on his blueprint. I put it right in front of his fireplace, where his skin would singe. Then, using the copier, I zoomed in on the beige sketch of the skin that I had drawn and printed off several color copies. After they were printed I taped them together to make a large 2' x 2' swatch of Danvers's skin. I put my drawing of the Danvers sofa and his blueprint with my added product placement in an envelope that was 8" x 11". I then wrapped the envelope in my Danvers skin paper and addressed it and walked down the stairs and placed the envelope in the public USPS mailbox on Sixth and Fourteenth.

As I slid the envelope into the blue metal slot I imagined Danvers opening the letter slowly, the seal of my skin package already broken by prison wardens who probably hated Danvers as much as I did, prison wardens who would relish letting my hate mail slide by. I imagined Danvers poring over my plans, poring over my drawings, with a confusion that slowly morphed into fear when he realized that I fully intended to cut off his ankles, if I had the chance, to make them into the footrests for kitchen stools, his knuckles the decorative knobs on the bars where I would rest my feet, and that in this house of my imagination he'd be murdered, murdered in the type of way that the murdered person's defining characteristic becomes how they were made into the dead.

I thought of him in prison, dismembered and inanimate, and imagined him finally realizing that he was no longer a man, just a thing in a house that would never be built, and would never be visited—a house that would disintegrate when I died because the mind that held it would melt into liquid and rot as soon as oxygen seeped inside.

This imagining hovered there for a moment, in the air above my head on Sixth and Fourteenth, and it felt good to look at it, and claim it, and acknowledge at least within myself that it was a creation that was mine. As I walked away from the mailbox I could feel the imagining following me. It hovered above my head. When I returned to the showroom to start my day at work, I could still feel it upon me, clamping the crown of my head as jewel settings prong a stone, and so when my boss called a meeting in the afternoon, I had trouble understanding what it was, exactly, he was saying, though I could hear his words perfectly fine.

There was going to be an overhaul of the company image, he said. We had previously carried many fine wood products, beautiful mahogany tables and chairs, beechwood outdoor chaises, but this was going to change. Within the interior design world, open-grain wood furniture is referred to as a living aesthetic, as in, the product's visual presence reveals that it did, in fact, come from a living thing. The living aesthetic is associated with rustic interiors, specifically those made by Scandinavian designers, who pioneered the realm of reclaimed wood. My boss said that this trend had become so popular that it had escaped the world of high design and invaded the mainstream. One could now buy wood-grain wallpaper at Target or pick up an open-grain table from Crate and Barrel on the cheap. This market, we were told in our meeting, was no longer something we were interested in serving. From here on out there would be no more open-grain wood, no more raw leather available from our showroom. The showroom would now exclusively embody a nonliving aesthetic. New lookbooks were already being made. There was going to be a lot more chrome, and a lot more white leather, and many more big glass boxes, which, my boss told us, were chairs.

The open-grain sample showroom furniture got lacquered over. I coordinated shipping the pieces to the workshop and they came back shiny, white, and gray. I could see myself in the reflection of their top coats. Chrome and lacquer scratch easily, my boss told me, so be careful of your rings. I wondered if the aesthetic change in the showroom demanded I now dress differently. Was there a way I could make myself look less living? Was my shaggy cropped hair too rustic, too suggestive that I too had once come from a living thing? How could I make myself more severe? I imagined my insides dissolving from their wet earth-tone tissues into a semisolid silver chrome matter. I saw a team of little men shaping the matter into a ball. They polished the ball into a perfectly shined chrome sphere that floated in the middle of my rib cage. All the little men looked at their reflections in my chrome sphere. They saw their faces fish-eyed, their body parts closest to the ball magnified. These drapes are horrid, I heard one of them say as he ran his fingers over the rungs of my ribs. Why do the curtains go so poorly with this chandelier? I felt my interiors breathing. As I brought fresh air into my lungs I could feel the chrome ball inside of me quivering.

Dorothea Lasky

GHOST FLIGHT TO THE MOON

You were never what I thought
Don Repo, you fixed the ovens
Where they put the people
And stirred their bones to ash
Flight to the mountains
Then the descent
Landing gear
Billowing silver
Like fabric acorns
We left at the corner of the sky
What or what I say to you
I wish I saw you more
Is what I said
To no response
But you probably
Were thinking of something
Like about your taxes
Or the way you could cheat
Others out of the pool money
My friend once came over
And read me her poems so freely
I wanted to
But I couldn't abandon her

The silent unabated
No oxygen delivery
The feeling of no air
In the room
Thick with white steam
She sat at the corner waiting for me
Adorned in pink crystals
A sound stage
She said
You never write
I say no response
I say to give no response
Is to respond
My friend says
He says nothing
To say something
Building heavy with meaning
She says,
You are on fire
I look around
I say,
I know

THE DREAM

A week after Max died I had a dream.

It was a late dream, after at least 5:00 AM.

I woke up after.

In the dream, I was getting some sort of therapy and went to this woman's house.

She had this big garden and someone told me to wait there.

At first it looked just like plants and flowers and stone things.

Then all of a sudden I realized there were monsters everywhere.

Large snakes and lions.

Mutated animals, with rough reptilian parts where there should have been soft ones.

I got very scared. I said, I don't think I want this kind of therapy.

The woman came into the garden.

She scooped me up like a baby and held me.

I closed my eyes.

A large animal came up to me and bit me on the left arm, but did not sink his teeth in.

He just held my arm and I said to her, can't you make him stop.

Weren't the animals ostensibly hers.

She said, he thinks you are his dinner. He is forgetting he has eaten.

Then she told me to slowly slide my arm from his mouth.

I could feel his teeth then go towards my side and I thought, oh no, the baby.

Yesterday when the ultrasound machine found the tumor, I thought of those summer
     days going to see her on my own.

Obsessions about him, who never did call.

Taking the subway to see her and then she was there.

When we saw into the machine now it was just a lush animal.

It didn't care. It had its own principle.

I woke up from the dream with the therapist still holding me.

But knowing that poems are things we can put on shelves.

I wanted to tell them: it's a miracle any of us are living.

But the moon and red stars had grown blasphemous.

The miracle had become the enemy once again.

The real life.

It's wild.

The monsters will bite you.

But only in dreams.

When you wake up she is holding you.

Corpse in the bath, with her disintegrating arms.

As lonely as the milk river.

That extends from here.

Deep feeding.

And far.

WINTER PLUMS

She's gonna die

We all are

Until then, the weather

The cold sweet fruit

That I kept for months

In the freezer

The vision

But not the skill

Is what I've mastered these days

Walking in the leaves by myself

To listen to the trees and what they say

Is more interesting

And more important

Than talking

Shut up

Live

People argue for the sake of daylight each day

Even they

Know more than the trees

And when you approach the house

Don't walk on by like you always do

Walk in the door

Take a seat

Unfasten your sweater

Uncross your legs

Remove your hat

Unfold your hands

Close your eyes

Hear them

You coward

Last Breath

The doctor said he would be fine. "It's just croup. It sounds scary, I know. You'll want to come back in to the office. But don't. Just give it a few days and it will go away."

My son was a year old. When he breathed, his chest rattled and whistled, and his coughing sounded like something heavy dragged across pavement.

None of us slept that night. My son couldn't stop coughing. I lay on the floor beside his crib and fit my hand between the bars so he could hold it. When he cried—from pain, frustration, exhaustion—the mewling gave way to a choking sound.

I put a hat on him and wrapped him in a blanket and carried him outside. This was March, in Wisconsin, and winter hadn't given up. Snow fluttered around us like moths. The cold was supposed to reduce the inflammation in his throat, and I paced the driveway for two hours, while he wheezed in my ear.

When dawn brightened the horizon, I brought him back inside. To warm up, I ran a hot shower. Eventually the hot water ran out and I tried to lay him down in his crib, but he at once started coughing again. And his lips—we could now see in the new light—had gone blue.

Benjamin Percy

"The doctor said it would be all right," I said to my wife. "But this isn't all right."

We drove back to the clinic. When the receptionist saw us, saw him, she ran for the doctor. And when the doctor arrived, she immediately dialed 911.

I heard the word "steroids." I heard the word "tracheotomy." I heard the word "emergency."

I stood outside the clinic, watching as the EMTs fitted my son with a tiny snouted oxygen mask, set him on a stretcher, and hoisted him into the ambulance. My wife climbed in with him before the rear doors closed. Then lights swirled away from me. I followed them to the hospital, not knowing whether my son would still be alive by the time we arrived.

He was. He still is. So is my daughter. So is my mother. So am I. Even though none of us breathes easily. We have low VO$_2$ max, underdeveloped airways, asthma. We get croup. We get bronchitis. We get pneumonia.

Sometimes I don't realize I'm having trouble breathing and my oxygen will get so low I have difficulty speaking, with big gaps between my sentences. I have an inhaler that I suck on several times a week. I finger the release, take a deep gasping breath, hold the spray inside me, and then blow out a misty sigh that leaves behind a chalky residue on my tongue. The inhaler is my constant prop, a charmed totem. I touch it often—in my pocket—as if for reassurance. In this way it is like Dumbo's magic feather. All of my confidence stored inside it. If I travel somewhere and forget it, I feel panicked and my throat instantly tightens as if gripped by a strangling hand.

In high school, I took an allergy test. The doctor made a grid on my back and then pricked each square with a different allergen. Down. Dust. Tree nuts. Melon. Dander. Penicillin. I don't know how many squares there were altogether but very nearly every one of them reddened into a painful hive, my back as lumpy as a toad's. I was told to be careful. Any exposure to triggers would worsen my chance of an asthma attack.

In college, I went for a run on a path that cut through a grove of flowering trees, the air so thick with pollen you could see the shape of the wind.

My breath sharpened. My eyes swelled. Hives rose from my skin with a needling itch. And when I stumbled back to my dorm room and collapsed into bed, I was barely recognizable, with slitted eyes and a swollen throat. My roommate called an ambulance and the EMTs stabbed me full of epinephrine and brought an oxygen mask to my face and told me I was coming with them, even though I tried to refuse their help.

My daughter reacts to the same triggers. If she kicks through the straw in a barn or if she sleeps with an old woolen blanket, she will lose her breath. We keep an orange prescription bottle full of little green pills nearby—one at school, one at home, one in my wife's purse—and when she has an attack, we crush the steroids and sprinkle them into honey that we serve to her on a spoon.

Every time a few months pass without incident, I stupidly think that we've outgrown it, escaped it. The danger has passed. We're cured.

But it always comes back. We're never safe. From the cough, the wheeze, the rasp that makes me cringe as if a knife has screeched across a plate.

When I was a kid, I tried to swallow an oozing mouthful of peanut butter but it lodged in my throat. I was alone in the kitchen. I didn't gag or cough. I choked silently until the edges of my vision fluttered and blackened.

I staggered around and knocked a glass onto the floor and it shattered and my mother ran into the kitchen and propped me over her knee and raised her hand and beat on my back until I expelled the mess all over the linoleum.

That's what it feels like to have asthma: choking on peanut butter. You're drowning on dry land. You're breathing through a straw. Your chest is a rotten beehive.

In the kitchen, my mother held me while I cried into her chest. She said, "I'm sorry, I'm sorry," which is what I want to say to my children for their broken-lunged, blue-lipped inheritance whenever they struggle for the air their lungs are robbing them of. 🜚

Red Army 3rd Rifle Division soldier

ON THE
EASTERN FRONT

Photos by **Peter Crabtree**

Vladimir Nabokov said that the word "reality" is the one word that should always have quotation marks around it. This tidbit of lodged knowledge came back to me when I first saw the remarkable photographs by Peter Crabtree of World War II reenactors, but since then my mind has become a hornet's nest, incapable of distinguishing or discriminating, which is, perhaps, precisely what Nabokov had in mind. Looking at the photographs I was enamored, chilled, and confused. I was enamored because Crabtree's portraits are ravishing, chilled because they are all of soldiers ready to kill or be killed, and confused because although I have long known of the American mania for Revolutionary and Civil War reenactments, I had not known that there are First and Second World War reenactments. After all, neither of these wars was fought on American soil. That might be one of the reasons we don't shy from reenacting them; as a European friend said of such reenactments, "How grotesque, how absurd, how American." I try to imagine a reenactment of Verdun (300,000 dead) or Gallipoli (the Ottoman command *I am not ordering you to attack, I am ordering you to die.*). These battles of the First World War seem beyond imagining, yet the equally horrific Gettysburg is reenacted every year, on the original battlefield. Europeans *do* stage reenactments, but they are mostly of medieval battles and result in a kind of pageantry, like a Renaissance fair. One exception are the Germans, who are keen on, of all things, American Civil War reenacting; most want to be Confederates and are disappointed when they have to fight for the Union.

These photographs were taken in Stamford, Vermont, in the summer of 2016; "it is August 1944 and the Soviet forces have smashed through the German lines near the Vistula river in Poland. Several German units have been cut off and are trying to get back to the main German lines before the counterattack can begin. Soviet forces are trying to hunt them down and find the new German lines. There are local Polish resistance units working in the area, but they have to be careful—the Germans would kill them, and the Soviets aren't much better." A late summer afternoon in Vermont. These are not stills from a film, these are not actors but *reenactors*. These are ordinary middle-class Americans with a passion for discipline and camaraderie, for re-creating and reliving a small tactical maneuver in a great war that was both atrocious and heroic. Why do I watch films that re-create that war, films that can be good or bad, but have no desire to watch a reenactment, which, I am sure, can be good or bad as well? Actually, I saw one once, the Revolutionary War Battle of Bennington, reenacted in my own hometown, but walked away from it when I heard that later in the day awards would be handed out to those soldiers who died the most "lifelike death" on the battlefield. Yet plenty of people die in films; some of those films win awards, some of the actors too. Is this a question of high or low? Art or life? What is the "reality" here? The original battle, the film, the reenactment; questions of "reality" permeate our culture, now more than ever, and none of it is for the faint of heart, but neither is war, or genocide, or demented oppression at any time. And so these photographs turned my head into a hornet's nest, testimony to the photographer's art, and also to the reenactors themselves.

Crabtree told me that this particular reenactment was not staged for an audience—none watched but the photographer—and that the smallest detail was not overlooked: the men and women did not use sleeping bags but slept on top of straw under wool blankets, ate only what the soldiers would have eaten, and that one night while the disciplined Germans patrolled the forest, the Russians sat drinking around the fire! You are looking at Russian soldiers and sailors, two German soldiers, a Nazi officer, and one Polish partisan who looks as if he is holding not a rifle but a potato and a paring knife. Suddenly I am reminded that in our own lives we fight the same battles over and again, often not understanding we are reenacting an old war; if we are all reenactors on a daily basis, find yourself among these faces. And that baby-faced boy? He is sixteen years old. Innocent, adorable, ready to go forth and fight, inexperienced, clueless, and I don't know what that dark spot on the bottom of his jacket is, but it looks like blood to me.

—*Mary Ruefle*

Russian sailors

Red Army Infantryman

Red Army soldier

German second-line security soldier

Sicherungs-Regiment 195 soldier

Sicherungs-Regiment 195 soldier

Waffen-SS Untersturmführer

Polish partisan

INJURY AND INVITATION

Kara Thompson

Concussed—more fun to say than be

I didn't intend to adopt a dog with three legs. But when I walked by his kennel at the Sacramento SPCA, on my way to meet a different dog, Sylvan (then Fred) showed off his sense of rhythm with a pink squeaky ball and several nimble backward hops. His stump, once host to his right rear leg, was shaved close and I could see the puckered, slightly red borders of an incision. His reddish-brown ears, folded over in front to form perfect velvet triangles (hypotenuse on top), bounced in perfect time.

Sylvan wears a red heeler's suit on a border collie's body: red merle fur with a white star on his forehead, long legs, a slight forty-five pounds. He is bookended with patches—a tiger-striped chestnut one circles his right eye and a mahogany rectangle anchors the base of his long, plumey tail. He is a tumble of perfect geometry. But strangers always notice first what's missing. And then they want a narrative. After I tell them What Happened, they often praise me for being a "good person," sometimes even an "angel." Parents will occasionally use him as a teachable moment: *See, honey, we're all different* or *Look at that* special *dog*. In my eleven years with

Sylvan, from California to Ohio to Virginia, the script has never changed. Sylvan always manages his role exquisitely, but I've grown less patient with the theater. I resent that Sylvan's body is not simply his to inhabit, that he becomes a metaphor, a prosthetic device—his three legs transform onlookers into stewards of pity and compassion.

"When one speaks of disability," writes disability theorist Lennard Davis, "one always associates it with a story, places it in a narrative. A person became deaf, became blind, was born blind, became quadriplegic." And once disability becomes a chronotope, a time-sequenced narrative, one tends to sentimentalize it, to link it to a bourgeois sense of individualism. Disability, Davis goes on to say, becomes a story with a hero or a victim. Sylvan is always the victim, and I the hero. The next time someone asks what happened to his leg, I just might say, "We left it in the car."

. . .

Labor Day, 2015. I was in the middle of a set of fifty pull-ups—not the calm, controlled chin-up version, but the kind by which a body gathers momentum with a swing of the hips that syncs with a strong arm pull, a dynamic motion that propels the body upward so that your chest almost touches the bar. But then the skin on my right hand started to tear, so I tried to regrip, and somehow, at the top of my swing, both hands let go of the bar. Imagine flying backward off a playground swing

at its apex. I hit the ground several feet away from the pull-up bar with such momentum and force that my head snapped back and pounded my skull against the concrete floor.

I went home with an aching back and neck, but propped myself up on the couch and worked all day. By the time my Steadfast Companion got home, I had much progress to report—work on the book that would determine the fate of my impending tenure case, new ideas for my NEH grant application. But I woke up the next day on a non-Euclidean plane. All I could do was reach across the bed and ask to be taken to the doctor. Modest movements like meeting another's eyes confused my senses so drastically that I had to keep my gaze fixed on the floor and remain as still as possible. The right and left turns on the way to the doctor spun me like the teacups at Disneyland; I begged Steadfast Companion to keep the car headed on a straight path—doctor or no doctor, I desperately needed never to turn right or left.

The physician's assistant diagnosed me with a concussion and told me I was going to feel "pretty terrible" for a few weeks. Oh, and don't lift any weights for a couple of days, he said. I could only make out the shape of his shoes.

The word *concussion* had always brought to mind a junior high or high school student sitting out a football or soccer or hockey game, maybe two if it was really serious. I was also aware of the recent attention paid to NFL players who had sustained repeated head injuries during their careers and then ten, fifteen, twenty years later, committed suicide. But these were distant narratives. Until my own concussion.

In the immediate aftermath, synesthesia rearranged my world: my body registered color and current instead of pain. When asked if my head hurt, I wanted to reply, *No, my body vibrates blue*. For the first three weeks, my cognition was a slurry of water, sand, and some kind of toxicity my body had never before encountered. When I lay perfectly still and in darkness, the sand and traces would float to the bottom, and my body was cloudy water. But a shadow or a soft utterance would again roil the world into a tangle of incoherence. I lay for 23, maybe even 23½, hours per day with blackout curtains drawn, staring into darkness. Concussions cause insomnia, perhaps one of the cruelest symptoms of this injury, for sleep is not only what I needed to heal, but it also would have given me a respite from the loneliness that invaded and set up semi-permanent camp in my heart. I could not look at anyone, let alone carry on a conversation. The very presence of a human body, unless that body moved imperceptibly to me, shook the slurry. I couldn't look at screens, large or small. I couldn't read. I had no language. So for 23+ hours a day, I thought in pronominal repetition: my name, the name of the president, my street name, the street name of my childhood home, my parents' names.

The brain
is mysterious
and fragile.

And again. Some kind of self-designed quiz to test the boundaries of my cognition.

The brain is mysterious and fragile. In the instant before a fall, the body's anticipation of sudden impact, all body parts turn guardians of the brain. Though they bear scars to prove their valiant defense, my neck and back ultimately surrendered to air and ground. And after the perfunctory examinations for a skull fracture and a CT scan to rule out internal bleeding, my brain's injuries belonged to speculation—no scan or test will reveal the parameters of injury, or the prospects for recovery. Freud begins chapter five of *Beyond the Pleasure Principle* with the brain's vulnerability, not to external threats (like air and ground) but to "excitations from within" against which the "cortical layer... is without any protective shield." He later calls such excitations *instincts*, and while it would seem that instincts drive us toward progress and development, that they are crucial to the very preservation of life (think evolution here), Freud identifies a certain paradox at work: in spite of the brain's will, instincts want to return us to an earlier state of things, a form of life before life—that last moment of inorganic matter before animacy, and another temporality altogether, begins.

Freud asks us to believe in something rather profound here, that "inanimate things existed before living ones."

Animacy owes its very existence to its counterpart. Maybe this explains how, in that first month after my concussion, I fell in love with my couch. I do not mean my couch was a fetish, a substitute love object. I mean I fell in love with the couch in all of its couchiness. And this was not an object to love, really; it was the kind of couch that had many aspirations without much follow-through. I bought it at Value City Furniture in North Olmsted, Ohio, right before I started my first teaching job. It was a sectional, deeply atomized: every piece of it removable, separable from the other, except for the stretched faux leather that covered its two frames. These frames attached to each other via an inconspicuous hinge under the couch—which, if not put to good use, could gouge an inattentive ankle. But with the help of the hinge, the two frames came together to form a tenuous L. Then there were the cushions, toxic foam covered in a soft faux suede (this is leather, twice removed), beige. Those cushions were fault lines—stable ground until they weren't, at which point cracks opened up on all sides to swallow pens, a remote control or iPhone, or a part of one's body. The back cushions were simply large pillows that came with the couch, an autumnal collage of chocolate, gold, and beige. It was a couch that proclaimed transition: first my own from graduate student to visiting assistant professor (I bought it new, no more grad student hand-me-downs), then from Ohio to Virginia and a tenure-track faculty position, and now to a form of incapacity that threatened to upend it all.

But that couch held me tender. It introduced me to a form of life and love that thrives on stillness. I lived in the crook of the L with a shifting topography of pillows. I stared at the bookshelf in my direct line of vision, and came to despise the faded orange spine of *Infinite Jest* that lived somewhere between *Angle of Repose* (yes, really) and *Fingersmith* (I know). To relieve me of this visual field, Steadfast Companion propped up a calendar, but not oriented to the record of days and weeks to which I had lost all accountability. She chose a misty scene of Spearfish Canyon, the sight (and site) of my childhood in South Dakota. I stared, now, into a memory.

The therapists are well aware that their actions make patients feel worse in the moment.

• • •

Weeks after the fall, once I could move—or better, once I could endure the movement of another human body—I started physical and cognitive therapy twice a week at a clinic called Sheltering Arms, a metaphor I initially took too far and imagined *arms* meant weapons. Only after several weeks of therapy would I notice the bronze-hewn message emblazoned above the front door:

"Behold What God Hath Wrought." Weapons down. This was penance for all my sins. With hat, sunglasses, loose clothes, and a guiding shoulder or hand, I endured the outings and the therapists' rigorous itineraries. The logic of post-concussion therapy is to repeatedly push the brain beyond its present capacity in order to rebuild the neurological pathways that were damaged or destroyed by the violent meeting of skull and concrete. The therapists are well aware that their actions make patients feel worse in the moment. They try to strike a certain levity, but how awful it must be to inflict upon already-fragile brains and hearts more confusion or pain.

Once I improved enough to register desire again, I discovered that the world of my body and mind had become a ruin. Caverns and tunnels full of remains where there had once been something smooth and vibrant. This was the beginning of my depression.

For the entire autumn into winter, my days consisted of physical therapy, drawn curtains, audiobooks, and dog love. I counted the hours until Steadfast Companion came home, but once she arrived, I longed for solitude again so that I could fully control the amount of light, noise, and movement my brain had to filter. I craved narrative, but then she would tell me a story using too many gestures, or with too much animation. She's always been a fast mover, a swift thinker, characteristics that I've long admired but that my concussion drove me to resent. She'd try to fill me in on the faculty meeting, or on a chance conversation with a neighbor, but I couldn't care about any of it. Disembodied podcasts became my sole, safe access to a story. And only Sylvan knew how to be with me in space and time.

He was my protective shield. He took one hour off per day to eat and take hasty walks, and then he was back, curled into a comma, chin on my feet. With great effort, I could glide the tips of my fingers across his swirls and tufts. My favorite zone of fur covered his left hip—a landscape of fluffy, defiant, impossibly soft cowlicks. Without his diligent administration, loneliness would have overtaken me like an unbreakable habit, like a habitation. Home.

Sylvan had been struck by a car as a stray near Sacramento when he was only a few months old (thus, the amputated leg). The first time I ever took him for a walk, he tried to climb inside a dense hedge when a car passed. I thought he was afraid that it would happen again, that this big machine was back for more, but maybe his brain simply couldn't register the motion. About three weeks after my fall, I started to walk outside, just down the block and back. But if a car drove by, I wanted to dive for cover.

The neurologist assured me that my brain function would improve—but degree was a matter she could not predict. She drew the blinds and spoke softly to me. She moved slowly, deliberately, and held on to me when she asked me to stand. She said I needed to rebuild and repair those damaged neuropathways. I wanted to ask, But what about my pathways to love and desire? Those were damaged too.

I would sit with friends and loved ones and listen to them talk. I felt nothing, but performed amusement or contentment, for their sake. To *rehabilitate* is to restore to a former capacity or status. Rehabilitation requires a memory, however distant or even unconscious, of a before time. It also requires the desire to return, to revisit, this former self. But the self that I once knew was gone. "I" was some other being looking out from the same (more or less) body.

. . .

Mirrors perform a trick of time for infants, a kind of magic that provokes much delight. Mirrors present *already* the image of what a child will eventually, only later, become: imagine a child who cannot yet sit upright, unassisted, but with the help of an adult or prop, the child assumes an upright position and then sees the reflection of this posture in the mirror. Immediately, instantly, the child meets the image of a whole self, independent and unencumbered. Before entering the mirror stage, so named by Lacan, infants know only drives, fragments of desire that must be met by another. But when they glimpse, for the first time, their singular image, they instantly believe the fiction of coherence. The mirror projects a self (an ego, a subjecthood) outside the body who looks right back. The infant understands this other *as* self, and this trick confers a sense of integrity.

Lacan emphasizes the fiction at work in ego formation whereby a projection, an exteriorized image, comes to form our (interior) selves. Identity is a performance, an elaborate gesture of negation, what he calls *méconnaissance*. My version of queerness: to grow up inside multiple and competing times and spaces, to transition from one to the other without notice. My version of ability: to meet every deadline, no matter what; to be always on time; to train my body to tolerate pain and discomfort. My version of a brain injury: an inside-out sea, like when sinkholes open and gobble up a world—houses, cars, people, whatever—and manage to take a whole topography of life underground.

. . .

Christina Crosby's memoir *A Body, Undone: Living On after Great Pain* was one of the first books I read when I could read again. It begins with a bicycle ride a month after Crosby's fiftieth birthday. A branch catches in the spokes of her front wheel; the impact of her chin against the pavement breaks her fifth and sixth cervical vertebrae; the broken bone scrapes her spinal cord, and "in an instant," she tells us in the first paragraph, "I was paralyzed." Despite it all—my intellectual and political commitments to disability identity, to rights of access, to neurodiversity—these words caught my breath. Even though my sense of self was gone, my neck was only sprained, my brain only concussed. And here I was, composing myself whole against the body that Crosby recalls from those months and years after her accident. I don't want to admit this now. This frisson of *méconnaissance*.

A few days after I let go of the pull-up bar, I assured students and colleagues that I just needed a week or two to heal (although I was on research leave, I still felt deeply beholden to the institution's itinerary). Granted, Steadfast Companion had to write all of these e-mails on my behalf because I could neither look at a screen nor type, but I was certain my recovery wouldn't take long and I would soon be back in the game. I even considered concealing my injury, because professional decorum states—perhaps tacitly, but still—that one shouldn't project weakness or admit to illness, especially not so close to the tenure deadline.

During my first meeting with the physical/cognitive therapist, which occurred in a nearly pitch-dark room because I couldn't bear the light or a human face, she asked me what my job entails. I simply said, "Complex thinking." Now, instead of writing a book, I moved my eyes between two targets posted twelve inches apart on a wall as the therapists had instructed, and for the rest of the day, I could barely move. My research leave converted to a medical leave. As the months passed, I graduated to sitting in a chair in front of a word search printed in giant black letters on a whiteboard. The therapists left me alone, dry erase marker in hand, to find all the capital cities or names of fruit. I stared at that board for several minutes before finding

> Rehabilitation requires a memory, however distant or even unconscious, of a before time.

one word, and the longer I searched and found nothing, the more anxious I felt. I was a professor, and everyone at Sheltering Arms knew it; they would often preface a new form of therapy with *This will be easy for you, but . . .* , because they assumed I had a certain kind of intelligence, or access to language and cognition, that maybe some of their other patients didn't—mainly because almost all of their other post-concussion patients were under sixteen. One of the therapists said, tactfully, "You're, uh, a bit outside the age range of our patients," before she asked me to respond to something that was clearly meant for a junior high or high school student who plays sports and can't legally make life decisions without parental consent. Each week, the therapists sent me home with exercises and prescriptions stuffed into a folder they had handed me on my first visit. Once, when one of them said, "Did you bring your folder this week?" I was downright humiliated—the question sounded to me like something a teacher would ask a first-grader. On top of that, I struggled to find "pineapple" and "Helena." Nor could I walk down a hallway while nodding my head from side to side.

Some weeks into the dark curtains and audiobooks, and after the academic conference in Toronto where I'd been scheduled to present came and went, I sat at the kitchen table with a paint-by-numbers propped on the portable writing desk that used to hold drafts of chapters and essays in progress. Steadfast Companion had bought me a tableau of dolphins (ages 8+) and one of wolves (no age listed—it was another caliber altogether). I started with dolphins. I mixed the colors with meticulous care, but the paints were so cheap I had to apply several coats. A cetacean palimpsest. On the outside, I was painting a dolphin's belly for the eighth time; on the inside, I cultivated sadness, anger, and resentment. The depression that had once frightened me, that early on in my concussed state I wanted someone to take away, started to feel like pleasure. My own secret, a habit to hide.

Most days started with the question *Do I want to live today?* On better days, the answer was *I don't know.* More often than not, it was *no.* This was the center, the core, of my depression.

At some late point during my medical leave, my doctors cleared me for moderate exercise—a crucial element of recovery, they explained. The brain needs other parts of the body to move, and the other parts depend on the brain to do so—an infinite relay that really messes with the phrase "mind *and* body," as if they are distinct. The impact of foot to pavement jostled my brain too much, so I locked my bike into a trainer and set it up in my study.

> Rehab is a form of haunting, really—the ghost of wellness and ability stands by.

I had become predictably obsessed about my weakened muscles, and about everything in my life that had come to such a startling halt. I rode the stationary bike. Faster and faster without moving an inch.

I listened to Maggie Nelson's *The Argonauts* every evening while I exercised. I would later discover her central role in Christina Crosby's rehabilitation. Nelson had been Crosby's student and then they'd become friends, still many years before the accident. "I loved Maggie before the accident, and two years of intensely heightened intimacy profoundly confirmed that love," Crosby writes. "Neurological destruction made a wilderness of my body. I was in an agony of grief. Being Maggie's friend in this time took me out of myself, and I will be forever grateful." After the bike accident, Nelson drove from New York to Middletown, Connecticut, to sit with Crosby, to read to her, to relieve her partner for a few hours, to write poems. Only months after those evenings on the bike, in my study, would I register the interplay of injury, friendship, art, academia, and queerness in these two writers I admired—and these would become my pathways to rehab. An invitation to return.

While I was at first caught up in *what happened* to Crosby—the disability as narrative—I soon followed another set of coordinates: Our brothers each died out of generational sequence; and though we both love our brothers in life and in death, we recall the quiet flames of envy of their easy claims to masculinity while we were left to deal with the ongoing, conscious and deliberate, work of gender performance. Our fitness and athleticism, a shared love for cycling. The way she shapes an argument with her hands, in gesture, when she teaches. Crosby threw out a tether, made of language and theory, queerness, loss, and metaphor. I grabbed hold.

• • •

When I returned to campus for the spring semester—to a full teaching load, graduate and honors students who'd been left in limbo while I was gone, curious colleagues, and concerned friends—I wore a new suit and cried in my office. Some people would ask me how I was doing, and before I had the chance to speak, they would respond to their own question with a declarative, almost demanding, "You look good!" Unlike Sylvan's amputation, my injury was entirely invisible. Others would wait for a response, but seemed impatient; their eyes would dart around the room, as if looking for a way out of the question. Or maybe they were (understandably) impatient as I searched for language. I learned to say, "I'm okay!" Or "Great, eighty percent back to normal!" in an upbeat, assuring tone. Post-concussion therapy taught me that pain signifies best in ratios. The therapist would ask: "On a scale of one to ten, how dizzy [or confused or in pain] are you?"

The question always confounded because zero was a precious *before* to which I no longer had bodily or affective access, and who's to say what ten is, especially when sadness is ever expansive?

Narratives of disability, and of queerness, fulfill a drive to make sense of bodies that otherwise exceed the boundaries of *normal*—they promote progress, a sense of overcoming, despite it all. They assure an eager audience that *it gets better*. The questions *what happened?* or *how are you feeling?* beg for a simple narrative in return. But when someone asks how I'm feeling, I want to say, *Let me tell you about my couch*.

My loved ones counted on a clean and progressive healing process—that my brain's transition back to its former capacities would be at once seamless and notable. That each day would be better than the next, an exciting new recovery of what I had inexplicably, but only temporarily, lost. Rehab is a form of haunting, really—the ghost of wellness and ability stands by, never to be embodied again, at least not in the same way. My abilities and capacities shift constantly, still, all these months later. Just after I manage to pull off a lecture on political theory, I can't remember the name of a dear friend's cat, or I-64 west from Williamsburg (where I teach) to Richmond (where I live) appears entirely new, as if while I was on campus for ten hours, someone lifted the lanes and plopped them onto an unfamiliar landscape. And it isn't just a matter of an elusive name or title, or uncanny geographies: whole episodes of my life are gone, and some days I feel a terrible bout of the flu or depression or fatigue, and then realize it's just (yes, *still*) the concussion. I've always been an introvert, content to stand slightly outside a circle of conversation, or to let my extroverted companion carry the weight of banter and small talk. Now, for reasons I don't quite understand, the company of others provokes a resounding silence inside of me.

· · ·

On September 7, 2016, a year to the day after my fall, I sold the couch on Craigslist. I didn't even mean for a poetic circumference. It just happened that way. But I couldn't watch it go. I disappeared upstairs while Steadfast Companion managed the transaction. Later, she told me that the buyer asked many questions about the couch, and was impressed that I'd steam-cleaned it before he arrived. He even asked if she could spare some trash bags to protect the cushions in transport. I hope they're happy together.

A month after that, I loaded Sylvan up and drove to Sheltering Arms on a Sunday. We sat in the car, in the parking lot, with the windows down. The air was like the air of the year before. Virginia holds fall at arm's length, but in October, it makes its presence known at the edges of an afternoon. Automatic sprinklers watered the pavement according to the wind's direction. And I cried with my head on the steering wheel, suddenly overcome with a sense of nostalgia, a wistful longing for a past that, when it was present, I only desperately wanted to undo or escape altogether. Those intimately involved with my rehabilitation reminded me constantly to focus on the present. But my obsessions—fitness and work—were in the past and (I hoped) the future, so these were the only tenses I chose to occupy. Then, I only wanted to be the person with the body and mind I'd had before the brain injury; and every act I had to perform to help me get back there, like the therapy at Sheltering Arms, felt like a betrayal of that former self.

But now, on that Sunday afternoon in the car, with a view of the slight curve in the sidewalk that used to make me dizzy, the familiar plot of withering flowers and fresh mulch, the useless sprinklers—all that God hath wrought—I longed for a return. Nostalgia is an acute longing for the familiar, for home. *Nostos + algía*: homecoming and pain, always hand in hand.

Queers have a way of *feeling backwards*, to borrow Heather Love's phrase. That is, queerness is constituted by injury: a long history of being characterized as *inverted*, with impossible and incoherent desires. Those of us who manage to survive remember, in both personal and collective memory, those who did not. We are haunted by loss and rejection. In turn, queers embrace the abject, the parts of ourselves and our lives that are allegedly barriers to progress and growth. I have always felt caught in this embrace: between communing with ghosts and reveling in the pleasures and perversions of backwardness, and the sheer work of pressing on, of moving forward, of imagining potential futures.

"Your body has and is a history," Crosby writes. In the car with Sylvan on that Sunday, I glimpsed a version of my body's history that is, still, to come, and it made me nostalgic for a past I've never known. I sat back so that I could reach around my seat to touch Sylvan's swirls. I looked toward the water feature at the entrance to Sheltering Arms, a murky pond with a constant skyward spray of water from the middle. I noticed for the first time a small sign next to it, white with black letters rendered in a serious font, all caps: NO FISHING. It was time for us to go home. 🝔

A Spot in the Pinewood

Ariel Djanikian

My sister was born when I was three years old. I don't remember life before her, which is my loss. Our little house in the pinewood was a modest jumble of rooms. It had a triangle roof and walls the color of gingerbread and a chimney that puffed white clouds that found a second home in the sky. The forest pressed right to the edge of our yard, encircling our house in a cupped hand. The trees interlaced and the needles were thick, though between the boughs there were deep black pockets: gaps that smoldered with a formless potential. Sometimes, when I was playing outside, my body would tense, observing them. My chin would rise slightly and my corncob doll would collapse in the grass, forgetting her next move in our game. It was easy to become transfixed, and I was sure it was dangerous. Look too long into that dark vacuum, I thought, and it might gather the power to pull me through.

We never saw people, because of my sister. On the day she was born she opened her mouth and emitted a cry that put spiderweb cracks in the windows. As an infant, she clamped down on our mother's breast and ripped off the nipple, leaving a flat strip of raw gore. When our mother cooked, the fire exploded inside the drum. When our father dipped a spoon into the broth for a taste, the pot disappeared and the boiling contents fell out of the empty air and splashed across our father's legs as he howled.

They were like two people being slowly crushed, my parents. Though they never complained or tried escaping their child. They were old-fashioned in their resignation, and took full responsibility for what they'd inadvertently called onto earth. In any case, what choice did they have? They would sell a crate of vegetables at the town bazaar, and for a decent price. But at home, when they reached into their wallets, the bills would crumble to green ash at first touch.

Our lives took a turn when I was eleven and my sister was eight. A family showed up at our house one late morning. They had built a cabin in the woods nearby and had taken off for a day of exploring. It was a mother,

ARIEL DJANIKIAN

a father, and a girl a bit younger than us, wearing a ruffled pale dress that she and her mother had constructed themselves. We carried the table outside and fixed sandwiches and ate in the shade. The girl and I were making homes for our dolls in the ivy when my sister emerged from the house. Our father's camera hung from her neck.

"Come on," she said to the girl, catching her hand. "I want to take your picture." And she led the girl into the woods.

Until this day my sister had hated only our parents. Even I had been invisible to her: her gaze would slide over me as if I were some benign obstruction, a sapling hemlock or a poorly placed chair.

But when they found the girl that afternoon she was sliced into neat pink pieces and arranged on a crest of forest floor. Her dress, even, was cut along the same clean lines as the rest of her, as if by a giant pair of shears. The report from my sister was that a rogue grizzly had done it, and in a placid voice she recounted the facts. She was annoyed, I remember, in the moments she felt we didn't believe her, her grip pulsing around the plastic lens cap in her hand. But mostly I remember the wrinkled faces and screams of the parents as they threw themselves down beside their child, and how the dirt stuck to them all.

> **When they found the girl that afternoon she was sliced into neat pink pieces.**

Afterward, my sister seemed to hanker for a repeat performance. She would put the camera around her neck and tug our mother's hand and say, "Come on, this way. I want to take a picture of you in the woods."

For years our mother demurred. She would crumple her fingers and slip away. She would wander through the house, gaze averted, like someone escaping from judgment. Later hours might find her hunched over a workbench canning tomatoes, or kneeling inside a broad oval of suds, methodically scrubbing the floor. When I grew tall enough to look them in the eyes, I would hold my parents' shoulders and try to reassure them. "Maybe if we wait a long time," I'd venture, "she'll discover something in us that she loves." More helpfully, I took over the maintenance of the vegetable gardens. I tarred the roof when it leaked. I did my best to care for my parents even after a chance encounter with a salesman of prefab chicken coops left me heavy and burdened with a child of my own.

But finally one afternoon, when my sister reached for her camera, our mother, exhausted, did not try to escape. Her spine dipped, her mouth bowed. She began to shuffle her feet toward the door. And, as if she were the daughter, and not the other way around, she allowed herself to be led toward the trees.

I ran to them. I slapped the place where their two hands joined, breaking the hold. I screamed at my mother:

"She's going to kill you!"

My sister swiveled her head. She regarded me with blank surprise. I was eighteen when this happened. No longer so young. In fact my little boy was on my hip, holding my hair. His hot face pressed into my neck.

My sister's expression narrowed. Our gazes, in all our lives, had never lined up as they were lining up now. I remember those eyes, molten brown. I remember her braids pinned in two neat rows, ear to ear, taut on her skull.

It took the three of us to restrain her on the mattress.

Slowly I realized what I had done. It overflowed in me as if from a turbulent stream: the danger.

A period of uncertainty followed. Months passed, then a full year. My mind did not drift. My child never left my hold. I did not lie in a bed. When I dozed off, often I'd do it standing up, my shoulders digging into a wall.

My parents tried to deflect her; they could because, toward them, she had changed. She'd ceased her entreaties for a photograph. The pots of boiling broth held their shape. Once, when our mother opened her wallet, the twenty-dollar bills had all transformed into forty-dollar bills. Useless, of course, but it was the gesture that stunned us. I was so surprised that I spoke:

"You love mom now."

My sister looked at me and laughed.

"I know," I quickly retreated. "Now you hate me."

But it wasn't just that. She waited for me to finish the thought. I clutched my son's head.

"You want to hurt him too."

I began to slink down the hallway toward the front door, step by step. My son's fingers wound through my hair, pulling it hard. He was a sturdy toddler and as long as a fox, but fear had stunted him, and he didn't speak yet.

"We'll leave," I said. "We'll find an apartment in town and never come back."

My parents seized upon the cause. They wanted to open the safe and give me some money. They offered to call into town for a ride. They wouldn't so much as look at me as they said these things. That's how afraid they were.

"Wait." Her clear voice halted us. "I want an apartment."

"That's right," I cooed, reversing course. "You should. I don't know what I was thinking. You should get all the money. You're the little sister."

This formulation pleased her. She smiled.

"We'll walk out of this house as we are," I said. "We'll walk. It's fine. I'll figure out something."

I was almost to the door, my fingers outstretched toward the knob, when she lunged. I dropped the child and for once in our lives we counter-attacked, my parents and I. We pushed her down the hall, all the way back to the bed. It took the three of us to restrain her on the mattress.

She was looking straight up as we braced her, wiggling her face. Above the bed was the glass globe of the overhead lamp. The seconds progressed, emptying out.

"You can't do it, can you?" I said, amazed. The shards should have rained down on us and lodged into our backs like spears. "You're trying to shatter the glass and you can't."

She gave no answer. But the little muscles in her face went still. We took our hands off her. We retreated down the hall and I scooped up my son. For years we had tried resisting my sister, but only with obsequious words and ducking sidesteps. We had accustomed ourselves—and she had accepted it—to living as playthings between her paws. Now she sat up on the bed, like a person startled out of a dream. She considered us briefly, through the wide doorway, then looked away. Her expression was inward and slightly confused.

After that, she changed. She wanted to play with my son—she played with him as if she too were a child. They chased each other around in the yard; they drew with sticks in the dirt. The only nasty things that happened took place when we asked them to pause from a game. Once when they were moving toy cars around on the rug, I said to stop, because dinner was ready, and the next thing I knew my parents and I were in the dark, under the floor, in the root cellar. But we only had to climb out; it wasn't as if she had locked us in there.

In autumn, she went outside with the boy to play at falling backward into leaf piles. But it was too much. A thickness of orange leaves enveloped the yard. The piles she made were orange hills and when the boy fell into them, he fell into a five-foot-deep black outline of himself. I had to rescue him and tell her:

"Easy now, you're getting carried away."

One day she took us on a walk through the pinewood. The same direction in which she had taken the girl who had lain in slices on top of the dirt and leaves, the same direction in which she had tried luring our mother for years. The underbrush was cleared away. Nascent grass, skinny and firm, sprung up where we stepped in open patches of sun. The rugged pines, with their crooked and gnarly boughs, were now majestic giants like trees in a storybook: Big green canopies like clouds. Round trunks that you couldn't have reached around the half of, even with your arms fully spread.

One tree had a heart carved into the bark. Inside the heart, pinned to the wood, was a photograph of our mother and father. They were smiling in it, gently embracing. Our parents saw it and collapsed to their knees. Their rush of tears dropped straight to the dirt, eluding their skin. The tree with the picture was the Tree of Life, my sister said, as its bright leaves rustled and flipped in a breeze. From now on she would be their guardian. They would live and grow old together, both.

I was standing next to my sister as she spoke, my arm resting over my boy. I was surprised, but I told myself, what did you expect? She is your little sister after all, it had to be a happy ending. Even the child she had made mincemeat of was there again, restored to herself in her homemade dress. The diaphanous folds in the skirt billowed once, dispersing the light, showing a flash of newborn legs. A gasp and she was sprinting away from us, darting between the trees, toward her home.

"What will her parents think?" I wondered aloud, watching her go. "It's been ten years."

An arch glance from my sister. "What's ten years?"

She had changed: from the devil among us to benevolent God. But throughout these happy days, my pulse, which ran at all times, even in sleep, about double the rate of a normal person's, never let up. The tightness like an extra muscle wrapped around my guts and clenched—no, it would not loosen its hold. We lived in that squat three-room house, the five of us, and we live there still. I have never tried leaving. Good or bad, it's alarming how close the feelings rub, when your faint life, your careful breaths, exist at the grace of her power. ⚜

LAZARETTO

Without a shipboard morgue,
    we kept the dead Iraqi
in the dairy box—his corpse
    supine beside the eggs

and sour cream—a figure
    draped in cotton sheets,
stretched to keep the still alive
    from witnessing the mouth

and eyes of the nameless
    drowned, whose tongue,
embalmed in wind and ocean
    brine, capsized between

his teeth and, like a ruined
    clementine, hung low: a thick
inch of fruit on the branch
    of his throat. Yet every look

I stole revealed some skin
    still beautiful: oil slick,
sulfuric-sweet beneath a shroud
    of faded sheets, quiet

as a mezzo note. Forgive me:
    I saw the man as meat—

     ~

Paradoxically, I think of light
    as an obscurity, the way night
arrives, but shouldn't. Stars crowd
    every inch of graphite sky—

above, below, and beside
    each needle-prick light—
like waves blown flat and pacified
    as mortuary tables. Night

should burn like the inside
    of a bulb, the sun's umbilical,
but how, then, would the dead
    hide? How could he appear

to me? Pitiful body, devoured
    by sea, everything's a mystery:
on cloudless nights, the naked eye
    sees nothing of our galaxy.

~

What has left returns to me:
    O-dark-thirty, my father
wakes his sons from sleep
    to augur pupils in the creek.

Beneath our feet, their blue
    hearts beat in syllables of blood,
condemning them to breathe. I slip
    two fingers into gill, remove

what life the water holds,
    and like some lone memorial,
circle fish around the hole
    we tunneled through the snow.

I dream, now, when I'm still
    enough to sleep, that the sunfish—
unmoving—are Iraqis.
    I could not look away. Still,

I cannot pray to what I cannot
      see—I refuse to believe
there's a ghost inside me,
      satisfied to praise the trees

or find the sacred in their leaves.
      Forgive me—I don't believe
in loss: every tree can be remade
      into a coffin or a cross.

AFTERWORLD

Once, an Iraqi spoke of a bird asleep
on his throat before he opened his mouth
    to that white rush of waves. Believing
he'd turn into a tree from his grief,

    he planted his tongue-seed into the sea;
a hundred birds fell into his branches.
    The whites of his eyes were black with flies.
Heaven is nothing how the living describe:

    the roads, paved with gold, burn like white
phosphorus—you wear what killed you
    on the outside: Your lungs are two
overturned bells filled with water—

    your wounds are still warm to the touch.
Beneath you, the earth burns so brightly
    it looks like the head of a nail hammered
into the darkness of a palm.

Wyoming

J. P. Gritton

I'll tell you what happened and then you can go ahead and decide. This was like a year ago, around when the Big Thompson canyon went up. That fire made everybody crazy. A billboard out toward Montgrand reads: HE IS RISEN. And we weren't ever the church-going type, but seeing fire wash down the mountain in a crazy-ass wave made me think twice about All That. Like maybe He's already here, and maybe you can read Him in flame and flood.

Day it started, my crew was working an addition for this guy Ronnie, lived up Left Hand Road. Now *that* was a job: big timber penning us in on all sides, keeping the sun off our backs. Around one in the afternoon, Ronnie would come a-prancing down the porch steps, big smile on his face. Then he'd get in his car and drive to town. Don't know what he did for a living, but it didn't look like he was working too hard. When Ronnie come back around five in the afternoon, we'd pack it in for the day. Sometimes he even brought us beer. He'd float downstairs, a case of Bud in his hand, grinning like jolly ole Saint Nick. He'd hand the beer out to everybody on the crew, that big smile on his face. Some kind of bonus, I guess. He always had a line of bullshit, like, "Don't you gentlemen get sore, working all day like this?" And you'd laugh, cause you knew you had to. I didn't mind Ronnie. It was just he wanted poke so bad you could smell it on him.

Anyway, that was a good job. I made seven grand in three months, and I don't think I broke a sweat that whole time.

Then one morning the thunder come, loud enough to scare shit out of you. These clouds wash over the mountains and I turn around, "Get ready for a rain delay, boys!" and everybody laughs cause we all know this is about the downhillest contract we ever worked. But then I get this weird feeling. For one thing, it doesn't hardly rain. Then the lightning starts flaring. Then I see this bolt come down and just *kiss* the tree line.

We seen the red start in the brush by a hundred-year pine, and then we watched it creepy-crawl its way past bark and branches. Took about ten seconds for the fire to swallow that tree *whole*, and then it jumped: I swear to God, it jumped. And just like that it swallowed another great big pine. We must have looked like holy rollers at a revival: all slouching and slack-jawed, watching and waiting. I guess a minute went by before my best friend backslash brother-in-law, Mike Corliss, hollered, "Pack it up, fellas!"

So we did.

We got the chest onto the company truck and then we piled all the little stuff inside: skill saws and quick saws, pneumatics and drills. We had two compressors, a new one and an old one, and I hauled the new one into my back seat, I don't know why, I knew I had no cause to. But it was chaos by then: the whole time we're packing, we can see the fire chewing up the mountainside, coming right at us. It was raining a little, but that wasn't slowing it down any, near as I could tell.

Took about ten seconds for the fire to swallow that tree whole.

One by one, everybody takes off: Mike Corliss in the big F-250 marked "Lundeen Construction LLC," then Tiny Tim and Eric-from-Boston and Eric-from-Phoenix, then the Mexicans. I don't know why I didn't haul ass out of there. I don't know why I just stood in the lot, looking around, trying to think of what we forgot. Then it hits me that nobody's told Ronnie.

So I hustle up the stairs, fast as I can, and when I get up to the door I pound on it like crazy. I guess the fire was about a mile off, maybe more, but it seemed closer. Maybe I imagined it, but I could feel the heat against my face. When he opened the door he was in a pair of jogging shorts and a tank top, all barefoot and sweaty. I don't know what he was doing in there and I sure as hell don't want to. I pointed west. I told him, "Get your ass out of here!" Motherfucker just *looks* at me. I can see "White Trash" ticker-taping over his eyes.

"Fire!" I shout, and I'll be goddamned if I can't help smiling. "Fire, you dipshit!"

Kind of seems like the Big Thompson going up was the beginning of the bad times for me and Mike. First of all, the work dried up. You'd think all them houses burning would mean a lot of building. Well it didn't. Now they were gone, wasn't anybody wanted to build up there. Plain scared, must've been. We did a reno out in Erie, we built a rich lady's deck in Boulder. That's about it.

By the time the boss man—Jake Lundeen, I mean—called me in, I hadn't worked in a month and a half. That was the first time I ever been in his trailer. Only reason to go in there is Lundeen wants to chew you out or you're picking up your paycheck. Account of he was my best friend, Mike Corliss picked up my paychecks for me, and I never gave Lundeen no reason to chew me out.

It was about the kind of office you might expect a guy like Lundeen to have: had his contractor's license from the State of Colorado framed and hung on the wall, alongside photographs of himself looking cut in jungle fatigues, smiling with some other dudes. He had his POW/MIA flag in the far corner, next to a steel shelf where the company's books were lined up, each with a year wrote down the side in yellow: 1975, 1976, 1977, all the way up to 1984. Apart from that, I remember he kept some Indian shit in there. A little guy with a mohawk playing a flute cut into a hunk of flagstone. Drums. Eagle feathers. He had a piece of rawhide about the shape and size of a dinner plate, strung up with rabbit fur and feathers and beads.

> Even in Vietnam, the dude seemed like he'd never had to worry about anything.

"Dream catcher," he told me when I asked him what it was. "Keeps all the bad dreams out. Anyway, it's supposed to."

"I need one," I said. I don't know why. Pretty much right away I wished I hadn't. I was nervous as all hell. When I'm nervous, I talk foolish.

"Well I guess we all need one," he said after a while. "How you doing, Shell?"

I said I was all right. I said I wished to hell the work wasn't so slow. See what I mean? Foolish.

"It's about to get a whole lot slower," he said. "It'll be winter soon. Actually—"

He gave me this *look*.

"That's kind of what I want to talk to you about," he said. "Because it's been awfully slow. And when the work's slow, the money's slow. And when the money's slow, people will sometimes get dumb ideas that seem like good ones."

I nodded, to show him I got his drift.

"I'm not singling you out," he said. "I'm not accusing. But there's a few things gone missing."

"Like what?"

"There's a bunch of little stuff," he said. "I'm not worried about the little stuff. But then there's one big thing I am a little worried about."

I asked him, "What's missing?"

"We seem to have had an air compressor simply vanish. Into thin air."

Now he'd said it, I didn't feel half so nervous anymore.

"Which one?" I asked. "We got a few."

"Not 'we,'" he said. "I. I have a few."

He figured he could flush me out, but he was dead wrong. I didn't say anything at first, then I figured I'd cut right to the chase: "I guess you think I did it."

"I never said that. I'm talking to everybody."

"Well I don't know about it," I said. "Maybe it went in the fire."

"I thought about that," he said. "It's possible. But I doubt it."

I didn't ask him why he doubted it. I said, "You asked Hector and Luis?"

"I know Hector and Luis," he told me. "I don't know you very well."

"So you think I must of did it."

He put his hands up and said he never said that. Then we were quiet. I looked around his office, waiting for Lundeen to tell me I could go. I looked at the picture of him in the army. Even in Vietnam, the dude seemed like he'd never had to worry about anything.

"I don't know you very well, Shelley," he said, "but I do know Mike, and I know that it hasn't been an easy time for you, these past few years. I'm not accusing anybody: just saying that I could see how it might seem like a good idea, even though it was a bad idea, to take something that belongs to me. I could understand it, I think. And if the guy who did it returned the air compressor to me, then I could probably see my way to not getting the police involved."

Time kind of stumbled along.

"Because the thing is," he said, "it'd take me hardly any time to figure it out. Tell you what I'd do. I'd take a day off. I'd go to every pawnshop between the Springs and Fort Collins. I'd ask to see their air compressors, and then when I found mine, I'd ask to see the pawn slip."

It was about the dumbest thing I'd ever heard. If he checked every pawnshop from Fort Collins to the Springs, he still wouldn't find the fucking thing. I knew cause, maybe a week earlier, I'd got a little drunk and drove up to Cheyenne and hawked the air compressor there. Five hundred bucks. It was almost all gone.

Wish I could help you, I kept telling Lundeen. Maybe I overdid it. I guess it doesn't matter: he knew I'd ripped it. It's like he said: he trusted the other guys on the crew, but he didn't trust me. When I walked outside, there was cold in the air, and I wondered what I'd do about supper.

It must have been Mike told my brother about me getting fired. That fat bastard come swinging through the front door, didn't even knock. It was cool out, but apart from sweats he didn't wear anything but a tee shirt, and in just that he was still panting and red in the face.

"You run here?" I said, just like always. I didn't even get up to shake his hand. From the couch I watched him do his Godzilla march over to the easy chair I kept in the corner. It was leather with three settings (sitting, laying, reclining), and the truth is I hardly sat in the fucking thing. I don't know how to explain how come I didn't, except to say I never felt clean enough. When Clay sat down, the chair groaned like an organ bellows.

"Heard about Lundeen's," he said.

I said, "Yeah, well."

"How you holding up?"

"Oh," I said, "you know."

I should've told him scram, but now he was here I figured hell with it. I even went and got him something to drink out of the fridge.

"You got no Pepsi?" he said, when I handed him Coke. It was like him to razz me when he hasn't been in the house but five minutes.

"There's Pepsi down the road," I said, meaning the 7-Eleven on Main. "You want Pepsi, go there."

He said, "No use us fighting already."

I thought about getting one last dig in, but on the whole I figured Clay was right: there was no point.

"Anyway," I said. "I'm okay. Had a little scratch saved up."

He smiled: "I bet you did."

I guessed he must mean the compressor. Well, fine. If that's what he thought, let him think it.

But still. Wasn't any of his damn business.

I don't know what it is, I just can't concentrate when my brother is in a room. The TV was on, but my brain didn't know what my eyes saw on the screen. They were just shapes and colors, twisting on the glass like ghost acrobats. My whole life was passing me by.

"I guess I'll get something together for the winter," I told him.

"Something like what?" he wanted to know.

Which is when I smelled a rat. It wasn't like my brother to wonder. Matter of fact, it wasn't like my brother to come to me like this at all. Tigers don't change their stripes. Neither do jailbirds. I could see his, plain enough.

"Don't worry about it," I told him, getting sulky. "I'll find something."

We watched the TV a while. Then I guess Clay must've got tired of beating around the bush.

"I come here as a favor."

"No favor to me," I told him. "Tell me what you want before you break that chair."

He didn't say anything for a second. Then he said, "I didn't mean you. May told me to come."

That fat bastard come swinging through the front door, didn't even knock.

May is Mike's wife. Me and Clay's sister.

"We heard about your trouble, is all," he said. "Kind of figured you could use some help."

I just about messed myself, laughing. Help, my ass.

Anyway Clay didn't stay much longer, a half hour or so. Just enough to catch his breath, I guess. The TV just thundered: pure noise. When he stood up finally, he didn't say goodbye. He walked right on out the door. When he'd gone, I stood up and turned the deadbolt.

The day I went to visit Mike, this was the middle of October or so, the whole house stunk of what was coming. I forgot to tell you that Mike's little girl had got sick in the summer. I do not like children but I almost liked Layla. She was a quiet thing, but not so quiet she made you nervous. She looked a lot like Mike, matter of fact: golden-haired, with big blue eyes and a sad mouth. I guess it was end of September they figured out she was about rot-through with the cancer.

That girl was *bad* sick: stumpy little skeleton, and the sheets pulled up to her chest. It did something to me, seeing the fingers that were just like matchsticks, and her eyes set deep in bruisey sockets, and what was left of her hair all damp and twisty on her forehead.

May sat there next to her on the bed. My voice had gone and she had to tell me, "Say hello to your niece."

I said, "Hi, Layla."

She was a polite girl but she didn't make no move, not even a tilt of her head to show she'd heard me. Veins ran crooked in her skinny neck. She watched me standing in the doorframe, thinking whatever she thought. Fuck all. I wondered does she know I'm a bad man.

May bent to the girl, whispered soft: "Say hi Uncle Shell, Layla."

The girl lifted her skeleton's hand. She had no voice to speak to me. And maybe if she had, she still wouldn't have said anything. I don't blame her. The poison they ran into her veins made her weak: cure's worse than the disease, like they say. But then again the disease seemed pretty god-awful.

> I wondered does she know I'm a bad man.

"I just come to say hello to your daddy," I told her, and the thought went through me like a blade: I got to do something about this.

Them two on the bed seemed to wait. They must want me to leave, I thought, but I couldn't. I just stared at that kid, into the blue-black eyes where her life was fading and flickering like a bum lightbulb. Even half-dead, you could still see how much she favored Mike.

I said, "She's a little angel."

"She sure is," said May, and she almost smiled. I didn't get any kind of pleasure from watching May suffer like that, I'll tell you. I was grateful to her when she let me go, nodding her head at the door:

"Mike's out in back," she said.

I went through the den, where old magazines had been stacked into crushing towers, and the radio played so low that all you could hear was a slanty buzz. I pulled the black doorknob and stepped back into the cold I'd just come from. Mike and May live out almost to Loveland. They got a nice place, bought when the land was still cheap: about two acres, and the Saint Vrain Creek runs right through it.

Mike was a ways off, at the edge of the property, sitting on the cutting stump and smoking. He had a pushcart and in the pushcart there was some firewood. I guess he must have heard me coming through the door, but he didn't turn around when it shut.

"Hey," I called. Still he didn't turn around. My guts sunk when I thought he might be having himself a cry. Nobody could fault him for that.

I sure as hell wouldn't. I slowed up my pace a little, I guess to give him a chance to get himself together. But when he stood up and turned to me, his eyes were dry.

"That chimney's got something wrong with it," he said. "Gets smoky as hell in there."

"Seemed all right to me," I said.

"That's cause May put the electric on."

I nodded.

"It's like living in a muffler. That kid, like she ain't got enough problems." Mike was quiet for a while. Then he said, "This is a bad deal here."

"It sure is," I told him. "Y'all can stay with me, you don't like the smoke."

Those days I rented a house in Montgrand from this old lady. It was cheap account of I did the mowing and the gutters and things like that. She liked me, too. There was gas heat and plenty of space there. Layla and her momma could stay in my room. Me and Mike could camp out on the living room floor.

"Thanks," Mike said, "but I guess we better leave Lay be."

Probably he was right about that. I thought about her waving at me. I said, "How are you all fixed?"

Mike said, "What do you mean?"

I said, "For cash."

He gave me a funny look: "That an offer?" he said, and I knew what he meant. He meant: What happened to the air compressor?

Mike had worked for Jake Lundeen for a long time. Since it was Mike got me the job there, I knew I had put him in a jackpot. I didn't like it, but that was how it was. When I didn't talk, he said, "Anyway, we're all right. I had some savings, so did May." Then after a while, he goes on, like it isn't any kind of big deal: "Clay's been helping some."

Boy, it spread through me like wildfire. I couldn't keep my voice straight cause I felt like I was choking.

"He's been what now?"

"He's helped us some," Mike said. "We've got a hundred-dollar copay ever time we go in that fucking place. Clay pays."

"He pays for the *hospital*?" I said.

"And other stuff."

Turned out Clay gave them money for all kinds of things: helped with the groceries and the electric, a down coat for Layla.

I said, "I don't know where to hell he gets the money."

It was a dumb thing to say, considering, and I guess Mike couldn't help smiling at me. We were quiet, and then he said, "You better bring it back, Shelley."

I said, "Bring what back?"

When he quit smiling, he looked as awful as I felt right then.

"All right," he told me, "your funeral."

I stood out there with my friend Mike Corliss, watching him chop the wood slow and steady. He pulled the axe over his head. He drove the bright edge into the heart of the wood. The kindling fell around the stump with a clatter, and I stooped to gather it into the pushcart.

While we worked I thought about Clay, wondering what his game was. On the face of it, he was helping Mike. But I knew Clay too well, and I knew help from Clay was no help at all.

"When's he want the money back?" I asked.

Mike set a big white block of wood up on the stump, drew up the blade, halved it.

"I don't think it's a loan," he said. "I think he just means it as a kindness."

And it didn't sound right: didn't sound much like Clay, anyway. Maybe he didn't want anything now, but that didn't mean he would want nothing later. It was a loan, even if Mike didn't know it was. And the devil was to pay.

"Come on," Mike said when we'd done. "You ready?"

I piled the last bit of the kindling into the cart and we headed on in. We were busy for a while piling the firewood against the wall of the house, where Mike had a strip of plywood cantilevered against the wet. It was good work, I could see that. When we'd got through, we took a few of the bigger wood blocks and went inside.

In the house I could hear the girl's voice all soft and crumpled-sounding: "I'm not thirsty," she kept saying. "I don't want it." She would die soon and everyone knew she would die and Clay was liable to come out the better for it. Drove me crazy, thinking about it.

After we'd set the wood against the claws of the stove, Mike walked to the kitchen and pour his little girl a glass of water. I followed him.

"Sit on down there," he said, poking his chin at the kitchen table. I did. With the glass of water in his hand he made for the little girl's room. I just sat there, listening. I could hear their voices, low. May laughed and then I heard Mike laughing, too. Maybe the girl was laughing, but I couldn't tell.

When Mike come back to the kitchen I asked, "What were y'all laughing about?"

"Nothing," he said, quick, so I wondered maybe were they laughing at me. It made me feel silly, and shy, like a kid hanging out with grown-ups. I didn't appreciate it much.

I said, "You needed help, you should've come to me."

We sat there quiet. I thought about them laughing in the next room. I wanted a drink bad but it was not the time for it. One of these days, it's all going to make sense. Like what exactly Mike meant when he said, "How can you hate him so much?"

"How can you not?" I asked, before I could think of a way around it.

"Cause he's my brother-in-law," Mike said. "And cause family's all you got, when it comes down to it."

You're all I got, I almost told him, but I knew it wouldn't sound right. He looked so tired all of a sudden. Some reason, I felt like apologizing to him: it was like I was the one who'd brought all this down on them. I knew it was crazy. I was Mike's best friend. All the wickedness in the world wouldn't change that.

> I was Mike's best friend. All the wickedness in the world wouldn't change that.

"Don't you know where that money come from?" I said, when I couldn't think of what else to say.

Mike just shook his head, like he couldn't believe my nerve.

"You can ask him yourself when he gets here," he told me, standing up and making for Layla's room. "Clay and the girls are coming for supper."

I wouldn't've stayed but that Clay and me had business.

Back in '72, a while before I come out West, Clay married himself a piece of redheaded Arkansas trash named Nancy, and then Nancy had two girls by Clay named Erin and Aileen. Them girls were redheaded trash just like their momma and you could see a reckless future playing out when you looked them in the eye. The one called Erin already had tits even if she was just twelve that year. Aileen was ten but she had as foul a mouth as you ever heard. She was prettier than her sister, and knew it.

When they showed up, the dark was already edging in on the plains. They walked in and seen me sitting at the kitchen table, and I heard that little bitch Aileen mutter, "Oh, *shit*."

Clay had on a jean jacket over his tee shirt, and a pair of sweats. I'm pretty sure they were the same sweats he wore when he come to see me that day in October. I told him, "I guess the whole family don't bother with knocking."

Nancy laughed and stooped down to kiss my cheek: "Family don't have to knock," she said. "How you doing, Shelley?"

"I'm all right," I said. I don't like being rude, but I couldn't stop thinking about Clay trying to get my best friend Mike Corliss over a barrel.

"You look like you just sucked a lemon," said Nancy. Her girls smirked.

When Mike come in he put on a brave face: smiled and kissed Nancy and hugged Clay like the brother he sure as hell wasn't. He scooped Erin and Aileen into a hug, and you could tell by the way they looked at Mike they were kind of sweet on him.

I don't know what to tell you: I have what you'd call a mean streak.

"May'll be out in a second," he said. "Layla had a accident."

"Poor little bug," said Nancy.

We were all quiet for a while, and then Mike wondered if burgers sounded all right to everybody. He fetched a package of ground beef from the fridge and set it in the sink. He turned to the girls and asked were they hungry now, and even though they shook their heads he fetched down some potato chips from the cupboard and opened them up. That's just like Mike: trying to make everybody happy.

"How's she doing?" Nancy wondered, while her girls laid into the chips.

"She's all right," Mike said. "We won't know much until next month. That's when we see the oncologist. They got to see how everything's going."

"We'll be praying for you," said Nancy.

Mike didn't say anything. Maybe he was thinking it wouldn't do no good. Turned out, it didn't.

It was a solemn-type moment, quiet but for the girls sucking down them goddamn potato chips. I stared hard at the one called Erin. I said, "You keep on eating like that, you're liable to end up like your daddy."

Don't think I'm proud of what I said, cause I'm not. Matter of fact, I felt sorry as hell for saying it. The room went real quiet. Erin got this worn-out look on her face. Then Mike smiled at her and said she ought to have just as much as she wanted, cause we weren't liable to eat for another hour or so.

I don't know what to tell you: I have what you'd call a mean streak.

When May had finished cleaning up Layla's bedsheets, she come out and hugged everybody and they set around and visited in the den. Nobody talked to me or asked me anything, which I didn't mind. I guess Layla must've been sound asleep in the next room, cause she didn't make a peep that whole time.

"It'll be mighty slow this winter," Mike said, shaking his head. "Slump got everybody scared."

"I'll tell you who isn't hurting," Clay said. "The boss man. He isn't hurting one bit."

Mike shrugged: "Lundeen's fair."

"Fair, shit," Clay said. "Get your contractor's license. Then you'll see what's fair."

Never mind he didn't know the first fucking thing about it.

"I don't have time to study," Mike told him. "And that test cost money."

Clay said, "If it's the money, don't worry about it."

That was about as much as I could take. I stood up. I said, "Come on outside."

For a second Clay looked like he didn't aim to follow. Twelve years earlier, after he got out of jail, he wouldn't have. But I was big now, and strong from the work. I guess he didn't want to see what would happen if he stayed put. After a minute he got his ass off the couch and follow me outside.

I walked down to the woodpile and the axe face-first in the cutting stump. My breath was a ghost in the hard blue air. I watched him come. He was panting and drawing the collar of his jacket up around his wattle. I didn't want any part of this. I didn't want anything to do with him. And still I said: "Well go on and tell me about it."

Before he answered me, he took a roach out of the pocket of his jacket and lit up. He takes this big old drag and exhales: "Tell you about what?"

I might've figured he'd play dumb. I said, "Tell me about this job you've got."

He looked at me, the roach flaring red. I watched the smoke floating east on the cold wind, headed for night. He said, "Two thousand dollars."

I said, "That isn't much."

He said, "It's plenty for what you'll be doing."

I said, "What is it you think I'm going to do?"

He said, "Drive to Houston."

And I said, "What's in the car?"

And he said, "What do you think?"

And I just laughed at him: "Favor, my ass," I told him.

Well there we were. Two thousand dollars to run his weight. Okey dokey, forget it. I said, "You can kiss my ass, Clay."

He did not appreciate that. He said, "I'm trying to help you. It's either you do it or I find somebody else to do it. And it won't be hard to find somebody else."

He puffed away and I saw meanness at the edge of his eyes. He sort of chuckled to himself. He said, "Hell, I bet Mike'd do it. Sort of sounds like he could use the work, too."

I'll tell you right now, I wanted to swing that axe at him. I wanted to bring the bright edge hard against his goddamn neck. I might have picked it up and did it, but to tell the truth I seen this coming. After a while I just said, "What gets to me is you don't even know how evil you are."

He looked at me. And I thought to myself, No: he knows damn well. After a second I said, "All right. But I want three thousand."

He said, "Twenty-five."

"Okay," I told him, "but I need five hundred up front."

After something like that I couldn't abide staying for dinner. I walked around the far side of the house, past the garage, so they wouldn't spy me from the den. When I come around the edge of the garage, though, May seen me from the kitchen. She had the window open to let the grease smoke out and she called to me, stooping under the glass: Shelley.

I went over and nodded at her. I said I couldn't stay.

She watched me for a second before she spoke. Quiet like that, she looked just like Momma. She said, "You and Clayton are at it again."

It wasn't any kind of question so I just shrugged.

"Are you going to do it?" she asked.

I thought about telling her no, but I couldn't see any harm in them knowing: "Yeah," I said, "I'm going to do it."

Something soft and cold fell on my cheek. I looked up and saw the snow had started. Its smell in the air was heavy, like an animal's.

"Wait a second," she said. I watched her go to the counter and take out a bun and scoop one of the hamburgers onto it. Then she reached out and gave me the hamburger, the grease still running down the side. My stomach growled when I smelled it. I said, Thank you, and then I walked to my car and drove off.

It snowed fourteen inches that night, but by the morning they had I-25 cleared pretty good. I made Cheyenne in just about an hour. I always expect Wyoming to feel different, but it never does. When I got to the pawnshop and lay the ticket on the counter, the dude just squinted at me for a second. He said, I kind of didn't expect to see you again. Yeah, I told him, me neither. After a minute he hauled the air compressor from where he had kept it in the window with an $800 price tag and set it down next to the counter where he had the register. I took Clay's five hundred dollars from my wallet and handed it to him, then I picked up the air compressor and walked out the door. I didn't even look back, that's how mean I was feeling.

I'll tell you right now, I wanted to swing that axe at him.

Somehow it seemed longer, going south.

Lundeen's car was out front, by the trailer. He drove a 1983 Lincoln Mark VII with tuck-and-roll upholstery and a cobalt-and-silver paint job. It gave me a funny feeling to park right next to him. Opening the trunk, I said out loud to nobody or everybody: "I'm never going to have to do this again."

That compressor weighed about three tons. I guessed that's what it was like, being Clay: like having a great big stone hanging round your neck. I humped that thing across the lot, up the rickety two-by-four stairs. Don't think I bothered with knocking.

Lundeen was at the desk, all his books and papers around him. Just judging by his face, I don't think he was all that surprised to see me. I set the compressor down on the floor, and then I turned around and walked out. I must've been halfway to my car when I heard him come out the door of his trailer: "Hey!" he called. "Wait a sec."

Something about his voice made me stop and turn and wonder. He waved me back up the stairs. He said, "Cold out here."

I wasn't afraid. I did not even feel ashamed, all of a sudden. I walked up the steps and back into the office. He didn't try making small talk, which I appreciated. Next to the desk where his papers were, he had a blower going. I just stood in the warm, waiting. From the top of that steel book-shelf, he took down one of the books. When he opened it I could see that inside were checks, three to a page. He was busy a while, deciding how much to give me, and then writing it down.

"What were you getting here?"

"Thirteen," I said.

"Lucky thirteen," he said. Then he tore the check loose and walked over and handed it to me. Six hundred sixty-six dollars, made out to Shelley Cooper. The memo read "Severance Pay." You had to hand it to the guy, he had a sense of humor. I couldn't help it. I smiled.

Walking to my car, I told myself I'd never cash it. Driving home, I told myself I couldn't afford not to.

Two weeks later, I drove to Texas with Clay's dope.

Night before I left, I went to that site up Left Hand Road, Ronnie's place. I don't know how to explain to you why I went there, but it pulled me like the current of a river. Like one minute I'm turning the keys in my ignition and the next minute my headlights are carving the gravel out of the dark, and my hands are twisting the wheel. After the fire, that big old house was nothing but a patch of concrete and a couple black logs laid one on top of the other. The add-on was just *gone*, so were all the trees: fire plucked that mountain like a chicken. He is risen: See what I mean? Sometimes you'll get an idea of the size of things.

With the car still going and the headlights on, I walked around the lot. I had my work boots on and I didn't care if they got dirty. The snow had melted by then, but the ash must have been an inch deep. Unbelievable.

I got to wondering whatever happened to old Ronnie.

Last I seen him, he was standing outside his car, watching the flame coming: I don't believe he knew whether to leave or stay. I wondered did he have insurance. I wondered did he land on his feet. I thought about how funny it would look, him driving up right then, finding me at the spot where his house used to be. I couldn't think of what I'd say to him. Sorry about all this.

Nobody came, though. For a while I stood there, watching the snow make pretties in my headlights. Then I got in my car and drove back to town. 🛡

Not in the Eyes!

Yesterday I started looking at people in the eyes again. This was after a twelve-day period of ocular abstinence, a record for me. "Eyes are made to be looked from, not at." How many times have I heard this proverb, acknowledging its good sense, only to violate it at the first opportunity?

Twelve days ago I resolved to try again.

Things got off to a good start, as they usually do. When you have a conversation with someone without looking at their eyes, real empathy becomes possible. You participate in their words. It's the closest thing to reading a book. Everyone knows how much easier it is to empathize while reading a novel than it is in real life, staring at someone who's staring back at you with an alien and inexplicable hunger.

Just don't do it. Look at their cheek, or just to the left of their left arm. I'm not saying you have to close your eyes. Be safe. People can attack for no reason. Avoiding eye contact is in many ways the best safety measure. Most assaults happen as a direct result of eye contact. Eye contact itself is a kind of assault.

The first conversation I had after my resolution was with my neighbor Howard. It was a Saturday. I'd walked out in the morning to get the paper.

"How's it going, Michael?"

Michael W. Clune

Howard asked me this question two to three times per week. Normally, making eye contact, I'd be transfixed by the mesmerizing force with which his eyes hissed, *I'm the thing in Howard's face, I'm looking at you, I'm different from you, I don't speak, I look, look at me.* I'd mumble something inane about the weather, and then Howard's friendly voice would reply, a voice whose warm human tone bore no relation whatsoever to the mute thing gazing out from his eyes.

On Saturday, I abstained from eye contact. I looked just to the side of his head.

"Lauren and I are planning to go to Hocking Hills next week," I said.

"I love Hocking Hills," he replied. "Have you been before? It's wonderful. You must go to Old Man's Cave, it's really something."

We stood and talked for five minutes, the conversation circling the topic of caves—*I've never been to a cave but I'm fascinated, Have you ever seen that Herzog documentary about the cave paintings, Oh my God I love that, don't tell me Hocking Hills is like that, laughter, No, no, now if you want to see real caves . . .*

I was *participating* in Howard's words, it was real communication! We'd never spoken for more than thirty seconds in the six years I've lived here. By withholding attention from the brute fact of the basic structural difference between us—the segregation of our minds in separate skulls—the miracle of language connected a direct line between us. Our experiences mixed, we discovered parts of the other inside ourselves. It was fantastic. I love Howard, I thought.

And then I thought: One glance at his eyes would cut the line. I won't do it. Never again. What are eyes, I thought, but colored emergency lights constantly broadcasting the slow emergency of human social life? *I am in here, and *you* are over there.*

Just don't do it. There's no pressure. The only persons who are bothered by your failure to look at them in the eyes are persons who want to assert their dominance over you in the brute animal fashion of pummeling you with the secret source of their vision.

"*Look* at me when I'm talking to you!"

Eyes are made to be looked from, not at. When someone else looks at your eyes, can't you feel their vision *pushing*? I'm *me*, and you're *you*. This is the only thing eyes say when they meet. What kind of quality human relationship can you have when your eyes are constantly proclaiming this nihilistic doctrine to each other?

I didn't last twelve days. I lied. The truth is that I relapsed after barely five minutes. Oh God. Not again. It wasn't Howard's fault. I love Howard. I mean I love the memory of that five minutes of participation in each other's consciousness. The glass barriers smashed, our thoughts running on speech-lines in and out of each other's heads. I'll never forget you, Howard! The real you, the true, eyeless Howard.

It wasn't Howard's fault that I looked at his eyes.

"Well, I should get going," he said.

He was turning to leave. It was almost over, I'd almost won. What made me look? I've asked myself that constantly over the past twelve days.

It wasn't anything he said. And it wasn't what you might think, that I wanted to see what his eyes looked like. No. Every eye is basically the same. People who tell other people that their eyes are beautiful mean . . . I don't know what they mean. As an aesthetic object, as something to look at, they're nothing special.

I looked at Howard's eyes to find out if he was looking at mine.

The fear had grown in me the entire time we were talking. It started with a small nearly subconscious spark—*I wonder if he's wondering what I'm looking at*—and gradually spread to a conflagration of panic. By the end I couldn't resist. The idea that he was looking at my eyes. *He could be looking at my eyes and I can't see his eyes.*

Intolerable. Totally fucking intolerable, I thought. I envisioned his eyes *standing* on my vision, *stomping* on it.

Stop it, I told myself. I'm being irrational. I don't feel anything. Do I? No. I don't feel like anyone's staring at my eyes, let alone *stomping* on my *vision*. Let it go.

But then I thought that the fact that I didn't feel anything was the worst part of it. The devil's greatest trick is to convince people he doesn't exist. I looked.

Our eyes met. Howard's face flushed. I could feel mine flushing. Right away I knew I'd made a terrible mistake. ◈

MAKE YOUR
HEALTH
POINTS
GOOD
HEALTH
KREGER
GET YOUR TEST Now

ILLNESS IS METAPHOR

Jenn Shapland

Reevaluating the Valetudinarian

THE LUNGERS AND I

On their backs they made their way west. Frail. Asleep. Consumed. Americans in search of a cure. They came on stretchers loaded through the windows of Pullman sleeping cars. Sufferers of tuberculosis, their diagnoses comprised any and all pulmonary ailments and weaknesses of the lungs. In time, these pilgrims came to call themselves "lungers." Doctors back east, overwhelmed with patients at all stages of consumption and increasingly aware of the threat they posed to population centers, prescribed more healthful climes: away from the malarial swamps of the coast, the Midwest, the South; away from cities and crowds, sewage and factory pollution. An arid, elevated, sunny place outdoors. Fresh air. Colorado, New Mexico, West Texas.

I moved to New Mexico in June 2016 with my partner and, at the time, I didn't think of it as a cure outright. Certainly I was sick of the heat and the humidity that plagued central Texas. Sick and tired, as they say. I was also *sick*, though it didn't occur to me that it might be related to climate. That's not how I've been taught to think about illness. But from our first days in Santa Fe, each person we encountered made it clear that they chose this place, this climate, for their health—bodily and otherwise. The owner of our neighborhood convenience store, Owl Liquors, was delighted to tell newcomers why he left LA twenty years prior: "California is nice but the air is much cleaner here. You can see the sky." Over and over we heard from Santa Feans how they found their way out of some plague of traffic and smog, and once arrived in the Southwest never saw fit to leave.

In the same way, during the late 1800s and early 1900s—the height of consumption and the climate cure—the body was seen as vulnerable to its surroundings. Damp or stale air, life indoors, lack of sunlight, pollution, depressing and crowded conditions, overstimulating urban environments: all of these were understood by medical experts and patients to contribute to a consumptive disposition. Before Robert Koch's theory about the tubercle bacillus caught on, consumptives were considered highly sensitive to the world around them. And, like present-day sufferers of multiple chemical sensitivity, they headed to the desert.

It wasn't just the medical establishment that suggested the Southwest as a place of healing. The New Mexico Bureau of Immigration papered the nation with pamphlets and brochures affirming the climate of New Mexico as the one ideally suited to good health. "Here, he may pitch his tent with the certainty that no extremes of weather will force him to strike it, in a land of perpetual sunshine, kindly nature the while, exerting all her curative powers to restore him to health and strength, those greatest of all physical blessings," writes health seeker and Episcopal priest Reverend Edward Meany in his pamphlet *Santa Fe as a Health Resort* in 1890. He arrived in Santa Fe in the late stages of consumption, and within two months at high altitude, he was breathing easily, free of disease. He was one of many who celebrated tent life as the ideal cure for consumption. Before the sanatoriums were built, and after they proved too costly for the average consumptive, health seekers—mainly single men and women in their thirties—were advised in medical brochures and newspaper advertisements to camp out in the forests as treatment for tuberculosis. This advertising campaign was extremely effective, and soon lunger tent cities sprouted up around Santa Fe, Albuquerque, and Las Vegas, NM. From my twenty-first century perspective, the strangest thing about the climate cure was that it worked. After spending several months in a new environment, lungers were cured of pulmonary and respiratory symptoms. And many of them never went back home. They stayed out West and extolled the cure to anyone who would listen.

This influx of constitutionally ill pilgrims was no accident, but a calculated effort by the New Mexico territory to gain statehood. The population of New Mexico had been predominantly brown since its establishment, made up of remaining Native Americans and descendants of Spanish colonists. Back in Congress, this didn't really fly for statehood. To be American was to be, well, whiter. And so text was written and brochures printed and distributed in population centers, luring ill white people to the territory. The legend of New Mexico's salubrity stuck and still characterizes the tourist industry. It brings people in droves to visit Santa Fe, my new city, where they wear tennis shoes and high socks and walk around the Plaza with the tense faces of families spending extended time together on vacation. On Saturday they all flock to the farmers' market and collectively marvel at vibrant produce. In a way, I am one of these pilgrims myself.

While there's something leper-colony-ish about sending all the sick white people to the Southwest, out of sight and out of mind of urban centers, the effect was the establishment of communities content to live differently, at some remove from society. TB, a disease with long-standing cultural associations that has creativity, brought to Santa Fe an estimated third of the city's artists and intellectuals in the 1910s. A number of single lungers—who outnumbered married patients by six to one—found spouses or partners during their stay at the sans. One sanatorium in Santa Fe used well-known writers to attract lungers, hosting readings by Carl Sandburg and Mary Austin. They arrived

One sanatorium in Santa Fe used well-known writers to attract lungers.

seeking recovery and stayed for something else.

My first September in Santa Fe I go to the ninety-second annual Zozobra burning, in which a fifty-foot puppet of Old Man Gloom is set on fire before crowds of thousands from all over the state, an effort to burn away all of one's bad feelings from the previous months. The festival was created by lunger and painter Will Shuster, and is thought to be the inspiration for Burning Man. Santa Fe's Pueblo Revival architecture is the product of efforts by lunger architect John Gaw Meem after his recovery at Sunmount Sanatorium. He is the reason Santa Fe looks the way it does: all adobe or fauxdobe, after the 1957 Historical Zoning Ordinance. Poet Alice Corbin Henderson was a lunger, and so were photographer Carlos Vierra and painter Gerald Cassidy. Many health seekers in sanatoriums and tent cities eventually found homes in artists' colonies or started their own, in the process entwining art not with malaise but with jubilant health. As a newcomer to the state, I suspect there's a link between the health seekers and the collision of hemp, woo, art, and organic gardening that comprises Santa Fe today.

Before wellness and creativity brought them together, lungers were individuals defined by illness: their very constitutions—the makeup of their bodies—were considered weak and unfit for regular life. Because TB, unlike cholera and other epidemics of the nineteenth century, is a slow-acting, degenerative disease, sickness was no longer a sign of impending death, but a way of life. Sanatoriums were not so much treatment centers as intentional communities, equipped with their own vegetable farms, dairies, post offices, water and telephone systems. Sufferers of TB, respiratory maladies, or bodily debility became "consumptives," and lived their lives first as sufferers, then as health seekers. Primarily characterized by frailty and fatigue, consumptives had no comfortable place in society as they knew it. Whether intentionally or not, they eventually formed their own societies of lungers, loungers, chasers of the cure: pajama people. But first, they rested.

LANGUOR VS. MALINGERING

I am tired, Lou Reed sings, *I am weary. I could sleep for a thousand years.* Where oh where is the poetics of tiredness? Of exhaustion? I am a tired woman. I have been tired for years now. Bone-tired. Dead tired.

I have one of those made-up sounding conditions that largely affects young women, which is to say, an understudied disease the medical community doesn't even believe in enough to call a disease or sickness or illness. Rather, it is a "syndrome." My primary symptom is being tired. More specifically, it is extremely exhausting for me to go from lying to sitting, harder still for me to stand. My heart rate rockets but my blood pressure doesn't adjust, not enough blood goes to my brain, and depending on a number of factors, I may fall down in a dead faint. On the whole, it is a very Victorian-seeming condition, and this is a joke I often make about it. "I'm a swooner!" I crow. "Oh, my delicate constitution."

Leading up to the 2016 presidential election, candidate Hillary Clinton passed out. It wasn't the first time it's happened, and like the other public occurrences (which have coincided with infections), it sent reporters into a frenzy of diagnosis. But more than the suspicions of seizures and brain tumors, fainting suggested that the presidential candidate might not be strong enough, healthy enough, for office. As a woman, she is already presumed to be weak and untrustworthy, but to have her body confirm both of these qualities by suddenly losing consciousness? We doubt those who show signs of weakness or frailty, questioning their ability and often their worth. Then for Clinton to take time to rest and recover from what turned out to be pneumonia? Convalescence challenges everything we look for in a healthy adult, let alone a leader: strength, endurance, ability. If she were really presidential

> On bad days I am aware that my body is in pain but no one can see it.

material, this belief implies, she'd tough it out.

Rest is often an indication of failure—failure to be productive, to function—and exhaustion is not a quality that the world takes very seriously, at least not the worlds I have inhabited. Energy is the prized possession of the young and the deepest desire of the aging. It isn't attractive or interesting to be the yawner in the group, the one who heads home early or doesn't come out, the one who abandons the party to find a place to nap (I am sort of famous for this). But in the age of TB, illness and frailty were high fashion. As Susan Sontag writes in *Illness as Metaphor*, symptoms were worn like clothing, "a kind of interior décor of the body." Weakness and exhaustion were transformed into languor, a luscious and impressive idleness. To be consumptive was not just a diagnosis of specific physical illness but "sometimes an indirect way of saying you were tired and wished to be alone, or that you felt artistic, sensual, and vaguely dramatic," writes TB historian Katherine Ott. And at one time, these weren't negative qualities. They were signs of creativity, genius, or even holiness.

We tend to be suspicious of sick people, probably because we cannot feel what a sick person feels, cannot know another's discomfort. On bad days I am aware that my body is in pain but no one can see it. I look the same. To think or talk about being sick makes me feel unduly self-pitying, or self-aggrandizing, or self-obsessed. What in another era might have been called "vaguely dramatic." I once heard

Maggie Nelson describe the self as a seismograph for experiences: senses, feelings, and thoughts are facts only the self knows. When I am a body in pain, I have only self to turn to. Even well-meaning others can't see or know or feel the facticity of all my skin aching at a light draft. For this same reason, it is difficult to chart illness as a historical phenomenon in relation to illness today. Illness is both culturally constructed and subjective. It is both within and without, felt in our bodies but interpreted by the language we have been given to describe it.

The psychologizing of illness, which coincided with the rise of consumption, makes this relationship between self and body even more complex. Sontag points out that, on the one hand, to psychologize illness is to view "every form of social deviation" as illness: from criminal behavior to addiction to, say, homosexuality. But at the same time, if any malady can be interpreted psychologically, it follows that on some unconscious level people get sick on purpose, and that if they really wanted to be well, they could cure themselves. I am reminded of my mother insisting that a person well enough to watch television was well enough to go to school. This double bind instills a pervasive sense that illness is not real, that what the self experiences is not valid. The chronically ill person, thus: the "invalid." When the sick person wonders why she is sick, the only possible culprit is herself. As Franz Kafka wrote to his fiancée, Felice Bauer, "Secretly I don't believe this illness to be tuberculosis, at least not primarily tuberculosis, but rather a sign of my general bankruptcy." Harsh words, Franz, but I feel you. I question my worth daily when I sleep too much, or struggle to get up the stairs, or when my brain fogs out while doing basic things, like talking while standing up.

Here, let me try again: It's as if, waking up in the morning, I'm under water. I tell my partner I am at the bottom of a well. I'm gulping at air that I can't breathe. Or: It's as if waking up every morning is similar to having been steamrolled, and when I try to get up, I am trapped under a heavy object, flattened. When I muster the strength to sit up, my heart overreacts. When you think of your heart, do you do so with affection, gratitude for its continuous pumping? When I think of my heart I think of a feral animal my body is trying to domesticate.

For those with healthy bodies, living in Santa Fe, at 7,200 feet, is like preparing to be an Olympic athlete (the Kenyan cross-country team trains here). The city is surrounded by hiking trails and hot springs, and it's not uncommon to find yourself in conversation comparing the merits of nearby healing waters—Jemez Springs vs. Ojo Caliente, Montezuma in Las Vegas, New Mexico, vs. Santa Fe's own Ten Thousand Waves. In our first few months in Santa Fe, my partner and I tromp around the Santa Fe National Forest, the Dale Ball and Dorothy Stewart trails, the Sun and Moon Mountains. We buy Tevas. When friends come to visit, we take them on overzealous hikes through the aspen forests. Medical professionals in the age of TB insisted that elevation was a key to climate as a treatment for pulmonary disorders. Our friend Reverend Meany writes, "Great altitudes furnish a gymnasium where the respiratory organs are compelled to be exercised and consequently become larger and more efficient." I do not yet know if this is true for me, but I tell myself it is. I think I am making myself stronger, better, by living here, by walking and climbing mountains and moving as much as I can. But it seems just as likely that my desire to be well, to be among the well, overshadows how I actually feel. For the first time in several years, I am living with someone who witnesses how much I sleep, how often I lie down. I feel that my secret life has been exposed. That I am, perhaps, just lazy. Weak. Unfit for public office, certainly.

DIAGNOSIS

When it comes to health problems, we generally want and expect a clear answer: a named illness with a definite cause and a simple solution. We expect this of science, and we think of Western medicine as a science. In the United States, this perspective was born of the nineteenth-century conflict between doctrinal medicine and homeopathic medicine. For decades, different schools of thought had coexisted in health professionals and patients, and physicians drew on not just medical doctrine, but common sense, old wives' tales, and folk remedies. At the same time, consumptives tended to engage in their own version of WebMD: they "self-diagnosed, self-dosed, and seldom sought any trained advice," according to Ott. In part, this was because consumption itself offered a broad understanding of illness. TB, Ott writes, was "a romantic, ambiguous affliction" and at the time, "vagueness was essential to diagnosis." The precision we expect from biomedical thinking today was neither available nor desired when the best route to identifying an illness was a holistic examination of a person's "constitution."

Society's part in acknowledging consumption as a broad and comprehensive category of illness that called for a change in location and lifestyle allowed for the health seeker movement to exist—vague diagnosis was a key to formulating a treatment plan so elemental as rest and sunlight. Such a cure required a commitment that only the privileged could afford, and as more lungers came west, they exposed new populations of primarily indigenous and Hispanic New Mexicans to the disease without permitting them access to their cures. Sanatoriums were often staffed by native New Mexicans who were subjected to TB but could not afford treatment for themselves. Without federal support, New Mexico was unable to fund public health centers for its own population, and doctors at private facilities did not share their basic knowledge of the disease's spread to local communities. Many medical experts insisted, ludicrously, that Hispanic and indigenous people were immune to TB. Professional medicine differentiated itself from traditional remedies and holistic approaches with the barrier of expertise, which came at a great cost.

Diagnosis and treatment remain imprecise arts, but we'd rather not believe that. Then, as now, diagnosis was more a kind of agreement, consensus, or compromise than a clear decision. It is impossible to achieve even the appearance of precision when attempting to measure the health of a body in its entirety, but to understand disease as originating in specific organs, and then in specific parts of those organs, makes it seem as if illness can be isolated and eradicated by specialists, for those who can afford medical treatment. We love this kind of precision, we seek more and more to quantify our bodies. How many steps, how many calories, how many heartbeats per minute? Our obsession with hard numbers comes from a performance of precision that arose with the development of certain new tools in the late 1800s. The stethoscope, the thermometer, and the aspirator not only helped the physician know the patient's health numerically for the first time but also made the doctor's procedures less legible to the patient.

Rather than judging health by how a patient interpreted his or her body

> I feel that my secret life has been exposed. That I am, perhaps, just lazy. Weak.

according to how it felt, the interior of the body became accessible and interpretable only by an expert and his devices. And because feelings and sensory experience are deeply subjective and difficult to communicate and compare, patients were made to defer to hard numbers—surely numeric test results were more reliable and impartial than the seismograph of the self. In other words, the less we know or understand the instruments of diagnosis, the more we trust in them. Common sense and folk treatments were traded in for a medical establishment that quickly built up walls of accreditation and specialization around itself. Homeopaths were left out in the cold as hospitals and medical boards gained power and funding. In time, the growing population of lungers found themselves second-class citizens, and local hotels and businesses posted signs forbidding their entrance: No Sick.

It took four months to get my first diagnosis. I was living in Austin and starting graduate school. After fainting one night—the night before I taught my first college class—while sitting outside at a bar, I was taken to the ER for what my friends assumed was a seizure: head thrown back, body convulsing. This initial misdiagnosis started me down a long road of testing focused on my brain, the single organ presumed to be at fault. For four months, I was given to suspect my brain and its function, and through MRIs, EEGs, and a variety of tests involving flashing lights, we slowly but surely ruled out epilepsy. It was during these months when I first began to doubt diagnosis and question the array of specialists, none of whom talked to one another, in charge of my well-being. "I put the word 'diagnosis' in quotes," Joan Didion writes, "because I have not yet seen that case in which a 'diagnosis' led to a 'cure,' or in fact to any outcome other than a confirmed, and therefore an enforced, debility." Neurological explanations were discarded in favor of questioning the efficacy of my heart. Blood tests, EKGs, ultrasounds—all normal. I had my pulse taken frequently enough to get very tired of the joke I'd first heard in sixth grade from the paramedics when I fainted during the class fish dissection: *You have no pulse, so I have to pronounce you dead!* I thought it was odd that no one could find my pulse easily, but they also never questioned it or brought it up unless they wanted to tell me I had died. The exams and procedures went on; I shuffled from waiting room to waiting room.

The Tilt Table Test is as medieval as it sounds. I was assured by everyone involved that this test always came up negative, that in all likelihood absolutely nothing would

I just want to be sick like a normal person who can see a GP and get a prescription and get better.

happen and the mystery of my illness would continue. They strapped my legs, arms, chest, and head to a table and left the room for thirty minutes. Then they slowly tilted the table up in increments, leaving me alone for fifteen minutes each time. Finally, they tilted the table ninety degrees to the floor, a standing position. My feet rested on a ledge at the bottom of the table. I lost consciousness almost instantly.

I've never seen a doctor so excited. I waited for him to tell me what it meant, what I had. "You have an arrhythmia, you'll need a pacemaker," was all he had to say. He was ready to schedule the surgery, but referred me to an electrocardiologist just to be sure. This diagnostic moment, which I now know confirmed not just arrhythmia but also hypovolemia and orthostatic intolerance, did not lead to a pacemaker or a cure. Instead, it opened the process up to six years of doctors offering different descriptions of my condition and different prescriptions to help me, each of which made me understand my body differently.

First they tell me my heart is arrhythmic and insist that we need to install an alarm, in case of emergency. My heart is unsteady, my body is out of control and needs a machine to make it work. Next, I am a vessel: my blood plasma volume is too low and the only solution is to consume salt and water constantly, an equation I recall from chemistry sophomore year. The salt pills make me nauseous, but I go a year without fainting. And still I am so, so tired. I go to the University of Texas health center for blood tests—I don't want

to go back to a specialist, I just want to be sick like a normal person who can see a GP and get a prescription and get better. Every time I sit in the office waiting for the doctor, I fall asleep on the table. She prescribes vitamin B, vitamin D, iron. After months of supplements, the new doctor gives me a survey and determines it's a case of generalized anxiety disorder. My new prescription is yoga, meditation, and Zoloft. No wait, Prozac. Perhaps Lexapro. I try them all. I become less anxious. I get very good at yoga. I am still exhausted. At this point I return to the electrocardiologist. For a week, I wear a Holter monitor, with electrodes taped to my chest. I name him Toby. His wires trail out from underneath my clothes. My tiny heart bleats into the universe from an Airbnb in Houston, where I've escaped for a weekend with my girlfriend, daydreaming about a new life together—within a year, we will move to Santa Fe.

Dianna the RN at Texas Cardiac Arrhythmia in Austin takes over my case because she is the only one on staff who has experience with postural orthostatic tachycardia syndrome, or POTS, which is what they now call my condition. She worked with a specialist in Dallas who got funding to study the disorder when astronauts returned from space with it. They were fainting, they were exhausted. A syndrome that affects women over men four to one and had been typically misdiagnosed or treated psychiatrically suddenly got NASA funding and a new nickname: Grinch Syndrome. My heart is too small, they tell me.

Dianna is my coach. She insists on a recumbent exercise regimen. I believe in this regimen; I go to the gym every other day, I am certain I can row my way to health. I buy a heart monitor and work within zones. I quantify my body. I feel stronger. Dianna tells me I cannot put my feet up during the day and I should not nap. I struggle with this part. I now see it as the equivalent of what was called in the age of TB the "heroic cure," the prescription given to the earliest health seekers in the Southwest. They were told to find a ranch and work hard, to rough it, to exercise as much as possible. These early health seekers, for the most part, died by the thousands or sought alternate treatment. Luckily the heroic cure gave way to the rest cure, and eventually they got better. I am still tired.

All these different cures work and also don't work. All these different diagnoses and explanations, narratives of my illness, account for it but do not describe what it is to live with it as it changes from one day to the next. I've been trained to believe that when something is wrong, the solution is to do something about it. To fix it. To try something else. In needles and herbs, I feel as though I may have turned to magic at last. The acupuncturist tells me I am deficient in blood, but that we can build it back up. Acupuncture is the closest I've gotten to feeling as if someone else understands my body and to feeling as if I can actually care for it. I think this is because it approaches the body as a whole, because traditional Chinese medicine is essentially a constitutional and vitalistic understanding of the body, rather than a mechanistic or chemical interpretation. I can recognize how all the symptoms—the feelings—I experience relate to and shape one another: the fatigue, the migraines, the blurred vision, the dizziness, the heart palpitations, the inability to concentrate all stemming from a systemic deficiency, all requiring that I take extreme care with my body every day. The rest cure was founded on vitalism, and TB sufferers were thought of as lacking in vitality or life-force. They were told their bodies were weak and unable to participate in the changing world around them. Coming west, they claimed a new narrative for themselves in which rest, a positive attitude, and exposure to light and air would rejuvenate them over time.

To this day, traditional and homeopathic doctrines operate according to methods for diagnosis and treatment that do not rely on instruments of precision—they are, as my blonde friend insists, "junk science"— but instead take into account a person's description of how she feels. I think this is why I have grown to believe in them. Sontag was adamant in *Illness as Metaphor* that "the healthiest way of being ill" is one devoid of "metaphoric thinking." "My point is that illness is *not* a metaphor," she writes. If only it were so simple to rid our thinking and our language of metaphor, perhaps she would be right. But the truth is that illness and health are deeply narrative practices that depend on metaphoric understandings of the body. Illness *is* metaphor. The symptoms of the body are metaphor made literal, because already to call a feeling "symptom" is to dive fully beneath the sea of language, description, and interpretation. Illness cannot exist outside language, for to be ill is itself a description of something felt and shared by other ill people. The important thing I have learned from chronic illness is that we can choose how we interpret our bodies. And that choice affects not just our behavior or psychology but how we *feel* and how we rehabilitate ourselves. In my case, it meant a permanent adjustment to a slower existence.

WELL COUNTRY

Though doctors were beginning to understand TB as a disease spread by bacteria, antibiotics that could cure it would not be available until the 1940s. Health seekers in New Mexico continued to practice chasing the cure on their own and in sanatoriums, where they rested, ate heartily, and spent as much time outside as possible. The sans had large verandas where patients lined up to lounge, and many had screened-in sleeping porches so they could take the cure 24-7. Heliotherapy was popular too. Patients took sunbaths and some used mirrors to reflect sunlight into their throats: to allow the exterior environment to heal their insides directly. It's very different from how I relate to the sun here, slathering myself in sunscreen, wearing long sleeves and a giant hat every time I go outside.

To be ill is itself a description of something felt and shared by other ill people.

Gone were the days of roughing it: out with the manual labor, in with the communal loafing. Lungers had strict schedules to keep: eating, bathing, reading and writing letters, and, primarily, chasing the cure. The chase was absolute idleness. When I look at photos from this era, I see people gathered together outside, lined up in chaise lounges. They are horizontal; they wear pajamas in public. The Snuggie was first invented in this time period—it even had pockets. And the weird thing about the chronically ill people in these photos is, they're all smiling.

Sickness can be a form of idleness, if you allow it to be, and as such it stands apart from most of what we think of as living. It is still, horizontal, quiet, and unproductive. In this way, it is kind of queer: it takes you out of a number of normative loops, like work, family, procreation, getting dressed, exercise and fitness, socializing. I'm often troubled by the automatic divide between work and repose, because I am, clinically speaking, idle. Since the days of TB, it has been common to imagine artists as sort of fevered creatures, or ill, not quite active participants in healthy lifestyles. But what if being sick is also its own opportunity to work creatively on things that are slow and thoughtful? Is this why Sunmount Sanatorium in Santa Fe became known as an artists' salon? Is this why so many artists' compounds sprung out of the health seeker era? For me, being sick was the permission I needed to make a living as a writer. It was what made me realize that I can't work on my feet all day, which I tried when I was full time at a bookstore, nor can I go to an office and work for eight hours sitting up (when I do, I tend to spend the entire time imagining where in the building I could lie down with no one noticing). I had to find a way to work and earn money while keeping my body functioning. (Medicaid helps, for now.) At the very least, I can write while sleeping and wake up to the joy of a sentence fully formed. The half-waking state is when I am at my best as a writer, my most honest and most lofty.

After World War I, the United States decided that sickness was out and determined that rather than "the old-fashioned idea of getting sick and then getting well," people should operate according to "the new idea of staying well," as cultural anthropologist Nancy Owen Lewis writes, citing the March 1919 issue of *Herald of the Well Country*. I question this obsessive quest for perfect health, for endless wellness. Sickness shows us that we are not invincible. If I have learned nothing else from my illness, I know now that the body is perhaps more delicate than I thought. I have heard many narratives of my body but few of them accept what I know to be true: I am meant to move at a slower pace. Rather than try to fix my body, or interpret it with a written diagnosis or cure, I simply listen to it. I live according to its needs day by day. In New Mexico I don't go to the gym but instead I hike the mountain trails in slow motion, stopping sometimes every few steps. A haiku plays on repeat in my mind: *O snail / Climb Mount Fuji, / But slowly, slowly!*

Sanatoriums are long gone and the idea of giving in to illness is one very few embrace. I tried to visit the sanatoriums near Santa Fe, only to find that they have all been repurposed: a Drury Hotel, a world college, a Carmelite monastery. Places that were once built for convalescence have been transformed into places for vacation, study, and worship.

Like the lungers at the sans, I focus my life around health and rest. The connection is most obvious to me when I go to community acupuncture and recline in a circle of armchairs with other health seekers. What else are we doing but chasing the cure? For a long time I wondered if I would view these as lost years: years spent horizontal, years spent asleep. I wondered if, when I got better, I would miss it: idleness, repose, convalescence. Now I wonder if the rest of my life will unfold in a similar fashion, napping and waking at odd hours, occasionally encountering other beings, more often encountering myself, over and over again, in dreams. Perhaps I don't belong in well country. Or perhaps, as the lungers and I understand, the cure is the ongoing chase. 🜨

SARCOMA

When the doctor says the word sarcoma, I consider how
it might be a nice name for a daughter, that good feminine
a, the way parents name their children for all sorts of
inappropriate things—apples, for instance, or the place
where the baby was conceived—and I trace my fingers over
the barrow of my belly as he speaks, flesh distended beneath
the blue tissue I wear for a dress—an ideal grief frock,
throwaway—and he says something about life expectancy but
of course I expect my life, so plain I thought nothing would
ever take it, and while he explains I cup my palms around my
center—as if comforting a child, or covering its ears.

HOSPITAL FOOD

Jenni Ferrari-Adler

Don't order fish. Don't order salads.

Isn't it nice when someone brings you breakfast in bed? Even this flattened croissant whose ends touch to form a circle, these scrambled eggs that surely came from a carton, these two rectangles of cold butter wrapped in gold foil. Even if the night was long, and you're not allowed to shower, and you're not at home. You tear the croissant in half and spread every bit of butter with the plastic knife. You empty the packets of salt and pepper on the eggs and push the jelly packets and orange juice cup to the side of the tray. You tip water and crushed ice into your cup from the ubiquitous pink plastic pitcher. The coffee smells burnt (in exactly the way airplane coffee always smells burnt) and the milk only turns it gray.

Just outside these thick windows it's the end of September in Manhattan, a weekday morning full of people rushing to the subways at Columbus Circle. Here you are killing time in an air-conditioned shared room on the fourteenth floor of St. Luke's-Roosevelt Hospital (now Mount Sinai West) at 1000 Tenth Avenue. You are twenty-eight weeks pregnant and bedbound.

The nurses all call you Mommy. Thank God you have a Mommy to call. "Mommy, please bring me the largest hottest milkiest most-caffeinated beverage. And thank you. And see you soon."

In advance of each meal a nurse gives you a paper menu and a half pencil. There are a lot of nurses, tall and short, dark and light, young and old, nearly all female. The best ones proffer small kindnesses—a *Martha Stewart Living* on Halloween crafts, a shoulder pat, the question *How are you, Mommy?*—nearly bringing you to tears.

You choose your meals with checkmarks; just about the only choice you get to make about your day. You study all the options twice, holding each choice in your mind—meatloaf and a baked potato? chef's salad?—looking for maximum ingredients and contrasts. What might be interesting to eat? It's as if you are in a university cafeteria, stoned. Your decision is not about hunger or health or price, the usual factors when reading a menu. It's not even about what might taste good. It is only about distraction. You select dishes you would never consider in a restaurant, dishes you would never cook at home, like beef stroganoff with bow-tie noodles and peas, which you hunt and stab with the tines of your fork. (You will save for later the pair of circle crackers in a cellophane wrapper. There is a lot of cellophane.) Spaghetti with mushrooms and cream sauce is perfect for twisting into tornadoes, or scraping the cream off the mushrooms so you can see how far each mushroom bends before it breaks.

All the vegetables have been made with your three-year-old daughter's Play-Doh machine. They are the right shape and color but they are not right.

They are the right shape and color but they are not right.

You peel back the silver lids of vanilla pudding cups and lick them clean before digging in. Vanilla pudding is hospital food in its most perfect form. Your favorite nurse—supplier of the frankest reassurances and extra pudding cups—mentions that homeless people sometimes turn up late at night in the ER claiming injuries and pleading for pudding. You understand their nocturnal panic. You always want more. If you are on bed rest until this baby is fully cooked at thirty-six weeks you might become obese. Probably, you should start eating less. But the boredom is deep. It is hard to read. It is hard to sleep. It is hard even to watch TV. You are physically uncomfortable and freaked out. You don't want to have this baby three months before his due date. You make each velvety pudding last as long as it can.

The worst food to order in a hospital is the kind of food you love best, simple meals with fresh vegetables and strong flavors. Don't order fish. Don't order salads. The tomatoes will taste like Freon. The carrots will smell like plastic bags. The lettuce will taste like ice cubes that were dropped on the floor. The dressing will be sweet.

It is a fine idea to order soup—minestrone, onion, beef, Italian wedding—but your best bets are dishes like macaroni and cheese and lasagna. Foods that are thick and square, layered, congealed, dense. Foods that can be easily frozen and

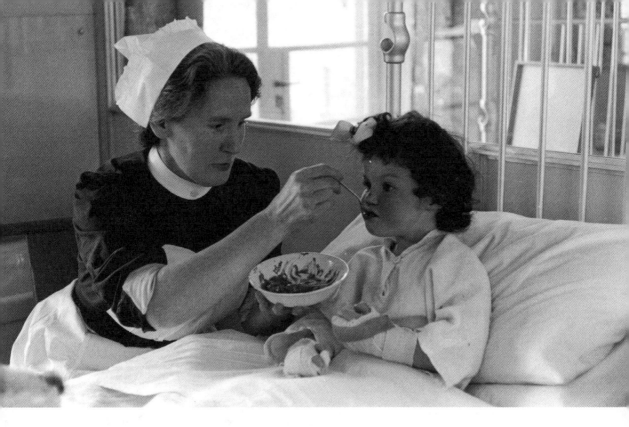

stacked on trays on trucks. Foods that can serve five hundred beds. Most big hospitals outsource their food entirely, ordering it from companies like Sysco, which has almost two hundred distribution facilities and serves more than four hundred thousand customers. Some hospitals have better food options for those willing to pay extra. A few hospitals—Oakland, Cleveland—buy local and organic foods and even have gardens. Most hospitals make multiple meal plans based on dietary needs: diabetic, cardiac, soft. The soft diet is often a literal blending of whatever protein is being served that day.

There is nothing crispy here, nothing bitter or sour or spicy. There is no garlic. There are no scallions. There are no hot peppers.

There is no kimchi. There is no stinky cheese! There are no red pepper flakes. There are no capers, no horseradish, no cilantro, no preserved lemons. This food has not known fire. It's been heated up in water baths. It's been defrosted over low electric heat in industrial-sized pots. Or maybe it's just been microwaved.

Bland food is for the sick but you aren't sick. You are only bleeding, a slow trickle from a source they can't find on their screens. It has been five days since you rode the C train up from work on your lunch break, concerned. They won't let you go home. You are an incubator in limbo and meals break up the days. You are overly aware of the categories at play: soft and softer, buttery and bland, watery, beefy, and sweet.

None of it is terrible, though. None of it is truly gross.

You are monitored, wheeled up and down the hall to different rooms to proffer your arm, your tongue, your belly. No one is weighing you anymore, no one cares that your prenatal vitamins are at home, that you never received the results to the gestational diabetes test. No one tells you to eat salmon or greens. It is only the end of the second trimester and you're back to basics, temperature and blood pressure. Beyond that, they check on the baby. Every day the baby stays inside of you is a good day for his developing brain, his lungs, his chances at making it, his chances at the good life. It is just you and him, holding out, taking things one meal at a time.

In the middle of your sixth night in the hospital—suddenly, swiftly—you deliver the baby. Two days after that you are home, your baby left behind to grow bigger than his two pounds. Have anyone's arms ever been so empty? Under doctor's orders you rest at home for two weeks, watching all the seasons of *Gossip Girl* and eating huge bowls of radicchio and endive with garlicky dressing and nubs of parmesan. Blue cheese. Salami. Sardines and onions on toast. All the sharp tastes you thought you wanted but of course nothing can satisfy you. You miss the mellow sweetness of the hospital, where at least you were watched and witnessed. Every night after putting your daughter to sleep with an elaborate story about a magical elevator, you lie awake in bed while your husband drives the West Side Highway

to the hospital. He texts you a picture. Your baby is covered in the white downy hair you associate with anorexics. Day by day there is a different, and eventually decreasing, assortment of wires, bandages, and tubes obscuring a delicate if slightly bug-eyed face. Your husband texts you the baby's weight gain—ounce by ounce—with exclamation points.

Two months later you carry your six-pounder—in his ten-pound car seat—down the elevator and out the revolving door to the world you've been telling him about. He turns one, and two, and three, and four, an almost outrageously rascally and winsome boy.

On sick days, when he cannot go to day care and therefore you cannot go to work, you buy six-packs of Swiss Miss vanilla pudding cups from the corner store. Comfort food, nursery food. It cools the throat; it's nice to swallow. It asks nothing of you. Sometimes you make it from scratch but its simple taste is not so simple to achieve. One must be patient for at least thirty minutes while it cools and that's after the pouring and the boiling and the vigorous whisking to yield the extreme smoothness you crave. Your pudding is rich, almost eggy, an elemental delight. Alas, neither of your children prefers it to store-bought, and your husband would rather it be chocolate. And truthfully you are fond of the packaging, the silver lid and the plastic cup.

All to say that when the corner store is out of pudding on a sick day you are not amused! Is it too much to ask for easy things to be easy? After sixty days of yellow robes, disinfectant, incubators, endlessly beeping machines, and pumping in that littlest room, you promised to never complain about little things again if only he was okay, and damn, that's turned out to be such a hard promise to keep. Every day there is so much to be upset about and so much to be thankful for.

You buy cream and carry it home. You make the slurry, the sugared milk, the pudding, assiduously whisking out lumps—the threat of lumps—at every step, while your son walks around the perimeter of the kitchen in his white-tiger pajamas, brushing loose curls away from his eyes, determinedly emptying every cabinet. 🏮

Vanilla Pudding
Serves 8

This recipe is adapted from the Rich Vanilla Pudding in Bakeless Sweets *by Faith Durand, who provides more thorough directions. If you want to make a perfect pudding from scratch, this is the one. I like to serve pudding in assorted small cups and glasses—sake, shot, espresso, and children's tea cups—with little spoons. Small portions justify seconds.*

INGREDIENTS:

¼ cup cornstarch
½ teaspoon salt
1 ½ cups cream
3 egg yolks
2 cups whole milk
6 tablespoons sugar
1 vanilla bean

DIRECTIONS:

1. Whisk cornstarch and salt in a medium bowl. Slowly add cream, then egg yolks.

2. Combine milk and sugar in a saucepan over medium heat. Split the vanilla bean and scrape the innards into the pan and then drop the pod in too. When the edges bubble and the surface trembles, remove the pod and discard it. Turn off the heat.

3. Pour 1 cup of the hot milk into the bowl of cornstarch, salt, yolks, and cream. Whisk until smooth! Pour this combined liquid into the pot slowly, whisking, whisking.

4. Over medium heat, stir mixture with a wooden spoon until it boils and for two minutes thereafter.

5. Pour into a shallow container. Cover with plastic wrap. Refrigerate for at least thirty minutes.

Reading Gordon Bowker's
Biography of Joyce

Peter Orner

JOYCE ACCOMPANIED HIS DAUGHTER, LUCIA, TO HER FIRST appointment with Carl Jung. Jung told Joyce that he'd need a month before he came to any conclusions. This was in Zurich in 1933. "As we talked," Jung remembered Joyce later, "by some effect of his glasses and the position of the light behind him, the enlarged pupils suggested that full-eyed concentration of a wild animal."

Seems like Jung was more interested in the writer than he was in the patient.

And a father's agony?

Twenty years later, Jung would write that in his opinion Joyce was a kind of schizophrenic by choice while Lucia was the real deal. At the time, Jung said to Joyce only that he simply wasn't sure of the best course of action in Lucia's case. Psychoanalysis might help. Then again, it might not. Who knows? The human shadow speaks with a thousand voices. Jung was a reluctant devotee of Joyce's work. Though *Ulysses* put him to sleep (twice) and he said that it would mean the same thing if read backwards, he was nonetheless convinced Joyce was a prophet, "an unwitting mouth piece of the secrets of his time." The bill for Lucia's treatment was 3,600 francs.

For a while, a few months, she was calmer. She began taking long car trips and playing billiards. Lucia was twenty-eight years old and told her father she was worried she might become like those hysterical women she'd met that time at Lake Geneva. She said what she really wanted was a quiet garden and a dog. Then she set her room on fire again. A day later she blacked her face with ink. They put her in restraints. They locked her in a room with bars. Friends of Joyce's urged him to have her committed. But he refused and took her with him to Paris. From there she traveled to Ireland (her father had no interest, he was through with Ireland) believing that a return to the homeland where she'd been so happy as young girl might—

Ireland was not what she expected or remembered.

In her lucid moments, of which there were a great many, Lucia once asked a doctor if there was any cure for her short of murder.

She sent telegrams to dead friends.

Doctor to doctor, clinic to clinic, sanatorium to sanatorium. One doctor in Zurich diagnosed her as having a curable blood disorder and Joyce clung to this for years, a desperate, ordinary father.

I don't want to know who died first, the father or the daughter. There's not much of the book left to go, maybe sixty pages.

PETER ORNER

Kaveh Akbar founded and edits *Divedapper*. His poems appear in *Poetry*, *APR*, *Narrative*, *FIELD*, and elsewhere. Born in Tehran, Iran, he currently lives in Florida.

Aimee Bender is the author of five books, most recently *The Particular Sadness of Lemon Cake* and *The Color Master*. She lives in Los Angeles.

Amy Bloom is a writer and teaches at Wesleyan University. Years ago, her daughter created stationery with Bloom's name in a fancy font and underneath: WILL WRITE FOR CASH.

Laura Bogart's work has appeared in *Salon*, *DAME*, *The Guardian*, *The Atlantic*, *SPIN* and other publications. She doesn't feel like herself without a dog around.

Rita Bullwinkel is the author of the story collection *Belly Up*, forthcoming in May 2018.

Leila Chatti is a Tunisian-American poet. She currently lives in Provincetown, Massachusetts, where she is a writing fellow at the Fine Arts Work Center.

Michael W. Clune's most recent book is *Gamelife*.

Brandon Courtney is the author of *The Grief Muscles* and *Rooms for Rent in the Burning City*, as well as the chapbook *Inadequate Grave*.

Peter Crabtree, formerly of the Bronx, now lives in North Bennington, Vermont. His website is petercrabtreephoto.com.

Meehan Crist is writer-in-residence in Biological Sciences at Columbia University. Previously, she was an editor at *Nautilus* and *The Believer*.

Ariel Djanikian's novel, *The Office of Mercy*, was published in 2013. Her stories are forthcoming from *Glimmer Train* and *Alaska Quarterly Review*.

Jenni Ferrari-Adler edited the anthology *Alone in the Kitchen with an Eggplant*. She is a literary agent at Union Literary.

J. P. Gritton teaches English and Creative Writing in Houston. His fiction has appeared or is forthcoming in *Black Warrior Review*, *Greensboro Review*, *Southwest Review*, and elsewhere.

Santi Elijah Holley has contributed to *VICE*, *SmokeLong Quarterly*, and other periodicals. A recipient of the 2017 Oregon Literary Fellowship, he lives in Portland, Oregon.

Marie Howe is the author, most recently, of *The Kingdom of Ordinary Time*.

Leslie Jamison is the author of *The Empathy Exams* and *The Gin Closet*. Her next book, *The Recovering*, will be published next spring.

Alyssa Knickerbocker is the author of a novella, *Your Rightful Home*. Stories and essays can be found in *AQR*, *American Short Fiction*, *Third Coast*, and elsewhere.

Peter LaBerge has authored two chapbooks, *Makeshift Cathedral* and *Hook*. He's an undergraduate student at the University of Pennsylvania. www.peterlaberge.com

Dorothea Lasky is the author of four books of poems, most recently *Rome*. She teaches at Columbia University and lives in New York City.

Sarah Manguso is the author of seven books, most recently *300 Arguments* and *Ongoingness*. She lives in California.

Alix Ohlin, a native of Montreal, now lives and writes in Easton, Pennsylvania.

Peter Orner is the author of two novels, two story collections, and most recently a memoir, *Am I Alone Here?* He currently lives in Windhoek, Namibia.

Benjamin Percy is the author of four novels and two short story collections. His most recent book is *Thrill Me: Essays on Fiction*.

Micah Perks is the award-winning author of a novel, a memoir, and many personal essays and short stories. More at www.micahperks.com

Mary Ruefle is the author of numerous books of poetry and prose, most recently *My Private Property*.

Elissa Schappell is the author of two books of fiction, a co-founding editor and Editor-at-Large of *Tin House*, and teaches in the MFA program at Columbia.

Jenn Shapland's nonfiction appears in *Pastelegram*, *Pushcart Prize XLI*, *The Lifted Brow*, and elsewhere. She is currently writing *The Autobiography of Carson McCullers*.

Kara Thompson is a writer and a professor of English and American studies. Her book *Blanket* is forthcoming.

Jennifer Tseng is an award-winning poet and the author of the novel *Mayumi and the Sea of Happiness*.

Adam Wilson is the author of the novel *Flatscreen*, and the collection of short stories *What's Important Is Feeling*.

Jerry Williams lives in New York City with his regrets and his small victories and his job.

FRONT COVER:

Liminal XVII, Oil on Canvas, 14″ x 14″, 2016
© Yang Cao. www.yangcaoart.com

SPREAD THE LOVE!

Tin House t-shirts, totes and koozies are now available at tinhouse.com

"A new classic for the collapsing political landscape of America."—**Kim Gordon**

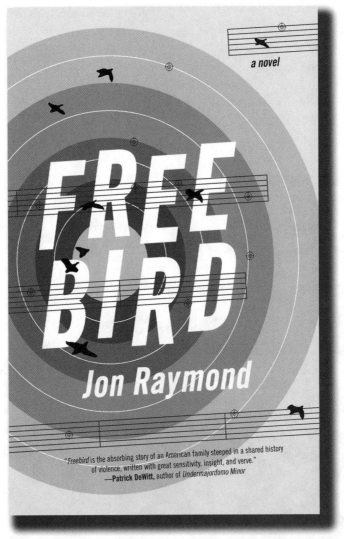

a novel

FREE BIRD

Jon Raymond

"*Freebird* is the absorbing story of an American family steeped in a shared history of violence, written with great sensitivity, insight, and verve."
—**Patrick DeWitt,** author of *Undermajordomo Minor*

"*Freebird* is the gripping story of a dysfunctional family through which we better understand these dysfunctional times."—**Benjamin Percy**

GRAYWOLFPRESS.ORG

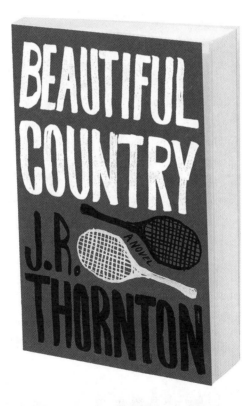

MASTER OF ARTS/MASTER OF FINE ARTS IN

Creative Writing

- Work closely with faculty through workshops and individual mentoring.

- Take advantage of the best features of residential and low-residency programs.

- Choose from specializations in fiction, creative nonfiction and poetry.

- Refine your writing skills in convenient evening courses in Chicago and Evanston.

RECENT AND CONTINUING FACULTY INCLUDE

Chris Abani
Eula Biss
Stuart Dybek
Reginald Gibbons
Goldie Goldbloom
Miles Harvey
Cristina Henríquez
Simone Muench
Naeem Murr
Ed Roberson
Christine Sneed
Megan Stielstra

sps.northwestern.edu/cw • 312-503-2579

Northwestern | PROFESSIONAL STUDIES

W

Chaos

MFA
CREATIVE WRITING
FICTION – POETRY

TEXAS ★ STATE
UNIVERSITY
The rising STAR of Texas

Our campus overlooks the scenic Hill Country town of San Marcos, part of the Austin Metropolitan Area. With Austin just 30 miles to the north, Texas State students have abundant opportunities to enjoy music, dining, outdoor recreation, and more.

Tim O'Brien
Professor of Creative Writing

T. Geronimo Johnson
Visiting Professor 2016-17

Karen Russell
Endowed Chair 2017-19

Faculty

Fiction
Doug Dorst
Jennifer duBois
Tom Grimes
Debra Monroe

Poetry
Cyrus Cassells
Roger Jones
Cecily Parks
Kathleen Peirce
Steve Wilson

Visiting Writers*
Elisa Albert
Lydia Davis
Stephen Dunn
Stuart Dybek
Jennifer Egan
Ross Gay
Jorie Graham
Terrance Hayes
Marlon James
Leslie Jamison
Adam Johnson
Ada Limón
Daniel Orozco
Mary Ruefle
Tracy K. Smith

Adjunct Thesis Faculty
Lee K. Abbott
Gina Apostol
Catherine Barnett
Rick Bass
Kevin Brockmeier
Gabrielle Calvocoressi
Ron Carlson
Victoria Chang
Maxine Chernoff
Eduardo Corral
Charles D'Ambrosio
Natalie Diaz
John Dufresne
Carolyn Forché
James Galvin
Amelia Gray
Saskia Hamilton
Amy Hempel
Bret Anthony Johnston

Li-Young Lee
Karan Mahajan
Nina McConigley
Elizabeth McCracken
Jane Mead
Mihaela Moscaliuc
David Mura
Naomi Shihab Nye
Kirstin Valdez Quade
Spencer Reece
Alberto Ríos
Elissa Schappell
Richard Siken
Gerald Stern
Natalia Sylvester
Justin Torres
Brian Turner
Eleanor Wilner

* Recent and upcoming

Now offering courses in creative nonfiction.

$70,000 Scholarship:
W. Morgan and Lou Claire Rose Fellowship for an incoming student. Additional scholarships and teaching assistantships available.

Front Porch, our literary journal:
frontporchjournal.com

Doug Dorst, MFA Director
Department of English

601 University Drive
San Marcos, TX 78666-4684
512.245.7681

Tin House Magazine

ABOUT THE COVER

This issue's cover artist, Yang Cao, focuses his paintings on the capricious nature of human emotion. He abstracts his realistic figures with crowns of clouds or he removes their heads altogether. The results are at once unsettling and relatable as the tone of each painting is uncertain and the audience is left to decipher the mood.

The mercurial subject of our cover painting, *Liminal XVII*, appears joyful, perhaps surprised: she's smiling, her cheeks are rosy, we can't see her eyes. The top half of d is swathed in a cotton candy cloud; flashes inside. The pink glow of nside sits at odds with the aus- of the background.

w with *Tussle Magazine*, Cao ns for the clouds. He said he "like[s] the unpredictability of the cloud. It's shapeless and changes all the time, it follows the wind and never stays in one form and place. Somehow I find this as a resemblance to our human nature and mind."

Cao works from life, using photos and models, but he takes a fluid approach to his practice. He considers his process to be one of trial and error, saying, "It's like looking back to the messy footprints and realizing that I'm making a track, but I don't yet know where to set my next foot." You can see more of his work at www.yangcaoart.com.

Written by *Tin House* designer Jakob Vala, based on an interview with the artist.